TOM HOWARD BEST MYSTERY
HONOURABLE MENTION

For

FIRST KILL

a Dr Kristina Melina mystery

LAURENT BOULANGER is the author of the critically acclaimed novel 'The Girl From France', winner of the 2014 Paris Book Festival awards, and 'Better Dead Than Never', 2014 eLit Bronze Winner for Best Multicultural Fiction. 'First Kill' won a Tom Howard Mystery contest Honorable Mention for Best Crime Fiction.

THIRD VICTIM

THIRD VICTIM

Laurent Boulanger

SNIPER BOOKS

Sniper Books

Copyright © 2009 Laurent Boulanger

First published in Australia by Sniper Books
Sniper Books is an imprint of Lake Ozark Press

Typeset in Garamond

Cover design © 2009 Lake Ozark Press

FOR
GAIL & CLINT

CHAPTER ONE

'She was found thrown over a high-steel fence, in the back courtyard of a group of flats, her armpit impaled on a spike,' explained Senior Sergeant Frank Moore when I questioned him about the location of the victim.

One elbow propped up on my blue pillow, lying in bed, the receiver tucked between my right shoulder and chin, I was scribbling down details, more from habit than reason, in a small spiral-bound notebook.

It was 6.26 a.m. on a grey, rainy June morning, and my head was heavy from lack of sleep. I'd given up my city apartment for a three-bedroom, brick-veneer house in Craigieburn, a small rural town thirty kilometres north of Melbourne.

In my new life, I had become accustomed to long lazy mornings, where the only urgency in getting up was to collect the mail from my postal box and make myself a cup of coffee. Thus, I was mildly irritated when Frank woke me up with his phone call, especially when I'd stopped being contracted to the Victorian Forensic Science Centre (VFSC) and the police six months prior. After my son Michael nearly died in a previous investigation, I'd threw in the towel and decided to work as a private investigator. Missing persons, insurance fraud, marital problems and white collar crimes were my bread and butter, but occasionally I also handled security, collection and child custody. Business was slow in the first two months, but now my income was steady enough to keep food on the table and to meet the mortgage repayment on my new dwelling.

The move to Craigieburn did me good, especially after having spent three years in the city. Noisy neighbours, tramways and emergency vehicles travelling up and down Chapel Street at all hours had contaminated my sleep to a point that no matter how many hours I spent in bed, I never managed a good night rest.

My first night in Craigieburn had been heaven-sent. I slept ten hours straight, and the only thing I heard when I woke up was the sound of my own breathing. Vast hills dotted with cattle and sheep adorned my bedroom window. I loved this town. Shop owners called me by my first name, the local bank tellers trusted my identity without asking for proof, and librarians engaged in private conversations as if they had known me all their lives. My faith in human nature was slowly being restored.

When I began my career in law-enforcement, armed with a Ph.D. in Criminal Justice and an eighteen-months training stint at the FBI in Quantico, USA, I had acquired the arrogance to think I could change the world. Years later, I realised that in fact the world was changing me, and I abhorred what I was experiencing. I was a forty-year-old, single mother with a teenage boy, who saw me mostly in newspapers when a crime of public interest had been committed. For two long years I contracted myself to the Criminal Investigation Branch (CIB) and the VFSC as an investigator and crime-scene examiner. I teamed up with Senior Sergeant Frank Moore on many cases, two of which nearly ended my life.

For the record, my name is Kristina Melina, born Kristina Dos Oliveira Melina, but I dropped the middle names of my Brazilian ancestors when I moved from my parents' home. I'm Kristina to friends and family, but Dr Melina to everyone else whom I need to impress, for one reason or another. I'm around one-seventy tall and grade an eight out of ten in looks, so I'm told.

I threw my pen and notebook on the side-table, nearly cramping one of the muscles in my neck from yawning.

'Okay, Frank, I understand the situation,' I said, irritation creeping into my voice, 'but you know I'm no longer under contract with you guys, so unless you have something better to offer me than a trip to the city at six-thirty in the morning when it's pissing out there, I think I'll give it a miss.'

There was a pause.

'Frank?'

'Okay, fine, I'll tell you now.'

'Tell me what?'

'What school did you attend?'

'What?'

'Ever heard of someone named Evelyn Carter?'

The receiver slipped from my chin and shoulder, but I caught it with my right hand. The name was as familiar to me as the sound of my own voice. Evelyn and I spent most of our last year of high school in the same classes and did our first year at university together. And although she had occupied only a small portion of my life, to cut it short, she was the sister I never had. I had mentioned her enough times to Frank over the years. Why was he asking me if I'd heard her name before?

'What are you saying, Frank?'

'The girl we found bears the same name as your bum-chum from high school. Somehow, I don't think it's a coincidence.'

I experienced an acute pain in my breastbone, which I eased with an applied pressure from the palm of my left hand. Fully awake, my pulse racing at double-speed, the ceiling in my bedroom seemed to have just caved in on me. My clammy fingers gripped the telephone receiver tightly.

I tried to say something, but no words came out.

'Kristina, are you okay?'

'I'm fine,' I muttered. 'Where are you now?'

'I'm at the scene. I've sealed the area off, taken names down and spoke to a few people in the neighbourhood. I'm going to begin collecting evidence, but I can keep the area under my control until you get here.'

'You've done well.'

'Don't make me wait too long. With this weather, it's hell. I'll do the best I can.'

'You do that. I'm on my way.'

I smashed the receiver down, stumbled out of bed and raced to the bathroom.

Down on my knees, hugging the toilet bowl, I regurgitated last night's chicken Florentine and three veggies

Forty-five minutes later I was in Toorak, an inner-Melbourne suburb just seven kilometres east of the city centre. Houses in the area cost more than ten factory workers could make in a lifetime. Toorak, along with its adjoining suburbs, South Yarra and Prahran, were the Beverly Hills of Melbourne. Some streets were adorned with three-to-four-storey mansions, Mercedes Benz and BMWs, and contractors constantly renovating someone's swimming pool, staircase or front yard Highly successful business people, movie stars, television personalities, lawyers, doctors and anyone who never had to worry about getting a job if they suddenly stopped working lived there.

I rode the recently-completed West Ring Road freeway, pushing my new white Hyundai Excell to 150Km/h in the pouring rain. The traffic was better-than-average at 6.46 a.m., but it was building up city-bound. The sky was painted in grey and white tones with no hint of blue whatsoever. It was as if God was mourning the death of my long-lost friend.

Tears streamed down my face during the entire trip, and I didn't try to stop them. Better to cry now then when I got to the crime scene. There was a lump the size of a ping-pong ball stuck in my throat at the realisation that part of my life and my childhood had been savagely ripped away from me. Even though I hadn't seen Evelyn Carter for nearly twenty years, her face was still fresh in my mind like the headlines in this morning's paper. She had been a pretty girl with freckles, green eyes and long blond hair, who later turned into a gorgeous woman with a voluptuous body and a personality to melt your heart. I had lost contact with her at university when she discovered she could make more in an hour's work as a high-class prostitute than in a week as a office worker. We kept in touch for a little while via phone, but then I got too engrossed in my studies, and she in her clients. Our vocations had taken us on different paths.

As I stepped out of the car and into the pouring rain, memories of times I spent with Evelyn over the years flashed in front of my eyes. We used to have lunch together at the same High School, and even dated and kissed boys for the first time on the same night. We spent endless hours talking about

4

sex, and who we would become when we'd grow up. We both wanted to become famous painters like Picasso or Van Gogh. Sometimes, we skipped classes to go to the National Art Gallery and spent endless hours in front of the one painting. We closed and opened our eyes for various periods of time, and got ourselves in a trance until the painting became as real as the world around us. Sometimes we would get drunk and laugh so much, we thought our bladders would burst. We hugged and walked hand-in-hand and told each other that no matter what tomorrow would bring we would always be friends, always be there for one another, no matter how far apart we would find ourselves later in life. In fact, there was little in my youth that wasn't associated with her. When eventually our lives drifted apart, I sometimes wondered what she would be like if I met her again. Never had I expected, not even in my worse nightmares, to find her in the condition I was about to.

Her body was found in a lane way, behind some shops and the back courtyard of high-rise flats, away from on-looking traffic. Two marked police cars, blue and red lights flashing like someone's Christmas's decorations, blocked both entries to the back alley, much to the annoyance of shop owners and delivery vans who had lost access to the rear of the premises for early deliveries.

I spotted Frank in the distance, busy talking to a local wearing a wool-blend sports jacket, but Frank didn't see me.

Frank was head of the Crime Scene Division at the VFSC. He joined the Forensic Branch in 1975, straight out of the Royal Melbourne Institute of Technology (RMIT) with a Bachelor in Criminal Justice Administration. He was tall and had little hair to speak of. He had a crush of me for years, which drove the both of us insane at times, but for different reasons.

Grey cobblestones filled the back alley. The rain had created puddles between the cobblestones, and rubbish was scattered at random. Cans of Coke, a bottle of beer, food wrappers. There was even a squashed, bloody pigeon metres from the body.

As I circled the car, careful not to lose balance on the slippery cobblestones, I dreaded going through collecting evidence in that weather. If you must commit a murder, this was the way to do it. In the rain where all trace evidence is washed away, leaving investigators little to go on with, other than witnesses.

I opened the boot. Carefully, I removed my Physical Evidence Recover Kit (PERK)—the necessary scissors, scalpels, brushes, tweezers and packages needed to recover evidence at a crime scene—in the shape of one large black carry-case. I also took with me a Minolta SLR camera with various lenses and filters to record the situation before too many people had the chance to contaminate the scene.

I clipped my pale green photo ID, which I had never returned after my last investigative job with the VFSC, to my breast pocket and proceeded along the lane way, rainwater dripping down my face. The scenery was grey with a purgatory-like ambience, which reminded me of one of the opening scenes of a serial killer movie I had recently seen on video.

I took in a deep breath, my mind alert but not ready to face the cruelty life inflicted on a chosen few.

Half way up the lane way, Frank noticed me.

I didn't immediately figure out what it was, but there was something changed about him since I'd seen him the previous Easter. It took me a full thirty seconds to realise he had shaved off his moustache.

He came towards me, a solemn smile on his face, eyes filled with grief and anger all at once.

'You look good without the moustache,' I said instead of greetings.

'Oh, that,' he replied, as if his moustache had been nothing more than a blackhead. 'How are you coping? You sure you want to go through with this?'

'Yes, I'm sure, Frank. Did you manage to get me clearance?'

'Yep, Trevor Mitchell is authorising it on paper this very minute.'

Trevor Mitchell was the Director at the VFSC. He had strong connections with the CIB and the Minister of Police and Emergencies. He had the authority to appoint whomever he deemed necessary in order to proceed with an investigation.

Frank went on: 'As of this minute, you're authorised to conduct collection of evidence and take control over the investigation.'

'What about the fact that I knew the victim?'

'Haven't told anyone. Thought I'd leave that to you.'

I balanced from one foot to the other and said, 'You knew I was going to agree with this, didn't you?'

He gave me a forced smile and raised his eyebrows as a reply.

I changed subject: 'What have we got so far?'

'Fuck all. I've spoken to a few people in the area. They haven't seen or heard anything.'

'Who was that guy you were talking to before?'

His eyebrows crossed.

I went on, 'The guy with the sports jacket? I saw you talking to him when I got out of the car.'

'Yeah, yeah, that was the owner of a bookshop on the other side of the lane way. Just wanted to know what was going on. You know what it's like? Can't keep curious minds away.'

'Did he know the girl?'

'Nope. No one did. It looks as if she's been dumped here for convenience. Nobody around in the early hours of the morning. Perfect place to dispose of a body.' He shifted half a turn. 'You want to see her?'

'Not really, but I guess I'll have to.'

We walked side-by-side towards a high-steel fence which separated the back of the flats and the lane way. There was a mass hunched over the spikes of the fence, something which I knew had to be Evelyn Carter.

'Is that how you found her?'

'Well, I didn't actually climb the fence to toss her across it.'

I shrugged. 'I'm sorry. I'm not thinking straight.'

'Hey, don't worry about it. Let's just go and see.'

We got within half a metre from the body.

Evelyn Carter was so battered that I didn't recognise her. Sure, the last time I saw her was some twenty years ago, but how much can a person change in twenty years?

Her body was hanging on the fence, her right armpit impaled on a spike, exactly the way Frank had described it. Rainwater was dripping from her long blond hair, forming a small pool of water and blood at the foot of the fence. If there were any fingerprints or other trace evidence on her skin, it would have washed away by now.

I half-circled the body with my hands behind my back, wondering how in the world she got there.

And why.

'How did you identify her?' I asked Frank, who was standing a metre to my right, observing my reaction.

'Found her car down the end of the lane way A '95 Saab. Ran the plates and her name came up. Also found a set of keys to the car down the far end of the lane way House keys, postal box, a whole collection attached to one ring.'

'How do we know it's really her? All you've got is a car.'

'Ninety-five percent sure. We'll have to run fingerprints, dental checks, you know, the works.'

'The Saab could be a coincidence.'

'Could be, but I doubt it.'

'Why is that?'

'I've already spoken to the various shop owners in the area. No one knows an Evelyn Carter. Also her residential address on her driver's licence is in Richmond, so what the hell is her car doing in Toorak at six in the morning?'

'Visiting someone.'

'Kristina...'

'You never know, Frank. There's been stranger coincidences in life.'

'Sure, with that kind of attitude, anything is possible. But let's try to stick to the obvious.'

Okay, now I was desperately hoping it wasn't Evelyn Carter after all. The body hunched in front of me could have been anyone. Her teeth were knocked out, and her face a bloody mess of bruises and blood smears. If not for the long blond hair and the lack of a penis attached to the body, it could have been a man. Flashes of the Evelyn I used to know came to mind. I tried to conjure similarities between her and the body in front of me. Her eyes were blacked and puffed as if they'd been filled with air and drawn on with a charcoal pencil. I couldn't even tell if this person had crystal blue eyes like Evelyn did. In the state she was in, I wasn't the one who was going to make a positive ID.

I swallowed hard, deciding it was time to put my emotions

8

aside, not matter how disturbed I felt, and get on with the job.

As the team leader, I had a lot on my plate. First I had to ensure the safety of personnel and security at the scene, which included monitoring the use of protective wear and the handling of blood or other human body fluid. And since Evelyn Carter seemed to be leaking from everywhere, my eyes would have to be kept right open. The last thing I needed was a police officer or forensic specialist suing me for negligence.

'We going to have to remove her from here,' I said. 'Have you called for backup yet?'

'I knew you were going to come. And I didn't see what difference it would make to wait an extra half hour, especially when the body has probably been here all night anyway.'

'Okay, we're going to have to change into our overalls and protective equipment. She's still bleeding, and I don't want to catch some damn disease.'

'It's in the car.'

'I want lighting assistance and a shelter build around the body large enough for us to be able to remove it with minimum fuss.'

'I'll call the State Emergency Services immediately.'

'Chances are we're going to be here all day. Can you arrange a post outside the crime scene with enough coffee and munchies to avoid any specialists or journalists infesting the area with their rubbish?'

'As good as done.'

I glanced around the front and back of the lane way There seemed to be a lot of people present at the scene.

'Did you seal the entire area?' I asked.

'Front and back of the lane way are guarded by two uniformed officers. They have instructions to not let anyone in the scene. Not easy since most of the shop-owners need access to the back of the shops either to park their cars or to bring in their goods for the day.'

'They can wait. It's not going to kill their business to close for one day. And no damn politicians at the scene. I don't care who they are or who they answer to.'

From the smile Frank gave me, he must have known I had Goosh in mind. The Deputy Commissioner of Police made it a habit to walk into a crime scene without warning, chain-smoking and contaminating everything in sight. Somehow that sonofabitch thought he was above the law, but in my books he stood where everyone else did. Behind the police line.

Although I didn't say anything, I was grateful Frank was taking my orders in a professional and diplomatic manner. Normally he would give me those looks as if to say *why don't you do it yourself?* But he must have sensed that I was highly strung, and I didn't need anyone getting in my way.

I went on, 'While we're waiting for the SES, let's do another walk-through with the video camera this time. I need you to fill me in on what you've found so far. Also, I'd like the Saab taken to the Centre for examination. But first, let's get changed.'

We made our way back down the lane way

'Are you okay?' Frank asked.

'I'm fine.'

'You look tensed.'

I turned around and faced him, 'What do you expect? I haven't done this kind of shit for six months. Yeah, yeah, I love the excitement, but somehow this morning it's different.'

'You want to go home, you just give me the go-ahead, and I'll take over. No questions asked.'

I didn't reply. He knew I wouldn't back away.

And that was why he called me in the first place.

Six months ago, I was determined to never investigate another murder.

Today I was back on the beat.

CHAPTER TWO

The State Emergency Services came within half an hour, just when I had finished videotaping.

Videotaping was challenging, especially when it's raining like a dog. But it would provide us with a perspective on the crime scene layout, which wouldn't be as easily perceived with photography or sketches. The medium was more reliable, and people, especially in a court-room situation, could readily relate to it. The other reason for using videotaping was that we might have missed evidence or picking-up clues during the walk-through. Once on tape, we would have time to cover the crime scene over and over again at our own leisure.

Once the video camera was switched on, I didn't stop filming until the thirty-minute tape ended. Everything was painfully shot in slow motion. Years ago, when I first began using a camera, I rushed through the filming, panning from one section of the crime scene to the other, not allowing the camera to properly capture details. Using a video camera was not something I had been taught, but something I learned from trials and errors.

I used a combination of wide angles, close-ups and macros to demonstrate the layout of the evidence and its relevance to the crime scene. I made sure to capture the name of the lane way and to use measuring comparable devices, such as a stainless steel ruler or a twenty cent coin, whenever necessary and appropriate.

When it came to filming the body, my hands were

trembling. I had to concentrate twice as hard on what I was doing. I've never had to attend a crime scene where the victim was someone I had been close to. My emotional nerves were raw and bleeding.

During filming, Frank was responsible for keeping everyone present at the crime scene silent. The last thing we needed was someone yelling out some smart-ass comment on tape and having to start all over again.

Filming in the rain was hell, but at 8.15 a.m., we got a lucky break. The rain had turned from a downpour to fine silver needles. It made the recording process much easier, not having to worry about humidity inside the camera and the film.

Frank was searching the lane way for physical evidence. I was busy overlooking the SES workers removing Evelyn Carter from the fence. It was a hell of a job, and not only because of the position she had found herself in. I ordered that the body should be touched to a minimum to preserve any trace evidence, even though I knew there would be little left at this stage.

Frank and I looked like cosmonauts in our white protective outfits and surgical gloves—a contrast to the SES workers dressed in bright orange overalls with sawn-on patches from the organisation.

'Can you guys try to be a bit more gentle?' I asked when one of the male workers pulled the body upward from the neck, trying to dislocate the impaled armpit from the fence. 'We don't want to cause any more injuries to the body than there already is.'

They proceeded, ignoring my request. Somehow they managed to bring the body down from the top of the fence. The lower part of her body hit the ground. I cringed but kept my mouth shut, trying hard not to come across like someone with an authoritative chip on my shoulder. These people were highly trained volunteers, and I guessed they knew more about removing bodies from unlikely places than I did. If I had been left on my own, the body would have been totally dismembered by the time I got it down from the fence.

By now, somehow, I managed to shut down my emotional channels, a natural defence mechanism which helped me deal with what most people considered unbearable situations. I knew that my stance was temporary, and although I looked tough on the outside, I was no different from every other human being. There was no doubt in my mind that I wouldn't be able to sleep that night. The face of Evelyn Carter would be flashing on the ceiling of my bedroom, that the cry of her desperate soul would ring in my ears for justice to be served.

After my last investigation, I had to go on Prozac for a while, just to help me face the challenges of every day life. It was during that three-month period that I'd decided to give up on homicidal investigations. For years I had predicted that eventually the accumulated horrors of what I had seen throughout the 90s would eventually get to me. Back at university, all those books and theories on crime sounded exciting and drew my curiosity to the point of obsession. But on site, things were different. Everyday we were dealing with real people—not only the victims, but also family and friends of the victims. And that was the difficult part. Criminology lecturers never tell you about the effects of attending a crime scene can have on an investigator. The focus is on the stress endured by victims' relatives and peers. The rest of us just have to grind our teeth throughout the investigation.

The body was gently rolled inside the mortuary van as Frank paced towards me.

'How's everything going?' he asked.

'Fine. Did you find any evidence?'

'Nope, apart from a witness who says Evelyn got here by cab, not in her Saab.'

I puzzled over this information for a few seconds. 'Why would she take a cab when her car was already here? This doesn't make sense.'

'Maybe she was meeting someone. Maybe she went somewhere and didn't want to take her car because of the traffic, and then she returned by cab and got attacked on her way back to the Saab.'

'That's a possibility.' And then: 'Who's the witness?'

'The guy from the bookshop.'

'I thought he didn't see anything.'

'Details came back to him. At first, he never associated the cab with the murder. It's only later that her recalled a car stopping near the shops during the early hours of the morning. He walked up to the bedroom window and saw this yellow cab pulling up. He thought he heard the driver and the female passenger argue, but now he's not so sure. He doesn't know if what he saw wasn't part of a dream he was having after he gone back to bed.'

'He lives in the bookshop?'

'Upstairs. A two-bedroom apartment.'

'Get his name and address, I'd like to talk to him before I leave the scene.'

'Done.'

He passed me his log book, from where I wrote down the details of the bookshop owner.

David Boyd was thirty-five, I found out later, but he could have been five years younger.

When I met him, I felt a churning in my stomach which I confused with hunger. He was behind the counter of his second-hand bookshop, surrounded by posters of various book jackets, including John Grisham's *The Partner* and Thomas Kennelly's *Schlinder's Ark*. The interior of the bookshop consisted of an assortment of pine and particle-board book shelves of various heights. On top of each book shelves were laser-or-inkjet-printed inscriptions, cataloguing books into subject areas—General fiction, Australian Literature, Science-Fiction, Crime, New-Age, Health & Nutrition, Science, Psychology, Philosophy, Hobbies, Films & Cinema, Sports, Autobiography & Biography, Textbooks, American Literature, Foreign Books, and Children. A fluorescent tube above each book shelf bathed the spines of the books in a bluish light.

The shop smelled of paper pulp and ink, a smell I associated with old libraries. I had spent countless hours in various libraries, losing myself into books, not strictly because of my study requirements, but because I had nothing else better to do. Books were the love of my life, and I would have rather spent an evening by myself with a Sue Grafton novel than in front of the television or at a dinner party with friends.

I approached the counter and spoke matter-of-factly.

'I'm Dr Kristina Melina, the person in charge of investigating the body we found behind your premises.'

David Boyd smiled in return, green eyes sparkling like

emeralds behind tortoise shell glasses. There was a touch of grey on his temples blending in with his black hair, giving him an air of wisdom and self-assertiveness. The lines on his face were thin but well defined and perfectly symmetric. A cute dimple sat in the middle of his chin, and when he spoke his voice was warm and soothing.

'I've already spoken to your colleague,' he said.

'I know, but I'd like to speak to you myself,' I said.

'Sure, as I said, I've already told him everything I know.'

'Sometimes we forget details. Maybe something will come back to you, something you don't remember right at that moment.'

He shrugged as if my persistence was the least of his worries in the world.

'You want to talk,' he said, 'I've got all the time in the world. Not many people buy books these days, so it's not like we're suddenly going to get a massive crowd storming in here.'

He was rubbing fine sandpaper along the edges of a hard-cover book.

Seeing I was curious, he explained:

'For those who do buy books, especially second-hand books, they want to get value for money. There are two main reasons why people buy second-hand books—the first is that they like the idea of saving money, and the second is to find a work out-of-print. Some second-hand book sellers just toss the books on the shelves and hope they will sell. Of course some do, but by presenting a book in its best light, the price is justified.'

He grabbed a book from a pile next to him and continued.

'See the marks and browning on the edges.' He slid his finger lengthwise along the pages of the book. 'It's grey, dull and stained in a few places. Now watch this.' In a swift motion, he gently applied the sandpaper against the pages of the book, leaving a white dust of cloud behind. 'Now look.' He turned the book towards me. The pages were white, like those of a brand new book.

'That's interesting,' I said. 'I'll keep that in mind if I ever want to open a second-hand bookshop.'

Before I had time to add another word, he asked, 'Do you read?'

I wanted to get on with my questioning, but because of the genuine look on his face, I couldn't help being polite. 'Now and then, whenever I get time.'

'What do you read?'

'Mostly crime books.'

'Fiction? Non-fiction?'

'Both. It helps me with my own investigations.'

'Who's your favourite fiction author?'

'I don't have one. I like Grafton, Patterson, McDermid, Cornwell, Reichs. I read Garry Disher as well. His Wyatt series reads like Richard Stark's novels.'

'What about John Camp?'

'Who?'

'Pulitzer Prize-winning journalist, John Camp. He writes under the pseudonym John Sandford. The *Prey* books. *Rules of Prey, Silent Prey, Mind Prey*—'

'Don't like the protagonist. He can be a bit chauvinist.'

'I agree. Lucas Davenport. You're right, he does treat women like objects.'

He was mentioning the character of Stanford's novels as if he was a real person.

He moved from behind the counter and went on, 'Let me show you our crime section. I'm sure —'

'Look, I know you mean well, but I'm not here to buy books. Maybe another time. I need to talk to you about the girl we found in the lane way behind your shop.'

'Oh, sure, I'm sorry, I just get carried away sometimes. You know, I love books so much, I assume everybody else does.'

'You don't have to apologise. Not enough people read nowadays.'

He shifted from one foot to another. 'So, what is it you wanted to ask me?'

I found myself staring at the green irises of his eyes for a few seconds too long. 'I just want to know exactly what you saw last night.'

'Like I said to your colleague, not much. I heard a car screeching outside, got out of bed, looked across the street from my window and noticed a taxi. The passenger and the driver were arguing.'

'About what?'

'Hey, I don't know. I was two floors up. I just heard this male and female voices screaming at each other.'

'And then?'

'And then she left the taxi.'

'What did the woman look like?'

'Long black hair, slim. That's all I can tell, it was dark out there.'

'What about the cab driver?'

'Never left his taxi.'

'Did you get the cab company's name?'

'Black Cabs. It was written on the side of the taxi.'

'My partner says you're not sure whether you heard the cab driver and the woman argue or whether it was your imagination. Can you explain?'

He puzzled for a few seconds. 'Well, that's true, I was asleep when the taxi woke me up. I walked to the window and returned to bed immediately. I was still thinking about what I'd seen outside when I went back to sleep. And at that moment, you know just when you're about to fall asleep, but you're still conscious...'

I nodded.

'...well, that's when I remembered they were yelling at each other. Or were they? Maybe my imagination took over then, I don't know. When I woke up in the morning, I remembered them yelling, but I'm aware that it might have been my imagination.'

'Okay, that's still good. Anything else you can tell me?'

'Like what?'

'Was the girl injured? Was she limping?'

'Hey, look, I wish I could be more helpful, but I only looked for a few seconds. It didn't seem like a big deal, people always argue about nothing.'

'That's true. You married?'

He looked at me surprised.

I blushed. 'Oh, no, I didn't mean it that way. I thought someone else in the house might have seen something.'

He smiled and said, 'I'm not married and never have been, which is not to say I'm not interested in marrying the right person.'

I couldn't hold back a small laughter. 'I really didn't mean it *that* way.'

'Freudian slip. It's all right, I think you're quite attractive too.'

Now he did it. I knew the churning I felt in my stomach when I first saw him was definitely not hunger. Somewhere upstairs, Cupid was playing with his chemicals again.

He went on, 'Maybe you'd like to go on a private tour of my bookshop when you have the time.' He handed me over a white, crisp business card with no-nonsense Roman fonts. *David's Bookshop.* How original.

'I'd love too.'

I took the business card and slid it in the inside pocket of my jacket.

'Just give me call, and I'll close the shop just for you.'

'Are you always this charming?'

'Only when someone interesting and beautiful comes along.'

CHAPTER THREE

The police complex at 412 St Kilda Road in Melbourne houses the Homicide Squad, the Arson Squad, the Burglary Squad, the Drug Squad and the Fingerprint Branch.

The Homicide Squad is found on the ninth floor of the twenty-storey building. It deals with investigations resulting in death in connection with criminal violence or assault; accidents, including criminal negligence, vehicle, rail road, aeroplane and boat accidents; suicides; drowning; any sudden death, or death which occurred under suspicious or unusual circumstances; and all deaths during confinement in jail or in detention cells.

Without any doubt, Evelyn Carter's death had been classified as assault and murder. Her body was resting at the mortuary, waiting its turn for the necessary autopsy, which I would be forced to attend straight after lunch.

I was sitting at the end of a mahogany table designed to sit up to twelve people.

Frank was over-looking through a large bay window at an unlimited view of South Melbourne and beyond.

Behind my back was a white board with several colour markers, which were used whenever something complex had to be explained, and the spoken word wasn't the best medium to convey ideas.

A half drunk cup of coffee stood next to my yellow manilla folder. I sipped from it, filling my mouth with lukewarm, cheap-brand instant coffee.

'How long is Goosh going to be?' I said, 'I don't want to be locked in this room all day.'

'He said he'd be here in five minutes,' Frank said.

'That was five minutes ago.'

'Be patient.'

'No, Frank, I'm not going to be here all goddamn day, five more minutes and that's it.'

Just then the door of the conference room was pushed open without warning. Goosh, the Deputy Commissioner of Police, came into the room. He held a clipboard in his right hand. His lips were tight and his eyes showed no expression whatsoever. He looked like a pallbearer who'd just attended a funeral.

Goosh was against the idea of having civilians performing sworn officers duties. When I left the VFSC a few months back, he'd been relieved. After all the insults we had traded over the past three years, he surprised me by giving me a top-notch reference. My guess was that he did it in the hope that I would find a fascinating job somewhere else and would never re-consider being contracted to the VFSC.

But here I was as if I'd never left.

Goosh had a round face and small dark eyes. His suits were expensive, but because he was short and shaped like a pear, it was a waste of money as far as I could tell. He would have looked better in a dress. Today, he wore a two-piece, black, cotton-blend suit. His tie was yellow laced with pale brown stripes and his shirt plain white. While he took a seat, I realised I had never seen this man smiling and wondered if he was in fact capable of doing so.

Frank turned around and said, 'Commissioner.'

'Okay, let's get on with this,' Goosh said. He glared at me before I even opened my mouth. 'I don't make it a habit to get involved in every homicide investigation. I've called you up because I want to know what *she*,' pointing at me, 'is doing here.'

I rolled my eyes and said, '*She* has a name, sir.'

'Kristina, shut up!' Frank said.

I felt heat on my face, wondering where the hell that was coming from. I tried to say something, but no words came out.

Frank turned to Goosh: 'Trevor Mitchell wants her on the team.'

'And why is that?'

'Because she has the experience, the knowledge and the background. You know that as well as I do. We haven't had time to find someone else, and frankly I'm not sure we need someone else.'

'Right, so what does Dr Melina have to say about that?'

He turned to me.

'Dr Melina said yes,' I said.

'You said yes? But I thought you never wanted to work another homicide? Weren't you going through some kind of nervous breakdown six months ago? Aren't you on some sort of medication?'

'This case is different.'

'And how's that?'

'I knew the victim twenty years ago.'

Goosh formed an O with his mouth. He rubbed the back of his neck and passed one hand through his hair. 'So, this is a personal quest for revenge?'

'Not really, sir, I'd just want to do my job. I believe in justice. Is that so hard for you to understand?'

'But this is not your job.'

'I was offered the job, I'm taking it.'

Thirty seconds of silence followed.

Goosh turned to Frank. 'And you said Trevor Mitchell authorised this?'

'Yes, sir.'

'Why?'

'I don't make the decisions. Like I've already pointed out, Kristina is the best in the business. Her track record is impressive. Surely, I don't have to give you details.'

'Looks like I'm going to have to have a word with him. I'm sure this is all a misunderstanding. Dr Melina will be relieved from her duty ASAP. I don't see how she can be impartial to the investigation when the victim is someone she knew. If this ever goes to trial, the defence is going to have a field day pointing out Kristina's past relationship with the victim.'

I shook my head, ready to say something, but Frank threw

me darts with his eyes.

'I'm sure Trevor Mitchell had good reasons to assign Dr Melina,' Frank said. 'I certainly don't have any problems working with her.'

Goosh was scribbling god-knows-what on a white pad attached to his clipboard.

I stood there, grinding my teeth, angry at not being able to express myself. I hated being talked down to, but I hated even more the inability to say what was on my mind. This was absolutely ridiculous. I was the one in charge of the investigation, but everyone else had something to say about me. I wondered if things would have been the same had I been a man.

'And what's the name of the victim?' Goosh asked.

'Evelyn Carter,' I said, refusing to sit quietly like somebody's pet.

'Evelyn Carter?'

'Yes, sir. Did you know her?'

He shifted uncomfortably in his chair.

'Why in the world would I know an Evelyn Carter?'

'So, you didn't know her?'

'No, I didn't know her, *Dr* Melina. It seems the only person who knew her so far is you, which is why I'd like you to pack your bags and forget about the investigation. I don't think that your grounds for working on this case are legitimate.'

'Well, yes, sir, I understand you don't like me, but if we keep this meeting at a strictly professional level, maybe we won't have to get too personal.'

His face picked up colour.

Frank took over. 'So, we found the girl at the back of an alley. It looks as she's been beaten to death at this stage. We still have to confirm her identity, but a Saab registered to her name was left not far from the body.'

'Any suspects?' Goosh asked.

'A witness saw the girl arriving by cab. We're tracking down the cab company. The dispatcher was Black Taxi-cabs.'

Goosh fiddled with his silver pen. 'Okay, I don't want any of this to go to the media yet. I'd like someone else to handle the case. I'll be ringing Trevor Mitchell this afternoon to make suitable arrangements. In the meantime, let's not get Kristina too involved. Anything she handles right now might jeopardise the investigation.'

My hands were shaking. He was talking to Frank as if I wasn't in the room. I pictured myself stabbing Goosh in the eye with my pen.

'Well, sir,' Frank said. 'You do what you have to, but Trevor Mitchell seemed determined to have Dr Melina investigating this homicide. And at this stage, I'm all the way behind him. I'll continue to work with her until I hear any different from Mitchell.'

'I'll do what I can to get rid of *her*. Don't burden yourself with this problem. I'm sure you've got enough to keep you busy at the moment. You leave it to me.'

I stood from my chair and threw both hands on the table.

'You guys are a real bunch of arseholes!'

Goosh dropped his jaw, but no words came out. I thought his eyes were going to pop out of their sockets.

Frank said, 'Kristina, sit and shut up!'

I screamed louder than him, 'No, you sit and shut up, you stupid fuck! I'm not going to take any more shit from either of you! Listen to yourselves talking. It's like I'm part of the furniture. What about me? Aren't I the one who should be making the decision?'

Goosh and Frank looked at each other like a married couple trying to cope with a juvenile delinquent.

'And for your information,' I went on, 'the crime we're dealing with happens to be the handy work of a man, if witnesses are correct. So, since your guys are of the same gender as the arsehole who killed Evelyn Carter, you're really not in a position to open your mouth. You're all the same. You've only got one thing on your mind.'

Goosh raised his hands and turned to Frank. 'Do I have to listen to this? And then you're wondering why I don't want her working for us. She needs a doctor. She's clearly insane.'

I threw my pen at Goosh with all my force. The pen hit him just above the eyebrow. He brought his hands to his face, and for a spilt second I thought I got him in the eye. Too bad, I missed.

'Ah, Jesus,' Goosh whimpered.

Frank stood from his chair. 'Kristina, calm down!'

'Fuck you too,' I said.

I grabbed my notes and headed for the exit.

Just as I slammed the door behind me, I heard Goosh scream, 'I want her out of the building now! Get rid of that woman. She's more dangerous than the killers she's chasing.'

I stood in front of the mirror of the women's lavatory on the ninth floor of the complex. I wasn't crying. I was just so damn angry that I needed to gather myself before I hit someone else. I've never felt so much rage coming out all at once. The fact that the victim of the crime I was investigating happened to be someone I knew long time ago didn't help. Maybe that was the real reason why I lost my self-control in the conference room.

I turned on the cold water and splashed my face.

And then I began laughing out loud. I tried to imagine what happened after I left the room. Goosh had probably screamed at Frank, telling him how incompetent I was, explaining how women had no respect for men nowadays.

I laughed myself silly even more as I pictured someone walking in the wash room and seeing me laugh like a lunatic.

Tears came rolling down my cheeks.

Tears of joy and pain.

And grief.

God had to have a sense of humour, I thought, because from up there, this must have been the best show on the planet.

I dried my hands with a paper towel and headed for the door.

Half an hour later I was back in the conference room. This time it was only Frank and me.

'You shouldn't have spoken to him that way,' he said, fidgeting with his fingers.

'And why not? Did you see the way he talked about me?'

'Yes, but you know what he's like.'

'What he's like? What about you? How dare you tell me to shut up in front of someone else, especially Goosh? What's the matter with you? We're supposed to be partners. I thought you respected me. I never treat you like shit in front of other people.'

'You called me a stupid fuck.'

'That's because you deserved it.'

'I was just trying to smooth things out. I knew how you were going to react.'

'How I was going to react? So, it's okay for Goosh to be himself, to insult me in front of you, but it's not okay for me to be myself? I have to be nice and docile. Listen to yourself. You're as pathetic as he is.'

There was a defeated look on his face. His eyes were sagging, and he reminded me of a cocker spaniel.

'Kristina, you know I care about you. I'm the one who called you to be on the investigation. If I didn't care about you, you wouldn't be here.'

'You only want to get into my pants. You know it and I know it. So, don't try to make it sound like you're the nice guy.'

He shrugged. 'Is it so wrong that I want to be with you?'

'Frank, I don't give a damn. I just want to get on with our work. You're not my type, I would never, never sleep with you. You might as well get that inside your thick skull.'

What a bitch!

For the next thirty seconds he stared at an empty spot in space.

'Okay,' he finally said. 'I'm ugly, bald, chauvinist and a pain in the arse. I can take it, I've lived with it all my life.'

'Frank—'

'Yeah, yeah, that's what you want to hear. Okay, so, I'll admit. I don't like myself. I hate what I see when I wake up every morning. I hate being single. I hate going bald. I don't like the way I dress, the way I try to save money on everything, the way I repulse women. I want to be loved, I want someone I can take care of, someone who loves me in return. But I might as well face the fact that I was destined to be unloved for the rest of my life. On one side you have the beautiful people, you, and then you have the rest, me. There's a line which cannot be crossed, and I'm stuck behind it. I can face it, Kristina, you're physically superior to me. I'm a specimen below you're minimum standard, and for that I can only blame myself.'

I hadn't expected such self-depreciating verbal diarrhoea.

'Frank, I'm not going to hold your hand and say how sorry I am. Your looks don't have much to do with why you're single.'

'I know, it's my personality.'

Here we go. The maturity of some grown men really astounded me. I felt like I was talking to a five-year-old kid. The man sitting across me was forty-six years old and begged to be pitied. What he needed a good kick up the backside to set him back on track.

'Frank, I'm really angry at the moment. I'm angry at Goosh, and I'm angry at you for making such a dick of yourself. Can we just leave it for another time and get on with what we're supposed to be doing?'

He hesitated for a few seconds and said, 'Sure.'

He lowered his eyes as if he'd just received a blow on the side of the head.

I did my best to ignore his martyred mentality by spreading the contents of my crime scene material on the desk.

'Okay,' I said, 'We've got one suspect so far. The girl is so black and blue, I reckon it was someone who knew her.'

'How's that?'

'If someone wanted her dead, he would have just killed her. She was savagely beaten. This wasn't just a straight murder. You ask yourself, why would someone beat another person so badly?'

'Punishment?' He shuffled through the photographs on the desk.

'Maybe. Maybe even anger, and then you ask yourself why.'

'She didn't do what she was supposed to.'

'Okay, so she's a prostitute, and someone paid her to do a sexual act of one sort or another. Either she refuses, or she takes the money and refuses to do what she's been asked. The guy gets angry and beats her to a pulp.'

'You think that's what happened?' Frank asked.

'Common scenario. So far it's only speculation, but given her work as a prostitute, it's a very likely sequence of events.'

'What's the plan?'

'I have to attend the autopsy this afternoon. If you can track down the cab driver who dropped her off this morning, that would be helpful. Next I'll be going around to her place and see if I can find anything. Talk to her neighbours, see if she has any relatives she visited recently. We can only take it one step at the time.'

'What about Goosh?'

'I wouldn't worry about him right now. Let's try to get as much done as we can while I've got a green light.'

'Good idea.'

We both scribbled details in our log books.

'Have you arranged for the Saab to be tested for trace evidence?' I asked.

'It's at the Centre this very minute.'

'How long will it take for the car to be processed?'

'You know it's a big job. If I can get someone on it immediately, maybe a couple of days.'

I locked my eyes into his. 'That long?'

'It's not just a matter of recovering evidence. The car has to be tested for fingerprints, and forensic evidence analysed. Don't forget there are other cases running as well.'

We resumed our notes and closed our log books.

'I'm heading back home to get ready for this afternoon,' I said.

'Okay. I'll see you at the mortuary.'

I was just about to leave the room when he said, 'Kristina?'

'What?'

'I'm sorry.'

CHAPTER FOUR

I arrived home at 1.32 p.m., aware that I only had just under a couple of hours to burn before being present at the Victorian Institute of Forensic Medicine (VIFM) in Southbank, home of the mortuary.

I got to Craigieburn via the West Ring Road, exited at Tullamarine Freeway, took the next exit at Mickleham Road, turned right at the next traffic light, and drove all the way down Craigieburn West Road. I lived on the edge of suburbia and vast empty spaces of rural land where cattle and sheep spent the day just existing. Why couldn't human beings behave in the same manner? It was a wicked world, and at the age of forty, I still hadn't figured half of it out.

As I unlocked the front door of my three-bedroom brick veneer home, I wondered how my fourteen-year-old son Michael was going. The previous year, he had been involved in one of my investigations. A violent incident had left him emotionally disturbed. Since that day, we hadn't been able to communicate openly. I missed the bond we shared prior to the incident. It was hard enough watching him become introverted, aware of all the confusion he was experiencing as a teenager, but seeing us gradually growing apart made me feel like the worst mother in the world. Being both the mother and father in his life hadn't been easy. I single-handedly brought him up from birth, and yet felt that I had spent too much time focusing on my career. When I was contracted full-time with the VFSC and the CIB, he often complained about the little time we spent together. His lament had been the main reason why I decided to work as a private investigator. Having my business based from home would ensure that I would be around him so often that he'd probably tire of me rather than complain that I wasn't there.

I made a light lunch of fibre-enriched cracker bread and low-fat cheese. I washed it down with a glass of bottled water. Dr Pepper was out of my diet. I drank too much of the stuff for too long, and although it tasted god-sent, all that caffeine and sugar couldn't have been all that good for me. After my last homicidal investigation, my butt had blown into one the size of a brontosaurus's, no thanks to a diet of soft drinks, chocolates and treats from the Cheesecake's Shop. I was determined to get back into shape and joining the gym in the next few days.

After lunch I sneaked into Michael's room to snoop around as I often did. Unlike his other bedroom when we lived in St Kilda, this one was neat and tidy. The usual single bed, study desk and computer were there, like in every fourteen-year-old's bedroom. Apart from an X-Files calendar pinned above his desk, the walls were bare of posters or decorations usually associated with teenagers. I knew he was going through a phase, but it wasn't the phase I had seen with other kids. Michael was quiet and withdrawn when he used to be loud and self-opinionated.

Sitting on his bed, I tried to figure out what was going on in his head. I concluded that I needed to talk to him if I didn't want our relationship to deteriorate to a point of no-return. At least, whatever the outcomes, I would live with the knowledge that I had tried to improve the situation.

After a few minutes, I left his room and headed for the bathroom. Finally I indulged in a hot shower I never had the chance to enjoy that morning. The steaming water on my scalp soothed my nerves. Evelyn Carter came to mind, and suddenly I dreaded ever more having to attend her autopsy. In my life, friends and dead people had never been associated together, not as a single package anyway. Evelyn had been an important part of my childhood, and seeing her with her vital organs inside out on a dissecting table wasn't my idea of reminiscing with an old friend.

Then I thought about David Boyd from the bookshop. An

image of his face and his friendly smile appeared before me. He was damn attractive, I finally admitted, though I had tried so hard to deny the churning emotion I felt when I first saw him. This man standing in the middle of all this books was so sexy, and I bet he didn't even know it. A well-toned body never failed to turn me on, but a great mind was fascinating and alluring, and kept me interested in its owner long after the sex was over. And someone with such intense interest in books had to possess a great mind. No doubt. My idea of a perfect partner. But I had only ended a relationship six months ago and wasn't sure if I wanted to get into another one. The only reason I dumped my ex-boyfriend was because of my reluctance to commit to any one person in particular.

As I stepped out of the shower and dried myself with a large, white bath towel, I wondered if I should be making a move on David, or wait for him to get in touch with me. Or maybe better wait until the investigation was over. After all, he was a witness in the Evelyn Carter murder, and I didn't want to stuff up the way Frank stuffed up eighteen months ago when he got involved with the wife of a murdered victim.

I dressed in the usual white blouse, marine skirt and matching jacket. Even though I had shampooed my shoulder-length, brown hair, it was still a mess. It took me ten minutes to figure out what I was going to do with it. Finally, I settled for tying it up into a mini ponytail, something I seldom did during working hours.

I stared at my green eyes in the full-length mirror, still getting used to the idea that I turned forty years old two months ago. It wasn't something I cherished, but a truth I tried to accept like everything else in life—a little surprise which crept in without warning. I feared growing older without anyone by my side. Commitment frightened me, but loneliness was more terrifying. After being independent for so long, I figured a woman didn't need a man to be happy and successful. But I also realised that one day I wouldn't be as busy as I am now. Companionship would become an essential part of my life. I had seen too many old people living by themselves and suffering from acute loneliness. And that wasn't my idea of a happy retirement. Michael wouldn't be with me forever. I would have to decide sooner or later to commit to the one man—the later, the more challenging it would be to find the right person. How would I adjust to his every faults and habits without driving myself insane? Trusting someone with your life seemed to take so long., and time wasn't something I currently possessed in abundance.

I applied a light foundation and make-up. Without a doubt, plainness was the safest way to go when interacting with male co-workers.

At 2.34 p.m., I locked the door of my home and headed back towards Melbourne.

Dr Charles W. Main was the Director of the Victorian Institute of Forensic Medicine.

The VIFM was a body corporate with perpetual succession which was established by the Coroners Act 1985 in the State of Victoria. The Institute was based at the Coronial Services Centre in Melbourne, a purpose-built facility in Kavanagh Street, Southbank. Its principle function was to provide timely, high quality and high value forensic medicine and related services, including teaching and research.

The VIFM was also the statutory body in charge of Forensic Pathology, Clinical Forensic Medicine, Forensic Toxicology and other forensic scientific services in the state. In addition, the blue-grey building housed the mortuary, where over 3000 autopsies were performed each year for legal or medical reasons or both.

Dr Main's office was located up on the first floor of the building, and down the end of a long corridor. Before an autopsy began, I usually met with him to discuss anything relating to the case.

Dr Main's office was three-by-three metres, cramped with a green, four-draw filing taxi-cabinet at one end and an outdated 486DX computer taking most of his desk. There was a degree from The University of Melbourne and various awards and certificates of merit hanging on the wall behind the desk.

I had already announced my arrival at the reception desk downstairs, and when I entered Dr Main's office, he smiled as if he had been expecting me.

'I'm glad to see you,' he said, passing one hand over his salt-and-pepper hair.

I admired his straight nose and fine creases under his eyes.

31

He was very handsome, but the idea of sleeping with someone who cut up dead bodies for a living didn't appeal to me.

He went on, 'I thought you no longer worked for the police?'

'I'm not officially,' I said, taking a seat behind his desk.

'So?'

'I knew the victim from a while back. I have a personal attachment to this case. Some people are not happy about my decision, but at the end of the day it's still my decision.'

'Understood.' He paused for effect. ' I'll be performing the autopsy in half an hour. You think you can cope with it this time?'

The last time I attended an autopsy, I walked out halfway through the procedure. Under the law, I was required to attend the autopsy, but Dr Main managed to discreetly bend the rules whenever he felt it appropriate.

'I can only try.'

'I'll have the autopsy videotaped this time, just in case you decide you can't stomach two hours in a row.' He puzzled for a few seconds and added, 'From what I've heard so far, she's in a pretty shocking condition. I haven't seen the body myself, but I understand it's going to be hell to work with.'

'Bruised and cut everywhere. I almost didn't recognise her.'

He shook his head. 'It always amazes me what people do to one another. No matter how many years I've been working in this field, the amount of cruelty humans are capable of is unbelievable.'

He didn't have to tell me that. I'd seen so much evil in my career, nothing surprised me. Any person was a potential killer, given the right circumstances. What was someone supposed to do when faced with the killer of his loved ones? I had no idea how I would react. I knew for sure that I couldn't just sit there and take it.

'Evelyn Carter was working as a prostitute,' I said. 'It's likely the killer was one of her clients.'

'Ah,' he said, as if this explained everything. 'Well, in that case I guess there won't be that much of an investigation.'

I wasn't sure what he meant. 'Why is that?'

'A prostitute. It goes with the job. These women know the risk they're taking when they walk the street. I mean, really, you can't be surprised by what's happening to them. It's almost like they're asking for it.'

'Asking for what?'

'You know, what's happening to them.'

I couldn't believe what I was hearing. 'Are you telling me Evelyn Carter deserved to die the way she did because she was working as a prostitute?'

At the tone of my voice, he started to lose his confidence. 'No, that's not what I'm saying. What I'm saying is that if you're going to work in that field, you should expect that such things can happen. You know, you become a high-risk factor. I mean that's just common sense. You get more prostitutes killed on average than your common housewife.'

'So what you're saying is that if I'm a prostitute, I should presume I will be beaten and killed, like it's part of my job?'

'Yeah, that's what I'm saying, but not so much in the way you're putting it.'

'So, it's Evelyn Carter's fault that she got killed?'

'Well, not directly, but in a way. I mean, if she wasn't doing what she was doing, it might have never happened in the first place. I mean, you know, what did she expect? It wasn't a desk job. Her customers already had a twisted sense of morality to be using her services in the first place. We're not talking about Catholic boys straight our of communion. They were grown men who were already sexually frustrated, otherwise they wouldn't be paying for it. Surely, she must have been aware of the risks when she decided to work in that field.'

I felt anger creeping all over my body.

'Dr Main, Evelyn Carter was a victim. The person who killed her is the criminal. Why is it that you men think a woman working as a prostitute has somehow contributed to her death? When did she stop becoming a woman and turned into a punching bag? Why is it that when a women decides to provide sex as a service, she suddenly becomes less than human? It's okay to beat her up, it's okay to insult her, call her a slut and everything else one desires. It's okay to kill and dispose of her when the service is not up to scratch—'

'You're losing the plot.'

'I'm losing the plot? When was the last time you beat your dentist to death because he didn't fix that toothache properly?'

'A dentist is not a prostitute.'

'But a dentist is a human being. So is a prostitute. And no woman should have to fear for her life when she's trying to make a living, no matter what her profession is. So, this case is not about whether she deserved it or not. No one deserves to be beaten to death. This case is about finding the bastard who did that to her, and that's that.'

I was completely worked up by now. Perspiration dripped down the small of my back. This was the most absurd thing I had ever heard, and the worst was that I knew Dr Main wasn't the only man who felt that way about sex workers.

'Fine,' he said, 'it doesn't matter anyway, what I think makes no difference. I'm going to do my job just as if she was any other victim. There won't be any corners cut.'

I shook my head in disbelief.

I stood from the chair and slammed my hands on his desk.

'She is *any other* victim.'

I met Frank at the VIFM canteen. We were sitting across one another at a table, drinking coffee and eating chocolate mud cake. I should have known better with those extra kilos I was carrying around, but chocolate was one of my many weaknesses.

'What's wrong with you,' he said, obviously realising I was in a foul mood.

'Ask your male friend, Dr Main.'

'What?'

'That sonofabitch tells me that Evelyn Carter deserves to have been beaten to death because she was working as a prostitute. Can you believe that?'

'I'm sure he didn't mean it that way. He probably felt she contributed to her death by working as a prostitute. I mean, there are statistics to support his point. Other than working as a prostitute, it's well known that if you're a woman who lives alone, on low-income, unemployed, if you live in dormitories, halfway houses, boarding homes or apartments with a large number of units, you're more likely to be a victim of rape and murder. There is evidence to support these figures. I think that's where Dr Main was coming from. You open any text on criminology, and you'll have to agree that what he said is a valid point.'

I gave him a deadly glare.

He continued, 'What? What did I say? You're going to dispute statistics as well now?'

'I'm not disputing the statistics, Frank. I just don't think numbers should be used as an excuse to put the blame on the victims. We turn around and say that because single white female prostitutes have a higher risk of been raped, then they should share in the responsibility of the rapist. That is absolutely absurd. No wonder our legal system is chaotic. White collar criminals get harsher prison terms than rapists and killers. How did we ever get to the point of devaluing human lives just to save a few dollars?'

Frank took a sip of coffee. 'You're a woman. And on top of that Evelyn Carter was your friend. Of course you're going to react that way.'

'And what way is that?'

'You know, all irrational and self-serving your gender.'

My mind was numb. I didn't have the time, nor the energy to argue with people who had detached themselves from their own emotional rationality at the expense of so-called common sense.

'I don't mean to insult you,' he said, 'but—'

'Just leave me alone,' I retorted, and stormed out of the lunch room

CHAPTER FIVE

The autopsy room consisted of a blue-green freshly washed concrete floor, a galvanised table with holes to allow water and fluids to drains, a small-parts dissection table with drains, a vertical mechanical scale to weigh each organ, and a tank for delivering water to the table and collecting fluids. The ceiling was white with various pipes criss-crossing like spider webs. Yellow plastic bio-hazard containers were scattered in various parts of the room.

Air conditioning hummed from the ceiling.

A sign told me to refrain from smoking, eating or drinking.

Next to the dissecting table was Dr Main's post-mortem instruments—dissecting and brain knifes, scissors, saws of various sizes, a skull key, forceps, scalpels and chisels.

I changed into protective clothing—blue, hospital pyjamas look-alike; green, surgical gloves; giant, white, rubber boots; and white disposable plastic aprons.

A mortuary technician rolled in a galvanised mobile cart with the bruised-up body of Evelyn Carter.

Dr Main followed five seconds later.

Frank and a police photographer moved into the autopsy room from a small viewing room attached to the east wall.

The mortuary technician set up a video camera and checked the focus and the cleanness of the lens. He played with the start and stop buttons to ensure everything was in working order.

At the same time, Dr Main arranged his post-mortem

instruments. He looked slightly uncomfortable as he handled his tools, while occasionally glancing towards me without saying a word.

I didn't feel all that at ease. It certainly occurred to me that this was his territory, and attacking someone on their own turf wasn't an enjoyable or comfortable experience. I felt like a stranger in a place reserved for club members.

'Would you like to move in closer?' Dr Main finally said, more from the need to break the ice than his concern for me, I gathered. 'You'll be able to see better.'

'Sure.'

I walked up the galvanised cart, observing the body whose face was almost beyond recognition.

'Since we're taping this,' Dr Main added, 'save any questions you have for when the autopsy is over.'

I nodded.

Dr Main addressed the mortuary technician: 'Ready?'

'When you are.'

'Three, two, one... roll.'

The technician began recording, the lens focused on the battered body.

The first thing Dr Main did was to examine the body step-by-step without touching it or removing anything attached to it. He took photographs of the entire corpse. Because it was badly bruised, Dr Main took a good twenty minutes to cover every inch. The mortuary technician helped him to turn the body over. The buttocks of Evelyn Carter were so badly bruised and bloody, they had lost their shape.

'Subject is a thirty-nine year old woman identified as Evelyn Maree Carter. Black hair, green eyes and fair complexion.' With the help of the technician, he proceeded with the weighting and measuring of the body. 'Subject weights sixty-eight kilos and is one-hundred-and-seventy-five centimetres tall. 'It is my belief at this early stage that the subject has been battered to death. Bruising has intensified and spread after her death. Time of death is estimated at about twelve hours ago.'

I looked on as Dr Main continued to make careful observations. Somehow I had managed to distance myself from the fact that this bruised mass of flesh lying on the galvanised cart was someone I knew. Maybe it was because she was in such an unrecognisable state that I could distance myself. If her injuries had been superficial, but resulting in death nonetheless, I probably wouldn't have been able to sit through the procedure.

Dr Main went on, 'Subject's abdomen is distended and pulpy, suggesting extensive internal damage.'

I noticed that her arms and legs were covered in huge purple bruises.

'Because the subject has been badly bruised and battered,' he explained, 'I am going to proceed with radiology to determine the presence of any bone fragments in the skull. The full autopsy will then be resumed.'

He made a hand signal to the technician to switch the camera off.

'Take five,' he said to me. 'We're going to conduct x-rays now. Give us fifteen minutes.'

'Sure,' I said, feeling like taking a break anyway, 'but why can't we do them once the autopsy is finished?'

'Too much risk of disturbing foreign bodies and fractures once the cutting of the body has begun. You know as well as I do that radiography serves as an excellent permanent record of any injuries. Often x-rays are more acceptable in court than photographs.'

'Aren't you worried about a break in continuity with the actual autopsy.'

'I make the decision to proceed with radiology according to the circumstances and issues of the particular case—this can be done before, during or after the autopsy. I wouldn't be too concerned, Dr Melina, she's in good hands. You'll have a solid forensic post-mortem report by the time I'm finished.'

I left the autopsy room and joined Frank and the police photographer in the viewing room. I told them what was happening, and we agreed to go for a coffee at the staff canteen.

We walked down the corridor on our way to the canteen

Frank said, 'I never got a chance to tell you before, but I've managed to track down the cab company which owned the taxi-cab Evelyn Carter took last night.'

'And?'

'A company called Sammy Taxis. Yes, they do have records

of who's been driving what cab on any particular day, but accurate records could only have been kept if Evelyn Carter rang for her cab. If she hailed the cab, there'd be no record whatsoever. We'd have to interrogate everyone who drove the graveyard shift on that particular day. And you're looking at around seventy drivers, give or take five each way. Shifts are from 5.00 p.m. to 5.00 a.m. the following day.'

I certainly wasn't looking forward to interrogate so many cab drivers, given most of them would probably have problems recalling every single trip they've made And if I did get the chance to talk to the driver who drove Evelyn Carter that night, there'd be no way of knowing if he's lying. If the driver was in fact the killer, he'd have no interest in helping us. If he wasn't, he'd probably wouldn't want any trouble by being associated with the murder.

'Couldn't we search all the cabs when the day shift is over today?' I asked as we reached the entrance of the staff canteen.

'It's a possibility. But you might piss off the owners. Without a warrant, they might be unwilling to cooperate.'

'It's worth a try.'

'I'll give them a call.'

We ordered coffees, and fifteen minutes later we were back in the autopsy room.

Before beginning the Y-incision, Dr Main ran past me a few items which came up on radio-graphs. He was careful not to get his fingerprints all over the four large, bluish negatives.

He held the x-rays up to the light and explained: 'Her ribs are broken on both sides. Most of her front teeth have been punched out. The roots of several incisors are sticking out through her gums. She's been punched in the face quiet a few times.' He supported his comments by pointing at the appropriate section on the x-ray. 'Her jaw and frontal bones of the skull are fractured. My guess is her head has been savagely banged against something solid, most likely a brick wall.' His index finger indicated at vault fractures on the upper and frontal section of Evelyn's cranium. 'As you can see there is also extensive facial fractures. That's why I wanted to do the radiology immediately. Doing the autopsy first might have caused disfigurement, and then it would have been hell to get good x-rays.'

I nodded, unable to really comment one way or another. Some bastard had butchered to my best friend from school. Even though I tried to distance myself from the fact I knew the victim personally, my emotions kept pulling me back to the reality. I felt heat at the back of my neck while staring at the radio-graphs. Unwillingly, I imagined the pain and agony Evelyn must have gone through. I wished I'd been there to save her from the butcher who had attacked her. It was so hard not to be angry at every man when involved in horrendous homicidal investigations involving female victims. Ninety-five percent of all violent crimes were committed by men—a fact in itself was basis enough to justify my anger.

Dr Main must have noticed anxiety crossing my face because he said, 'Are you okay?'

'Yeah, I'm fine.'

'If you don't want to stay for the rest of the autopsy, I'd understand.'

He was surprisingly friendly for someone I had argued with less than an hour ago about the rights of prostitutes.

'I have to go through this, even if it's just for the sake of it. It will help me to come to terms with my grief.'

'Sure,' he said and shrugged.

This was the first time I admitted to someone else and to myself I was inevitably going through a grieving process. It didn't matter if I hadn't seen Evelyn for twenty years—the pain was just the same.

Once the video camera started rolling again, Dr Main carefully examined the body for any foreign material, such as blood, skin, clothing fibres, or any trace evidence which may lead to the identity of the killer.

Each sample was bagged and labelled with the case number, the item number, date and a brief description.

He then proceeded with examination of the hands and fingernails. He commented at the same time for the benefit of the video recording:

'Scrapping from under the fingernails indicate presence of grass and particles of earth and clay.' He was puzzling at something else he removed from under the fingernails. 'Unidentified black sticky tissue recovered from nails. Organic in nature at first glance, but cannot tell whether it's animal or vegetable.'

He bagged and labelled the samples of the foreign substance.

I wondered if it could have been flesh taken from the attacker when the victim tried to fight back. Hopefully the killer would have fingernail marks across his face.

Once Dr Main had completed external gathering of trace evidence, he proceeded with the Y-incision, which consisted of a cut made with a surgeon knife across the chest from shoulder to shoulder, crossing down over the breasts, then from the lower tip of the sternum, down the entire length of the abdomen to the pubis. He then cut the ribcage and cartilage to expose the heart and lungs. With a large needle, he withdrew a sample of blood from the heart after opening the pericardial sac to determine Evelyn Carter's blood type.

He removed the heart, lungs, oesophagus and trachea *en bloc*, then proceeded with the weighing of each organ before making a careful examination of their surfaces. This was followed by slicing every organ into sections to evaluate the internal structures. Meanwhile, the mortuary technician prepared microscopic slides of tissues from the organs for examination of cellular change, while I could feel my black coffee churning in my stomach.

Dr Main commented while examining the internal organs: 'The subject has sustained a ruptured liver, ruptured spleen, tearing of the bowels in six places and fractures of six ribs. She been kicked severely, which has caused a broken rib to make a deep puncture wound into her left lung.'

He paused for a few seconds, contemplating the damage done to the body.

He then proceeded by examination of the pelvis, including examination of the genital area for evidence of injury or foreign matter. Part of the process was to take vaginal and anal swabs for seminal residues. This would not only confirm the victim had had sex, whether from rape or common intercourse, but also might help to identify the killer at a later stage through DNA typing and comparison. DNA typing is very specific for every individual, so much so, the chances of two people having the same DNA is about one to a million. Given there are not one million suspects in a homicidal investigation, it was usually a pretty straight-forward process to eliminate suspects and matching a DNA grouping to the killer's own. And since the law in Victoria had recently been changed in favour of the police, forcing suspects to provide blood samples for DNA comparison if requested in the course of an investigation, the process was a bliss.

Dr Main removed semen from Evelyn Carter's vagina— immediate microscopic examination by the technician confirmed the sample to be fresh. DNA testing and blood grouping would be performed within the next twenty-four hours.

After Dr Main finished the autopsy by sewing back the body, he, Frank and I adjoined to the homicide room in the same building for a briefing.

We sat around a plastic table, pads and pens ready to take notes.

Frank addressed himself to Dr Main: 'So what do you conclude she died of?'

Dr Main flicked through his notes and said, 'God, this is really a chance guess at this stage. Given the injuries found on her body, any of major traumas could have been the fatal one. Also because all her vital organs were damaged within a relatively short time frame of one another, it's impossible to plot a course of progressive damage.'

'But her death has to be certified. So, what will it be?'

'I'll put down the cause of death was from multiple injuries. Having received so many blows in such a small amount of time, I'd say her heart just gave out.'

Frank and I both scribbled into our pads.

'What about the semen found in the vagina?' I asked.

'Given she was a prostitute,' Dr Main said, 'it could have easily been one of her clients.'

I puzzled for a few seconds and said, 'But prostitutes are not in the habit of having unprotected sex. Am I right?'

'Good point,' Frank said.

'So,' I went on, my mind racing, 'assuming the semen isn't something left from one of her jobs, then it leaves only two reasonable explanations: either she had consensual sex with someone before she got killed, or she was raped in the process of been killed. Given the state we found her in, I'm somehow inclined to believe in the second scenario.'

'But, isn't it possible she simply had consensual sex with her boyfriend, and her death is totally unrelated to the semen found in her vagina?' Frank asked.

'Possible, but most unlikely. The timing just seems too close. If she was working, don't you find it a bit coincidental she happens to have engaged in sexual intercourse with her boyfriend, assuming she's got one, just before going to work. And in addition, why would she have had sex without protection, even if it was her boyfriend?'

'You just said before she might have had consensual sex with someone before she got killed—well, who are we talking about if not her boyfriend or one of her clients?'

We both turned to Dr Main.

'Hey, don't look at me,' he said, 'you're running this investigation.'

'Okay, let's leave it for the time being,' Frank said.

'How long will it take for the autopsy report to be completed?' I asked Dr Main.

'I can have it finished within forty-eight hours. Toxicology tests might take a little longer.'

'How much longer?'

'Four days at the most.'

I made a note of the dates in my log book and gathered papers and photos I had with me in a manilla folder. Four days was good. I had waited weeks for toxicology results in the past, wasting precious time on investigative leads which proved to be futile by the time the toxicology tests were in my hands.

There was still a lot of work to be done, and for reasons I knew too well, I wasn't looking forward to it. Maybe Goosh had been right when he said this case was too personal for me to get involved with.

And with Goosh in mind, I suddenly realised I had yet to hear from Trevor Mitchell.

Maybe I had already been pulled out of the investigation, and I didn't even know it.

CHAPTER SIX

'**Y**ou wanna search all the cabs?' John Thomas asked, the flesh from his face loosened with surprise.'

John Thomas was the managing director of Sammy Taxis. He was unhappy at the prospect of having his entire fleet of taxi-cabs searched for trace evidence, right here, right now, during the shift transfer. Frank had decided to come with me. We figured with the two of us there, we'd have more pulling power. It would also take us less time to thoroughly inspect every single cab.

It was just on 4.37 p.m., and a couple of cabs had already returned to the depot.

The depot was located in an industrial area occupied by small-to-medium factories, workshops and warehouses. It was a large block of land covered in dirt and pebbles. At the far back, where we were talking to John Thomas, was the general office and a large shed used as a mechanical workshop.

I noticed at least three mechanics dressed in greasy, blue overalls on duty. Whatever needed repairing with the taxi-cabs was obviously being fixed on the spot by the in-house mechanics. This place was a money-printing industry. I could almost smell the dough.

'I know this is inconvenient,' I said to John Thomas, 'but a woman's dead, and we have information which indicates she was last seen in one of your cabs.'

Frank was standing next to me, his Victoria Police badge prominently displayed on the breast-pocket of his jacket. He cut an impressive figure, his notebook open in one hand and his pen in the other, ready to take down anything of importance John might throw at us. I noticed the bulge of his Smith & Weston under his jacket.

The sky was overcast, and I smelled rain in the distance. I prayed to God to hold on to the downpour for a little while longer. A southern wind was cutting through my jacket and chilled me to the bone. I wished we were having this discussion in John's office, where he probably lodged a small electric heater at his feet, under his desk.

John shifted from one foot to the other. He was in his early fifties and wore a pair of dirty, grey tracksuit pants with a five-dollar, green flannel shirt. Not exactly what I would describe as a walking fashion statement. His salt-and-pepper hair was thinning on top, revealing a serious case of dandruff. His complexion was pink as bacon rashes, and I wouldn't have surprised if he'd had some booze hidden somewhere in his office.

'Jeez, look, no can do,' he said. 'You wanna search my cabs, you gonna have to come back later.'

'Mr Thomas, I don't want to make the situation more difficult than it already is. We only need a few minutes per vehicle. At this stage we're looking for the obvious.'

He shook his head vigorously.

'Fine. We'll get a search warrant and have your entire fleet taken to the Forensic Centre tomorrow. And don't expect to get them back for at least two weeks.'

'Bullshit! You can't do that.'

'Watch me.'

John rubbed his triple chin, obviously contemplating the disastrous situation of having his entire fleet off the road.

'The drivers are gonna get pissed with this,' he finally said.

'No more pissed than if their wheels are off the road for two weeks,' I said, 'not to mention the effect this is going to have on your business. I don't think you're in a position to be uncooperative, Mr Thomas.'

He glanced over my shoulder and said, 'I tell you what—when the cabs return from their day shift, they line up here...' He pointed at the petrol pump behind my back, '...and refill for the next driver. All cabs have to be in by five. It can take two to ten minutes for a car to move through the rank. Gets busier as we're closing in on the zero hour. Everyone is trying to make an extra buck at the last minute. Is ten minutes enough time to find what you're looking for?'

I glanced at Frank who shrugged in response.

'Okay,' I said. 'Ten to twenty minutes per car should do.'

Frank and I both knew perfectly well this was completely inadequate. But I wasn't going to stand here and argue with him when rain was just about to come down on us like an avalanche.

'Jeez, ten minutes, it's all I can spare per car,' John insisted.

'Ten minutes,' I lied.

Searching a car sometimes took up to four hours. We'll have to skip the vacuum sweeping and other invisible trace evidence.

'You gotta deal,' John said. 'You can stand next to the pump and tell the drivers what's going on. And don't give'em the shits. They work day shift. Nothing to do with the night shift.'

'And when do we get to see the night-shift drivers?'

'Most of them hang around the canteen or just out here,' he pointed to a spot not far from the petrol pump. 'After the day-shift drivers fill up their tanks, they park their car in the lot. If the night-shift driver happens to be hangin' around, he usually jumps in the car straight away without waiting for the car to be parked.'

A three-ring circus, I thought.

Frank scribbled details down in his notebook.

'And please, don't piss anyone off,' John continued. 'I'm the one who has to deal with these people on a daily basis. We like to keep a happy atmosphere. Once a cab driver, always a cab driver. I don't care whether you're unemployed or a doctor, once you've driven a cab, you'll always come back to drive one at some stage in your life. There's always going to be a moment when you're going to need the extra cash.'

Deep and philosophical.

'Thank you, Mr Thomas,' I said, 'we'll be as diligent and polite as it is humanly possible.'

He twisted his mouth in a smile which looked more like a cringe. 'Yeah, right, whatever. Any problems, I'm in the office at the back.'

He was about to walk off when I called out, 'Mr Thomas?'

'Yeah?'

'I'll need a print-out of all the drivers who were on the road last night.'

He looked at me blankly for a few seconds and said, 'Jeez, all right, I'll see what I can do.'

John Thomas disappeared back into his plywood construction, shaking his head as if Frank and I were a couple of kids who were planning a prank, and there was nothing he could do about it.

Frank waited by the petrol pump while I returned to the Ford to get the PERK. I had no idea what we'd be looking for. I hoped to God Evelyn Carter had left a lipstick behind or something with her fingerprints on it. The tiniest evidence could lead us in the right direction.

When I returned back to the petrol pump, two taxi-cabs were already lined up, one with the petrol nozzle hanging from the side. The drivers, one Asian and one Anglo-Saxon looking, were talking to Frank. Both men were dressed in blue shirts with Black Taxi-cabs insignia.

I approached the group, checking my ID was properly clipped to my breast pocket.

'So you guys enjoy this kind of work?' Frank asked.

The Anglo-Saxon, a man in his early twenties, answered first, 'Yeah, like I really like the excitement. You know, you never know what's going to happen next.'

Like you get stabbed in the back for a lousy ten dollars, I thought.

The young man went on, 'You get to meet so many interesting people. I mean, when I first started driving, I didn't realise it was going to be so much fun.' He elbowed the Asian man. 'Isn't it right? It's adrelin-pumping shit, isn't it?'

The Asian man rolled his eyes. 'The excitement kind of wears itself out after a couple of years.'

The young man swallowed, clearly disappointed that the fun wouldn't last forever.

'How did she die?' the Asian man asked.

Frank shot me a look, a kind of SOS., and then turned his attention back to the cab drivers: 'We're not at liberty to

47

discuss the case. All we're doing at this stage is establishing links. We know she was driving in a cab last night, and we're going to be looking through every single one of them.'

The chit-chat was getting on my nerves. A drop of rain hit me on the cheek.

'Step aside,' I ordered the two cab drivers. 'I know you're curious, but we don't have much time. Don't go to far. We might need to ask you a few questions.'

The Anglo-Saxon driver looked at me from head to toes, but I wasn't sure what the look meant. Either *who the hell does she think she is?* or *wouldn't mind fucking that one!* I choose to ignore him either way.

When doing a vehicle search, we divide the vehicle into five specific sections. This method ensures proper coverage of every inch of the car. Just like grid search, the vehicle is boxed and divided into nearside-front, offside-front, nearside-rear, offside-rear and boot. The offside is the driver's side of the vehicle.

I began searching the nearside-front and nearside-rear of the vehicle. Patiently, I collected trace evidence, such as hair, fibres and foreign objects, which were almost invisible to the naked eye. I also collected large and obvious physical evidence. In no time, I had several bags filled with empty cans, cigarettes buts, coins, chewing-gum wrappers, sand, matchboxes, magazines, a couple of trashy paperback novels, hair pins, an empty condom wrapper, and even a smelly pair of trainers. The driver of the cab, from which I recovered the shoes, was as surprised as I was; the shoes weren't his, and he'd never seen them before. Me, I couldn't understand how he actually managed to breathe in the cab with the foul smell of the trainers filling his lungs every time he opened his mouth.

Weather wise, we were lucky. The downpour I predicted had failed to materialise. I kept my fingers crossed. We were not even one third through yet.

Frank and I processed fifteen cars before we finally we found something dubious, nearly hidden under the floor matt at the nearside-rear section of cab number 95.

'What do you think?' Frank asked.

I kneeled down to scrutinise the suspicious-looking stain.

'Can't be one hundred percent certain, but it looks like

dried blood,' I said.

'Okay, let's get it.'

I stepped out of the cab and said, 'Better find out who was driving this car last night. We're going to have to take the car in for fingerprinting and to do a thorough collection of trace evidence. I'm going to conduct some basic fingerprinting first just in case the inside of the vehicle gets contaminated before it's taken down to the Forensic Centre.'

'I'll have a word with John Thomas,' Frank said, 'as soon as we've finished with the car.'

I removed a clean scalpel fitted with a new blade, and an envelope from the PERK.

For the second time, I entered cab 95 and I kneeled down. Gently I scraped off the small stain the size of a twenty-cent coin. I cautiously inserted the flakes inside the envelope.

'We'll conduct DNA testing on the sample ASAP,' I went on, 'and compare it with a blood sample from Evelyn Carter.'

The drivers waiting in the queue to fill up their tanks and those waiting to start their shift were getting agitated.

While I was dusting prints from cab 95, one of the night-shift drivers came towards me.

'Hey, you're gonna hang here long? I gotta make a living,' he said, brushing his greasy hair back with his fingers. He wore a five-o'clock shadow, and his brown eyes projected nastiness.

'Step aside,' I ordered, 'and let us finish what we're doing.'

'You gonna pay me for the wasted time? Five dollars for every fifteen minutes you keep me waiting. It's the going rate for drivers who return their cabs late. The way I see it, it's no different with you guys.'

I glanced at Frank and turned to the driver. 'You drive this thing, do you?' I asked, pointing at cab number 95.

'Hopefully I will one day.'

Frank stopped dusting for prints on the driver's side door handle of the cab, got back on his feet and said, 'Okay, stop the smart-arse attitude. You drive number 95 on the night-shift?'

'Yeah, what is it to you?'

'Police officer, arsehole,' Frank said, pointing to the photo-ID attached to his breast-pocket. 'Keep your attitude to yourself and show us some identification.'

The driver puzzled for five seconds and removed his driver's licence from his wallet.

'Peter W. Perezzia,' Frank read from the licence the size of a credit card. 'What's the W stand for?'

'William.'

'What's Perezzia? Greek? Italian?'

'What type of question is this? You're gonna arrest me 'cause I'm not a skip?'

'Okay, Peter William Perezzia, just answer the questions. Did you take a female passenger last night, dark hair, nice looking?'

'I take a lot of passengers. It's my job.'

'This one was let off in Toorak.'

'Like I said, I take a lot of passengers. It's the nature of being a cab driver.'

'Yeah, but this one had an argument with the driver. Did you argue with any of your customers?'

Peter Perezzia's brown eyes shifted from Frank's to mine and back to Frank's. 'Are you guys going to arrest me?'

I stepped in. 'No, Mr Perezzia, we're not arresting you. We want to know if you argued with a female passenger last night during your shift.'

'Nope,' he said immediately, without giving it a second thought.

'Are you sure?'

'Yeah, I'm sure.' He paused. 'Shouldn't I be speaking to a lawyer?'

'What about the blood stain we found in the back of your car?' I asked.

'What blood stain?'

'Near the left rear door.'

'I don't know nothin' about no bloodstain.'

'So, how do you think it got there?'

'Why ask me? I'm not the only person who drives the fuckin' car. The bloodstain could have been from weeks ago.' He glanced at the car and continued, 'Can I get my car back now? I've got to make a living. And talking to your guys is not paying the bills. You're wasting my time.'

'You're not taking this car,' Frank said. 'We're taking it in for testing.'

Peter Perezzia rolled his eyes. 'Evidence of what?' He threw his hands in the air and slapped both his thighs. 'Jesus Christ! What the fuck are you doing?'

'Hey, tone down the language,' Frank ordered.

'Fuck you, you bald prick. I didn't do nothin' and you taking my cab from me. You fuckin' pigs are all the same.'

Other cab drivers were chatting amongst themselves while looking in our direction.

'Okay, you're done.' Frank removed a pair of handcuffs from under his sports jacket. 'Turn around. I'm placing you under arrest.'

'What? Are you nuts?'

In a swift move, Frank managed to grab the driver's wrist and handcuff him.

Just then, John Thomas stepped out of his office. 'Hey, what's going on here? What are you doing with my driver?'

I paced towards John, letting Frank get on with his business. 'It's okay, Mr Thomas. We're just placing Mr Perezzia under arrest.'

'Abusive language to begin with. The rest we'll figure it out as we get to the station. We found bloodstains in his car.'

John Thomas looked mildly surprised. 'Jeez, bloodstains? Where? What?'

'Now, you don't worry about it, sir. We'll take care of it from here on.'

'You promised you were gonna be nice to my drivers.'

'We were, Mr Perezzia got nasty on us.'

John tried to move past me.

I pulled him back by the sleeve of his flannel shirt. 'Look, Mr Thomas, I wouldn't get involved if I was you. We're just doing our job.'

He locked his eyes with mine and said, 'I've got the list of drivers you wanted in my office. I'll go and get it.'

'Thank you, Mr Thomas.'

CHAPTER SEVEN

The interrogation room on the ninth floor of the St Kilda Road Police Complex was bare of furniture, other than a table, two chairs and a video camera mounted with a metal bracket to one of the walls.

Peter Perezzia sat at one end of the table, his hands crossed and his mouth shut. There was a solemn expression on his face. All the way from the taxi depot, he'd been insulting Frank and me about abusing his rights. Fifteen minutes on the road, and Frank snapped. He told Perezzia if he didn't shut up, he was going to pull the car to the side of the road and give him the beating of his life. Perezzia hadn't said a word since then.

I was to conduct the interview as usual. Frank was watching us from a monitor in a small room adjoined to the interrogation room. As per regulation, the interview would be recorded.

I placed a thick file held by a large, red elastic band on the table. The file was mostly filled with blank photocopy paper, other than a previous assault conviction. The idea was to intimidate the suspect by making him think we had more on him than we really did. It was a common trick I learned back in the USA, and in spite of its popularity, the method never failed to impress whomever was being interrogated.

Perezzia had been previously convicted and jailed for four months for attempted rape on a sixteen-year-old girl from Wantirna South. Had he succeeded in raping the girl, he would have had twenty years. If his solicitor hadn't effectively argued the attempted rape had not been committed during Perezzia's working hours and was not linked in any way to him driving a cab, he would have also lost his cab license in the process. The judge gave him one last chance, which to date he had respected with integrity.

I read him his rights and jumped straight into the interrogation.

'Okay, Mr Perezzia, your attitude towards the police doesn't really help the situation. My partner thinks you've killed the woman. Me, I'm partial. I want to hear your story first.'

'I didn't kill no one, for fuck's sake! You people are unbelievable.'

'It's easier to tell the truth now than in front of a jury. The press is going to be there, members of the public are going to be there, the prosecution is going to grill you. I don't think it's a situation you want to find yourself in. Why don't you make it easy on yourself?'

His eyes crossed mine.

I went on, 'I think I can help you. See, I think you must have had a good reason to kill her. Didn't she give you what you paid for?'

'What the fuck are you talking about?'

'Look, we've matched up the blood from your car with the one from the victim,' I lied. The blood sample was still on its way to the Forensic Centre, and DNA processing results would take another twenty-four hours before I would have access to them. 'There's no doubt she took a ride with you on that night.'

Perezzia went blank for a few seconds, shifting his buns on the plastic-moulded chair.

'It's impossible,' he said, 'I've never seen this woman before.'

'What woman?' I asked.

'The one who got killed.'

'I didn't show you a picture of the victim, so how do you know you haven't seen her?'

Fifteen seconds of awkward silence.

He hesitated. 'Well, I know I didn't see her because... I don't remember the woman you're describing.'

53

I played with my pen for a few seconds, letting his brain simmer in its own juice.

'You're lying to me, Mr Perezzia. You know and I know you're lying. I haven't described this woman to you.' I pulled a twelve-by-fourteen, black-and-white head shot of Evelyn Carter from the manilla folder. 'Have a good look.' I placed the picture on the table in front of him. 'You've never seen this woman before?'

He shifted his eyes away from the picture.

'Look at the goddamn picture,' I snapped, 'look at the picture and tell me you recognise this woman.'

He stared at me and then at the picture. 'All right, she was in my cab.'

I pursed my lips.

He continued, 'But I didn't say anything because you told me she got killed, and I didn't want to get in trouble. I knew it was going to end like this. If I told you I gave her a ride, you was gonna think I did it. And I didn't do nothin'. So, don't try to make me say I did it because I didn't do shit.'

I paused for effect then said, 'I'd like to believe you, Mr Perezzia, but so far you've lied to me, so explain how I'm suppose to believe you're telling the truth from here on.'

'Because I'm telling you, because I told you why I lied, because you guys scared the shit out of me.'

'Okay, then, let's both agree that from this point on, you're telling the truth. If that's the case, can you explain to me why there was her blood at the back of your cab?'

He puzzled for a few seconds. 'She was filing her nails and cut herself.'

That was a dumb an excuse as I ever heard. 'And how do you know that?'

'She told me.'

'She told you she cut herself filing her nails?'

'She did, she said, "Shit", and I said, "What's the matter?", and she said, "Fuck, I just cut myself with the nail filer, hey, you got a tissue or something? I'm pissing blood".'

'She talked like that, did she?'

'She certainly did, she was a hooker.'

Another judgemental prick, I thought. 'How do you know she was a hooker?'

'She told me.'

'She's told you a lot. Maybe she thought you were a priest, not a taxi driver.'

'That's really funny.' He threw me a hatred stare.

'What else did she tell you?' I asked.

'She had to meet someone in Toorak, her boyfriend I think, but she didn't really say so, it could have been a client.'

'And that's where you were took her there?'

'Yeah.'

'Did she say what the name of this person was?'

'Nope, what do you think? I was going to ask her everything about her life? As you pointed out, I'm not a *priest* for Christ's sake. I'm a cab driver, remember? He smiled, looking really proud of himself.

'You're story sounds fishy. You want to hear what I think happened?'

'Nope, I don't, but I guess you're not going to give me a choice.'

'I think when she told you she was a hooker, you started thinking you had some right over her. Knowing she was a hooker, you probably thought she wasn't really a woman, she was something men fucked, something you could use and toss away. That's what you thought, wasn't it?'

'Not true, absolute bullshit.'

'And I think you asked her to do something for you, and she didn't want to. She didn't want to for whatever reason. You felt rejected and couldn't accept the fact that some hooker told you where to go. You assaulted her, raped her, killed her and threw her down the back alley of some shops. That's what I think happened.'

He said nothing for a little while, then: 'This is absolute bullshit. You're making up all this crap, hoping I'm going to confess. But I'm not going to say shit because I didn't do anything. So save your breath cause you're not getting a confession out of me. I didn't do it, and you're not going to make me say I did. I would never think of doing such a thing in the first place.'

I opened the folder in front of me and retrieved records from his previous attempted-rape conviction.

'You're not exactly a saint, Mr Perezzia,' I said, browsing

through the case file in my hand. 'Sixteen-year-old girl on her way back from school? Does that ring a bell?'

'I didn't do anything, I wasn't even charged for rape.'

'Oh, no, I know that, you were charged and convicted for attempted rape. How could you have been charged for rape when she managed to kick you in the groin before you got to do her up?'

'That was a long time ago, and it has fuck all to do with this case.'

'It has everything to do with this case, Mr Perezzia. I'm trying to find a link between what happened to Evelyn Carter and your behaviour. Based on that, I don't see it as an impossibility that you were the one who killed that woman. The behavioural patterns are there.'

He stared at me silently for a few seconds, then his eyes shifted to the tabletop.

'I didn't do it, I'm not going to say any more.'

And that was that.

'I'm going to take a little break now,' I said. 'Want a coffee or something?'

'Screw your coffee. I want to get out of this place.'

'Not until you tell me the truth.' I paced towards the door. 'I'll be back in ten minutes.'

'Yeah, you do that.'

I shut the door.

Last thing I heard was his voice behind my back.

'Bloody pigs.'

I made instant coffee on the premises. There was a nice little place around the corner of the police complex where they brewed the best percolated coffee. Although I was dying for a cup, I had no intention of letting Frank out of my sight. While conducting an interrogation six months ago, I took a break to get some coffee from the shop downstairs. When I came back, Frank had stepped in the interrogation room and harassed the suspect without my authorisation. My trust in him had weakened from that day on. We had known each other for eight years and worked hundreds of cases together. Our friendship was built on mutual trust and integrity towards one another. He destroyed the unquestionable faith we shared when he double-crossed me on that particular day, especially when he knew I was in charge of the investigation.

I pushed the door of the monitor room with my foot, my hands carrying two hot mugs of coffee.

'Thanks,' Frank said as soon as he saw me.

'What do you think?' I asked, placing his mug in front of the monitor.

'Are you asking me if I think he did it?'

'Yes.'

'I've past sentencing prematurely in the past, and it's made some people upset, especially you. So I'm not sure you want to hear what I have to say.'

'Ah, come on, Frank, this is me you're talking to. If I don't want to hear what you have to say, I wouldn't be asking.'

He took a sip from his mug, pulled a face and said, 'All right. Having seen what we've got so far, I'm inclined to say he did it. Only because he lied to us from the beginning, saying he had never seen Evelyn Carter in his life. And now I'm not convinced he's telling the truth. You know as well as I do that his story with her cutting herself while filing her nails is a crock of shit.'

'I'll have to agree with you. Cutting herself filing her nails, that is. As far as him having done it, I'm not sure whether he has at this stage. Maybe he was scared when he learned the girl he had in his cab last night got killed. And maybe that was why he lied to us. But still, something doesn't ring right. I think he might have done something else, but he's scared to tell.'

'What do you mean?'

'Well, maybe he didn't actually kill her, but had a fight with her nonetheless. They argued in the cab, and that's when she got cut. Maybe he pulled a knife on her or something. See, David Boyd from the bookshop said he heard them argue in the car, and then she left the cab.'

Frank looked at the monitor. Perezzia's eyes were cast on the table.

Frank said, 'So what? He could have followed her. It doesn't take much to get out of a car and follow someone.'

'We're assuming that he was the last person who saw her when she left the cab. Mr Perezzia did say she was meeting someone.'

'Maybe he lied just to cover himself. I mean if he did kill her, do you think he's going to own up?'

I took a sip from my mug. Instant coffee tasted like cat's pee. 'Okay,' I said, 'if she wasn't meeting anyone, why was she riding in a cab in the middle of the night to go nowhere?'

'She went to get her SAAB.'

'Sure, we can more or less confirm that. But what was the SAAB doing at the back of the shops? Did someone else drive the car there to meet her? Could it have been the boyfriend Perezzia mentioned? See, maybe this boyfriend of hers drove the SAAB to the shops where they were supposed to meet. And they did, but something went wrong. They argued and he ends up killing her.'

Frank took another sip from his mug. He rinsed his mouth with the contents before swallowing. 'Maybe, maybe, maybe. Maybe anything could have happened. Maybe it was a complete stranger who saw her getting out of the cab and jumped on her. Maybe it was a crime of opportunity, and we'll never find a logical link between the victim and the murderer.'

I glanced back at the monitor. Perezzia was playing with his fingers, a desperate look washed over his face. I turned to Frank and said, 'I don't think we have enough to charge Perezzia with the murder right now. There's no weapon—'

'He used his hands. Of course you don't have a weapon. It's already been established that the victim was beaten to death.'

'There's no physical evidence left at the crime scene to support that Perezzia is the killer.'

'The blood in the taxi-cab. What do you call that?'

'The cab isn't part of the crime scene,' I said relentlessly, 'and we've got no proof that the blood was hers. We're still waiting for the DNA test.' I emptied my mug of coffee and went on, 'I'm going back in there, and unless he confesses immediately, I'm going to let him go. I want to talk to David Boyd. I want to know if there's anything else he remembers.'

Frank shook his head. 'What don't you grill him for another half hour?'

'I'm going to let him go, Frank. It's the best thing to do for the time being.'

'Jesus Christ, I don't know why I bother sometimes. You

leave me in there with him for half an hour, and I'll get the truth out.'

'Yes, well, I believe I've already experienced your so-called interrogation methods.' In a previous case we worked on together, Frank got the truth by beating it out of the suspect.

'Why do I have the feeling you're trying to run this investigation all by yourself?'

'You called me, Frank, you called *me*!'

'I *know*!'

I slammed my mug on the monitor desk and headed back to the interrogation room.

'Okay, Mr Perezzia,' I said, the palm of my hands flat on the table, and the crime-scene photographs of Evelyn Carter scattered in front of us, 'I'm going to ask you one last time. Did you kill this woman? Have a good long at those pictures and tell me you didn't do this.'

He glanced at the pictures and said, 'It's horrible. Get these things away from me. I didn't kill her, and I'm tired of repeating myself. I'm going to get a solicitor.'

'You don't need to do that right away, sir. You're free to go.'

He looked at me surprised, as if I was playing a trick.

'I can go?'

'You can go if you want. I have nothing else to ask you.'

'You're not going to arrest me?'

'No, I'm not going to arrest you. But we'll probably meet again in the course of this investigation. And if anything comes back to mind, I'd appreciate if you give me a call.'

I slipped a business card in his right hand.

'And Mr Perezzia...' He looked up, '...if you didn't kill that woman, then you have nothing to worry about. But if you did, I'm going to get you—don't doubt that for a minute. I knew this woman, so consider it a personal vendetta.'

He swallowed and said, 'Well, I'm sorry for your loss, but I didn't kill her.'

I watched him head for the door, suddenly conscious that our conversation was being taped, and I had just threatened him.

At the last moment, he turned around and said, 'If you fuck with me one more time, I'm going to sue you and that friend cop of yours.'

'Mr Perezzia—'

He gave me his middle finger and left the room.

CHAPTER EIGHT

David Boyd was even more handsome than I remembered. The last time I saw him was in the early hours of the morning, and I had been in a foul mood at the time, in spite of remaining diplomatic.

I stepped out of my car, umbrella in hand. The street was glistening as if painted with oil, the seven colours of the rainbow surging out of the road and the side walk It had been raining for two hours non-stop while Frank and I were in the St Kilda Road Police Complex interrogating Perezzia. The downpour had stopped, but the smell of rainwater was still in the air. Hot steam escaped from the bonnet of my car.

I crossed the road to David's Bookshop.

A sign on the door told me it was OPEN.

David didn't seemed surprised to see me when I entered the shop. A small silver bell attached to the top of the entrance door announced my arrival.

'I knew you would be back,' he said, looking up from his newspaper. 'Decided to go on that book tour after all? Perfect timing. No one's come in the shop in the last two hours. Sometimes I wonder why I bother staying in business.'

'No, I'm no here for a book tour, Mr Boyd.'

'Oh, please, don't insult me. Call me David.'

He circled the counter, walked straight past me, locked the door of the shop from the inside, and turned the sign around so that it read CLOSED on the outside.

He went on, 'Really, it's not a problem at all. I haven't had lunch, and someone's dropped in two boxes of second-hand books which I haven't put on the shelves yet. You can have a sneak preview if you want, but I have to hold on to them for seven days before making them available to buy. You know how it works. Could be stolen goods. Any titles you'd like, I'll put them on the side for you.'

'Thanks, David, but I'll take a rain-check on the book tour and the sneak preview. I'm actually here to ask you a few more questions about last night.'

'Sure, but I've already told you everything I know.'

'Yes, but sometimes details come back hours, sometimes days after an event. Maybe you know something which you think is irrelevant, but it might be. Small details can often lead an investigator in the right direction.'

He nodded absently and said, 'Can I get you a cup of something?'

The cold from outside was still trapped between my skin and bone, and I was dying for another hot brew. 'Coffee would be nice.'

'Sure, follow me.'

We stepped into a small kitchenette separated from the bookshop by a curtain in motives of stars and moons.

'How do you have it?' he asked.

'Black. No sugar. No milk.'

'Mmmm, just like me. A real coffee drinker.'

While he made the coffee, I glanced around. The room was small but clean. There was a table to sit two people in one corner and a small fridge from the early fifties in the other. The fridge reminded me of a Holden car from the fifties. It was off-white and had round edges.

David passed me my coffee and said, 'So, what is it that you wanted to know?'

'Last night you said you heard the cab driver and the woman argue. Did you hear what they were arguing about?'

'I told you before, it was too far away. By the time I got to the bedroom window, she had already stepped out of the taxi.'

'Did he follow her?'

'Who? the driver?'

'Yes.'

'No, not that I saw.'

'Did you see the car driving away as soon as he dropped her?'

'No, not immediately. To be honest with you, I didn't stay look enough at the window to check whether the taxi left or not. I just looked because I was curious. It didn't seem like a big deal, so I retired to bed.'

'So you've got no idea how long the cab stayed in the area?'

'No, like I've said, I went straight back to bed. Once she left the taxi and walked away, I thought she was safe.'

So much for safety, I thought, the poor thing got beaten to a pulp.

'And what about her car?'

'What car?'

'The SAAB was parked at the back of the shops. You didn't notice a SAAB parked there during the day?'

'No. I don't drive, so I don't usually go down the back of the shops. Only once a week when I have to gather the garbage for collection. But selling second-hand books doesn't produce much rubbish, frankly. In and out goods come through the front door.'

'Would you be able to recognise the face of the cab driver if I showed you a picture?'

'I doubt it, but you can always try.'

We stayed silent for half a minute, sipping our black coffees.

'So, you've got any suspects?' he said between two sips.

'One, but I can't really get into it at this stage. Plus it's a bit early in the investigation to derive any conclusion.'

He shifted on the spot. 'Why don't we sit down?'

'Okay.'

I sat at one end of the small table. He sat across from me.

He went on, 'What is it like to work for the police? Do you like this kind of work, you know, looking at dead people all the time? I mean, you're a good looking woman and everything. Why would you want to do a job like that?'

'Beauty is only skin deep and to the eye of the beholder— I'm sure you've heard both these cliches before. Crime investigation has nothing to do with looks. It's all about using your brain and your intuition. In fact, looks can get in the way.'

'How did you get into this line of work? You just woke up one morning and decided to chase criminals for a living?'

I gave him my life story in five minutes, how I had always been fascinated by crime, how I studied criminology at university, and how I ended up at the FBI Academy in the USA before landing a contract with the VFSC and the CIB.

He listened attentively without interruption.

When I finished, he said, 'Wow, you've certainly had an interesting life. You've seen more of the world than I have.'

'I wouldn't exactly call it seeing the world. Most of what I've seen, you wouldn't want to see for yourself. What about you?'

'Nothing much to tell, really. I was born in Perth and moved to Melbourne in my early twenties. I wanted to do something exciting, and I heard Melbourne had lots of opportunities. Worked in a second-hand bookshop for a few years, and I liked it. Not what some people would call exciting, but I've always been a reader, and working in a bookshop gave me plenty of time to read. After a couple of years, I was almost running the shop myself. I knew how everything worked. It wasn't that complicated, really, not like when you're selling new books, and you have to deal with book distributors, accounts and returns. I managed to save enough money and decided to open my own bookshop. And here I am. Ten years in the same place and nothing ever happens. But I don't mind. It's not like I'm complaining or anything. I quite like what I'm doing. I'm still an avid reader, and this is the perfect environment for a bookworm.'

'Have you ever been married?'

'No, never thought about it. I guess the right person never came about. I would consider it if I met the right girl. But it gets harder as you get older.' A pause. 'Why? Are you married?'

'I was once, but it didn't work out.'

'Oh, well, you know what they say, nothing lasts forever.'

'Yeah, I suppose. Still, they also say, never say never.'

He threw me a look. 'Are you proposing?'

'No,' I laughed, 'just curious.'

Our conversation was interrupted by an awkward silence. I liked the way he stared at me and made me feel important without saying a word. Normally, I couldn't bare to be stared at. But this time it was different. It's wasn't an obsessive stare, but a warm glance, like if we were brother and sister. And yet there was still something delightfully mysterious behind his eyes, something that made me want to know him better.

'Do you want me to show you those crime books?' he asked, standing from his chair. 'That is if you've got no more questions to ask me about the investigation.'

'No, thanks, I should really be going. I still have a lot of work to do.'

'How about dinner tonight? I know this nice restaurant not far from here. I've been in the bookshop all day. I need a break, and I'm sure you need one too.'

I hesitated for a few seconds.

'And I like your company,' he added.

'Yes and no,' I finally said.

He gave me a look of disappointment.

'It's not that I don't want to, David. I'm just tired, and you're part of this investigation. When things have calmed down a little, I'll take up your offer.'

'Sure, I understand. You give me a call if you change your mind.'

'Will do,' I said and stood from my chair. 'But I've really got to go now.'

He stood from his chair. 'Let me walk you to the door.'

We left the kitchenette and headed back to the front of the bookshop.

I slipped him another one of my business cards. 'If you do remember anything about last night, do give me a call, any time, even after hours.'

I left the bookshop, upset with myself. I was letting my emotions rule my head. I broke my number one rule. I knew now that the main reason why I went back to see David Boyd was not to question him about Evelyn Carter's death, but just to see him.

And that was damn silly for someone in my position.

I swore in silence never to do it again.

Just as I slid behind the wheel of my car, rain came down

without warning.

CHAPTER NINE

At 10.35 a.m. the following day, while I was typing a preliminary investigative report on the Evelyn Carter murder, the phone rang. I was in my study, feet up on the desk, peeping at black cows through the window in my study. The sky was overcast, and rain had been predicted for later in the day. The smell of an English muffin I had burned in the toaster an hour ago lingered in every corner of the house.

The previous night my sleep had been broken several times by high winds thundering against the pane of my bedroom window. Once awake, my mind kept on replaying the scene where we found Evelyn Carter bloodied and bruised, and left for dead. There was no going back to sleep. I speculated on the possible identity of the murderer. If Perezzia was indeed the killer, we would catch up with him eventually. It was just a matter of gathering the right trace evidence and matching it up with something that belonged to him. Whatever we collected from cab number 95 would be of little use. Hundreds of people had entered the cab in the past few weeks. The defence would have no problem in establishing reasonable doubt in the minds of a jury. I was trying to figure out under what pretext we would be allowed a search warrant for Perezzia's home. Once the DNA test on the stain we found at the back of the cab would be completed and compared with that from a blood sample of Evelyn Carter, we'd presumably be able to get a search warrant. There was little doubt that the polymeric sequences of the test results would match. Even if Perezzia didn't kill Evelyn, he did confirm that she cut her finger in his cab, and that would virtually guarantee the match I was hoping for.

After a hot shower and two cups of black coffee back-to-back, I retired to my study and focused on the preliminary investigative report.

Two hours later, the report was nearly completed. I was working on the conclusion and recommendation of my five-page document to Goosh. He had insisted on been kept informed during every stage of the investigation, much to my despair, until someone else would fill my shoes.

I waited for the phone to ring another five seconds before answering the call.

I snatched the receiver, tucked it between my chin and shoulder and returned my fingers to the keyboard.

'Melina Investigations,' I said absently.

'It's David.'

My mind did a somersault, and I didn't respond.

'It's me, David,' he repeated, 'from the bookshop.'

I lifted my fingers from the keyboard and grabbed the phone receiver.

'What's up David?'

'Are you doing anything tonight?'

I hesitated for a few seconds and said, 'Have you got something to tell about the murder?'

'No, I just thought I'd take you out somewhere.'

'We've already gone through this yesterday.'

'Yes, I know, but I'd really like to know you better. I'm sorry if I'm being a bit forward, but I'm not much for keeping it all on the inside. What do you say? A little tête-à-tête over the best lamb couscous in Melbourne?'

I smiled to myself. Since I'd stopped seeing Phillip a few months back, I missed the intimacy of a close relationship. Love made me feel whole, even though it always ended up with pain. I closed my eyes and pictured myself falling into David's arms, unbuttoning his shirt and covering his chest with kisses. I could almost smell the citrus aroma of his aftershave.

'Kristina?' David interrupted.

'Oh, yes, I'm sorry. Okay, sure, why not.'

We agreed for him to pick me up at my place at 9.00 p.m.

I hung up with a mixture of fear and excitement.

I broke my number one rule, but I no longer cared.

It was 5.32 p.m., and Frank and I were sitting across from one another at the staff canteen of the VFSC, two mugs of coffee steaming and hardly touched. We were winding down a conversation relating to the investigation.

'I've got Evelyn Carter's address, flicking through his log book,' Frank said. 'When do you want to search her apartment?'

'It's an apartment, is it?'

'Could be a flat. It's got a lot number: 2-33.' He scribbled the details on a small piece of paper and passed it over to me.

I read the address and said, 'We could head off now, if you're not doing anything. I don't want to wait until tomorrow morning. The killer is still at large, and the last thing we need is him getting to her place before we do. If the killer is the boyfriend the cab driver mentioned, there might be incriminating evidence at her place he'd like to get his hands on before we do.'

'You want to go now?' Frank asked, raising one eyebrow.

'Yes, but only if you're not doing anything.'

'Well, let me see... I don't have kids, I'm not married, I have no one to go home to... I think I can find the time to fit you in.' He grinned like an imbecile.

His attempt at humour fell upon dead ears. His seduction techniques were cliched and boring. I would never be romantically involved with this man. He knew it, and I knew it. So why did he persist so relentlessly? Was this part of the gene composition that came with being male?

'Great,' I said, 'we're also going to have to find out if she's got any relatives. They need to be notified. She probably has a phone book at home with her friends listed. I'm going to conduct door-to-door interviews in her neighbourhood during the next few days.'

'Sounds good,' he said. He gathered his log book and pen. 'Want to take my car?'

'Sure, whatever.'

We emptied our mugs and left the VFSC.

Evelyn Carter's apartment was in Richmond, a popular inner-city suburb of Melbourne. When we arrived, darkness had already fallen like a huge blanket over the city. I couldn't see the stars in the sky, and it smelled like rain. The showers they had predicted that morning would be upon us any minute.

Frank and I stepped from the white Ford Falcon and circled the car in order to gather the PERK and photographic equipment.

Frank glanced towards the apartments where Evelyn supposedly lived. 'Sure looks like she had a lot of money,' Frank said.

'If she owned the place.'

'Even if she rented it.'

Frank was right. The type of apartment I was looking would have cost her no less than $500 a week for a one-bedroom or a studio. The facades had strong, angular lines and an interesting combination of colour and materials—smooth, deep-blue walls contrasted with craggy, sandstone bricks. The crisp simplicity of the windows fashionably disagreed with the quirky art deco design of the steel balcony railing and the front security gate.

The security gate made it impossible for us to enter the courtyard, unless someone opened the gate for us, or we tampered with the locking mechanism.

'How we're going to get in?' Frank asked.

'Watch me.'

At the gate, I rang the doorbell of apartment 1.

In less than thirty seconds, a male voice came through the intercom, 'Hello?'

'Police,' I said. 'We need someone to open the gate for us.'

Silence.

'Who's this?'

'The police.'

'Hold on a sec.'

Nothing. We waited a full minute without saying a word.

Frank was about to press the doorbell again, but I held his arm back. 'Wait a minute.'

'What for?'

'Just hold.'

Fifteen seconds late, a man in his mid-thirties with thinning hair came towards us from the other side of the gate. 'You're the police, are you?' he called out. His nose was long, and his chin was weak. He wore jeans and a blue tee-shirt, and looked as if we'd just woken him up.

'Yes,' I said as I unclipped my ID from my breast pocket.

Frank did the same as the man approached us. We showed our Ids through the gate.

'All right,' the man said.

He fiddled with a set of keys and opened the gate. 'Is there anything wrong?'

'Could you tell us where apartment 2 is?'

'Sure, let me show you the way.'

We followed the man down the lane way and into the hallway of the apartment block. The hallway was painted a deep-blue, just like the outside walls of the apartments.

'Here it is,' he said when we reached apartment number 2. He stood there, as if we were going to invite him in.

'We'll be right now,' I said.

'Ah, sure, okay then,' he said and left.

I put on a pair of surgical gloves to avoid leaving my own fingerprints behind. As expected the door was locked, so I had to use my lock-picking kit. It took me a whole damn three minutes because the lock was jammed. Frank was standing behind me, checking if anyone was coming down the hallway.

'The apartments are set close together,' he said, 'and with the security gate, surely someone would have noticed if she had a boyfriend. All we have to do is ask the neighbours.'

'We'll do that later,' I said, while raising the pins of the lock to their opening point. The tension tool, placed directly under the pick, kept pressure on the pins while rotating. The pins were held in their open position by the pressure applied from the tension tool.

Frank became agitated. 'What's taking you so long? The neighbours are going to think we're breaking in.'

'We are.'

'Yes, but the last—

'Shut up, Frank. I can't hear what I'm doing.' I could feel the vibration of the pins. I listened patiently for a distinctive click, and then pushed the door open. 'Done.'

'About time,' he muttered.

We moved inside the hallway. The place was plunged in darkness. I flicked the light-switch and was surprised at the cleanness of the apartment. At the opening from the entrance we'd just came through was a sitting room overlooking the front courtyard through a large bay window. Beyond a central staircase was an open-plan living and dining room filled with little, but expensive art deco furniture. The colour of the carpet throughout the apartment was what a floor-covering expert would call salmon. I noticed at the other end of the room, a wall of windows and sliding doors which lead to a large, private courtyard.

'There's a woman who really knew how to look after her place,' I commented.

Then, without warning, a black cat sneaked in on us and rubbed itself against my leg. It let out a cry of despair, probably because it hadn't been fed for a few days.

'Hi there,' I said. 'What's your name little fellow?'

I kneeled down and read its collar.

Oscar.

I always felt it strange when people gave animals human names.

Oscar moved on to Frank.

'Go away,' Frank said, kicking the cat gently out of his way.

'Don't be mean,' I said.

'I don't like cats. They're lazy. All they want to do is eat and sleep all day. And they smell.'

'You're nasty.'

'A dog considers you his master. A cat considers you his servant. And that's a fact.'

I walked to the kitchen and removed a milk cartoon from the fridge, smelling its contents to make sure it wasn't out-of-date. I noticed a small, original still life painting, featuring a large loaf of bread and various salamis, above the kitchen table. It looked a bit tacky in the middle of the modern kitchen.

I grabbed a breakfast bowl from the pantry and filled it with milk. I kneeled down and placed it next to the fridge. Oscar drank from it as if it was his last meal before execution.

'I wonder what's going to happen to the poor thing now that the owner is dead,' I said throwing Frank a pitied look.

'Don't look at me that way,' he said, 'I'm not taking fur ball with me. I hate cats.'

'So you keep telling me. I wouldn't expect you to have any compassion to bother saving an animal from starvation.'

'Hey, come on, it's not my goddamn cat. If you're so holy, why don't you pay a visit to the city pound and rescue all cats and dogs?'

'You're an idiot, Frank,' I said matter-of-factly, not bothering with eye contact.

'Thank you.'

I noticed a telephone on a side-table next to a leather couch. Without saying a word, I picked up the receiver and pressed the redial button. That was one easy way to figure out whom Evelyn had been in touch with last. A series of touch-tone beeps were followed by a high-pitch sound, a bit like the one I normally get when I dial a facsimile number by accident. I placed the receiver back and looked around the room. No fax machine. That got me intrigued for the next sixty seconds.

We began with a walk-through of the apartment while Oscar drank his milk. Upstairs, there was a study and two bedrooms, one turned into a home office, both opened from a central landing. The bedrooms were at either end of the hallway, and separated by a large, clutter-free sitting area and a bathroom. First impression of the place was clinical tidiness, to the point that I felt we were visiting a display home. It was obvious Evelyn Carter had been making a comfortable living working as a prostitute. And maybe that was why she never let go of her job, even after working twenty years in the field. I wondered why she hadn't bothered completing her studies and moving on. Maybe she realised that no matter what studies she would undertake, she would never match the money she was earning as a high-class prostitute. And even if she did, she'd have to work long hours and have little time left to enjoy her freedom. Who could really tell now that she was dead? Maybe she even learned to enjoy her work. But at what cost?

The bedroom which she turned into a home office compromised a desk, a chair, a filing cabinet and a 686SX computer. There was no fax machine anywhere in sight. Her filing cabinet was unlocked. It was filled with empty files and folders.

I called Frank from the bedroom, 'Come and see this.'

Five seconds later he appeared from somewhere in the house.

'What's up?'

'What do you make of this?' I asked, the top drawer of the filing cabinet open, my hand flicking through the empty folders.

He took one look and puzzled for a few seconds. 'Someone might have got there before us,' he said.

'I was thinking that too.'

I flicked her computer on and waited sixty seconds for it to boot up. The Windows 98 display came up, followed by the usual icons associated with Microsoft programs. I checked her document folders under Microsoft Office, but it was empty.

'Well,' I said to Frank, who was standing next to me, 'nothing in here either. Looks like somebody's wiped out the whole lot.'

I checked Access, Excell, PowerPoint and her File Manager. Everything was empty, as if she had never used the computer.

I turned the computer off and resumed with the house search.

By the time we finished the walk-through, we had collected absolutely nothing that was going to help with our investigation.

Down on my knees, I was packing up my PERK and suggested to Frank, 'We'll have to dust for prints. Maybe her mysterious boyfriend has visited this place.'

Frank was about to answer, but instead he turned his attention to the hallway.

A short woman with dark hair stood at the door way. She wore faded jeans and a hand-knitted, green jumper. She looked about my age and was slightly overweight, but appeared to have spent most of her life in the country. Her face was speckled with freckles, and she wore little make-up. She looked at odds with the apartment we were standing in.

'Who are you?' she asked, surprise glowing on her face.

Frank and I looked at each other for half a second.

'Police,' I said, pointing at my ID attached to my breast

pocket. 'And who are you?'

She answered with a question, 'Where's Evelyn?' The tone of her voice indicated that she knew something was wrong.

I swallowed, knowing I would have to break the news to her. My first instinct was that she was a friend of Evelyn who'd just dropped in for one reason or another.

I stood up and said dryly, 'Evelyn Carter won't be coming home. There's been an accident.' I paused for effect and went on, 'What is your name?'

She puzzled for a few seconds before answering. 'Judith Kingman.'

'I'm sorry, Ms Kingman, but Evelyn Carter was murdered last night.'

Judith held on to the frame of the door. 'Oh, my God,' she gasped, 'I knew this was going to happen one day. I told her to be careful.' Her voice had gone up in pitch. 'Why, what, what happened?'

I hoped she wasn't going to go completely hysterical on us. I wasn't utterly at ease with having lost my long-time friend yet, and I wasn't sure I had the strength to morally support someone else over her death.

'We don't know what happened,' I said. 'All I can tell you is that she was killed. We've only begun the investigation.'

All along, Frank was just standing by my side like a mute.

I moved two steps forward.

Judith was almost in tears.

'Did you know Evelyn well?' I asked.

She looked at me, her eyes finally bursting into tears. 'She was my neighbour. God, of course I knew her, she was a sister to me.'

And when she said *sister*, tears welled from my eyes. Evelyn had been my best friend once, and although it was a long time ago, I could still feel how strong and important that friendship had been to me.

I moved forward and hugged the stranger. She sobbed on my shoulder. No one said a word for a full minute. I could feel her pain weighing on my heart and soul. Something was tearing itself up inside me. I let tears stream down my face. Even though I had never met Judith Kingman before, hugging her felt like the most natural thing in the world. It was as if we were long-lost relatives, like in one of those exploitative American television shows, who had finally caught up with one another.

Frank interrupted, 'Maybe Judith would like to come to the station with us.'

I separated myself from Judith, wiping my tears away.

'I knew Evelyn too,' I explained, 'a long time ago. We went to school together. We were best friends. She meant a lot to me, and I guess she still does.'

Judith nodded while sobbing.

I gave a full minute to let it out of her system and to compose myself.

'You don't mind coming to the station with us?' I asked.

'I live three apartments down,' she said.

I looked at Frank, then back to Judith: 'Okay, we can have a chat at your place, if you don't mind.'

'Sure.'

Frank passed her a paper hanky from the PERK.

CHAPTER TEN

Ten minutes later we were at Judith Kingman's apartment, an exact layout replica of Evelyn's dwelling, but a mirror image. It was as if we were in Evelyn's kitchen, but the world had been turned back-to-front. The furniture, however, was more cane and country style rather than art deco. There was a vase of red carnations on the kitchen table.

'Nice flowers,' I said.

'Thanks,' Judith replied her back to me. 'A gift from a friend.'

Judith made put some water on the boil and grabbed three mugs from a cupboard next to the kitchen sink.

'I told her to be careful,' she went on, talking to us but commenting to herself at the same time. 'How many times did I tell her to get a real job? How many times?'. She turned to me. 'How do you have yours?'

'Black, no sugar.'

She turned to Frank.

'Milk, two sugars,' he said without waiting for the question.

With her back to us, she continued her coffee making. 'This is not a job fit for a woman, or for anyone for that matter,' she said.

'It's wasn't her fault,' I said. 'It's never *their* fault.'

'I know, but who's fault is it then? Someone has to be blamed for her death.'

Frank glanced at me and raised his eyebrows as if to say *so, who's going to ask the questions?*

I put my hand up, telling him to be patient.

He rolled his eyes in return.

I waited for Judith to finish making the coffees before getting into the questioning.

She carried three hot mugs to the table, place one in front of me, one in front of Frank and one in front of an empty chair.

I sipped from my mug and said, 'How long have you known Evelyn for?'

Judith sat on the empty chair, across the table from me and said, 'Years. About ten years I think.' She paused for a few seconds. 'Yeah, she moved in only a couple of months after me. I thought she was very elegant. I would have never guessed she worked as a prostitute. Not that it really shocked me, but in my mind I had pictured a prostitute differently.' She sipped from her mug. 'She was so elegant, always well dressed. I thought she was a professional of one sort or another. You know, one of these corporate executive women. Tends to be the trend these days. Women climbing the corporate ladder.' She paused for a few seconds. 'She wore expensive clothes, so that's why I made that assumption. Of course, she could have also been self-employed as some type of consultant. My brother is a PR consultant, and he charges $150 an hour. It's good money. She had the looks and the style. She could have gone into something like that.'

'Being her best friend,' I said, 'I gather you knew her well?'

'I wasn't her best friend. We were very close, but I wasn't her best friend. I'm from the country. My father died ten years ago, and he owned half the town we lived in. I could have stayed, but I was an only child and my mother died two years prior to him. I didn't want to stay there. I lived all my life in a small town, and with a million dollars to my name and no family or attachment, I knew I had to move on. When I was a kid, my father took me to the city once a month. That's where I want to live, I told myself. It was a brave move for a country girl. Sure, now everyone moves away from the country. No job opportunities. So, I moved here and met Evelyn. She was nice to me from day one. She showed me around Melbourne and in no time I felt at home. But she was a city girl, and there were subtle differences between her and me, enough to stop us being best friends. You know, mainly our taste in clothes and food. She was into designer labels. I dress for comfort, not to impress.'

'So, who was Evelyn's best friend then?'

'Her best friend was Celia Pressly. She went back home to the US five years ago. She came on a one-year contract for some big business computer firm, but ended up staying four years. Evelyn and Celia met at a nightclub.'

I made a note of the name in my spiral notebook. I never heard of Celia Pressly. It must have been someone Evelyn met after we stopped seeing each other.

'Who was Celia Pressly working for?' I asked.

'She worked as a programmer for Foles & Sanders at the company's headquarters. Battlestar Gallactica, she used to call the place because of its size. It was at a time when there wasn't enough computer graduates coming out of Australia, so large corporations recruited them from US human resources companies. I went with Evelyn once to visit her at work. You wouldn't believe the size of the place. It looks like a five-star hotel with a restaurant-like canteen and fully equipped gymnasium. It was like, oh, my God, where do they get all the money from?'

I knew the place she was talking about. A huge, glass building, which was visible from the South Eastern Arterial just before crossing the Glenferrie Road intersection. I worked there for a month under cover two years ago to investigate mismanagement of the company's funds. The company's CEO was eventually charged for fraud. He had spent hundreds of thousands of dollars from Foles & Sanders's coffers to renovate his own home and that of friends. A million dollars missing through the system hadn't been easy to trace in a corporate financial maze like that of Foles & Sanders. The company owned hundreds of department stores, restaurant chains, specialised shops and boutiques all over the country, churning out billions of dollars of retail sales per year. That's where the money was coming from.

I stirred my coffee and said, 'Did Evelyn and Celia kept in touch with one another after Celia returned to the US?'

'Oh, yeah. Evelyn often spoke about her, what she was doing, so, she must have received some news from her. Maybe they were writing to each other. I don't know. She didn't give me details, and I wasn't asking. I did respect her privacy.'

Frank interrupted us. 'Did she have any other friends?'

'Not that I knew of.'

'Boyfriend?'

'Couldn't keep up. She changed and swapped them now and then. Never a two-timer, but she tires really quickly of the same man. She was going out with someone lately, but I never got a chance to meet him. She said he was very handsome. She said she was going to introduce him to me, but like I said, I never got a chance.'

'She mentioned his name?' I asked.

Judith puzzled for a few seconds. 'No idea. I don't think she ever told me.'

We sipped from our mugs. The coffee was strong and bitter and could have woken up the dead.

'What about her clients?' I went on. 'Did she ever talk about them?'

'Oh, yeah. All of them from high places. They wanted discretion. They couldn't afford to get extracurricular sex and being seen. It was better for them to have Evelyn cater for their needs. Her services were in high demand because of the guaranteed discretion, and obviously because Evelyn was simply a gorgeous woman. She didn't look cheap like all those street prostitutes. You could be seen in public with her if you wanted to, and you didn't have to worry about what people thought.'

'How did prospective clients find out about her?'

'By word of mouth. Written applications only. They were properly screened. She wanted to know who they were, where they came from, whether they had prior criminal records. Anyone who looked like a potential psychopath didn't stand a chance. She was extremely careful with all that. She must have listened to me. But now, look what's happened. It goes to show you never know.'

I took another mouthful of coffee while Frank recorded details of our conversation.

'Did she mention any names?' I asked.

'Names of?'

'Her clients.'

Judith locked her eyes into mine for a few seconds. 'She did, but I'm not sure if I can repeat them. She gave them her word that she would never tell anyone.'

If Evelyn told Judith some of her clients' names, she had already broken the confidentiality rule she set for herself. So, why stop here?

'I understand, Judith, but Evelyn is dead now, and there's a good chance that the person who killed was one of her clients.'

'And you never promised anything,' Frank added. 'She did. If we're going to find out who killed her, we need all the help we can get. I'm sure Evelyn would have wanted it that way if she was still alive.'

Judith took her time. 'That's true.' She paused for a few seconds. 'What's the name of that game-show host?'

Frank and I looked at her clueless. I seldom watched television, and whenever I did, certainly not game shows. My timetable was far too busy to bother with such trivial things.

Judith went on, 'You now at seven o'clock—weeknight.'

'Mind Wheel,' Frank said. 'Simon Garvey. He's been host for ten years.'

'Yeah, that's him,' Judith said, her face lighting up. 'He was one of her clients. Married with three kids. You can understand why it was imperative for Evelyn to be discreet about her services.'

Simon Garvey. Okay, the name did ring a bell. I'd never watched his show, but I must have read about him in *Who Weekly* or *TV Week* or another one of those celebrity magazines. I wrote the name down at the same time as Frank.

'Anyone else?' I asked.

'Politicians. A couple of MPs. Can't recall their names right now. But I'm sure I'll remember. Some cops in high places. A supreme court judge. Like I said, people in power with money to burn. They looked after each other, don't you worry. Everyone's always on the lookout to scratch somebody's back as long as they know they're going to get theirs scratched. Aren't that the nature of politics?'

'It sounds like common human nature to me,' I said.

Frank and I looked at each other. If Judith was correct, some people in high places were probably having a hard time closing their eyes at night. If their names became linked to the murder of Evelyn Carter, it would be the end of their career. I knew Frank was thinking the same thing from the look on his face.

'She did keep a little black book with all the names in it,' Judith said.

'Her clients' names?' I asked.

'Yeah, all of them. She bragged on about it. She said that if one day she wanted to make a million bucks, all the had to do was sell the book to a newspaper or magazine.'

'Where's the book?' Frank asked.

'Don't know. I guess she kept it at her place.'

Frank and I hadn't recovered a black address book of any sort.

'You're sure about this address book?' I asked.

'I saw it. She wouldn't let me look inside it, but I saw the book.' She made a square in the air about five centimetres by twenty centimetres in diameter. 'It was about that size. "My little black book of horrors", she used to call it. I thought it was rather sad. All the people in her book were men who cheated on their wives, men who lied to their family and friends, men in high places who probably lied about other things as well. I mean how can you trust someone who lies to his wife? Look what it's done to the American President. Such a disgrace.'

It was true that the President of the United States of America's affair with a young intern had tarnished his image forever. And it wasn't so much because of the affair in a way, but because he lied to everyone around him, insisting he never had a sexual relationship with the young woman. I hadn't made up my mind as to what to think of him because frankly every man cheated on his wife at one time or another.

Frank emptied his mug and said, 'Anything else you can tell us that might help with the investigation?'

Judith passed one hand over her round face. 'Like I said, she was going out with someone. You should try to find out who this person was. She must have disclosed his identity to another person. Someone must have seen them together somewhere. It could have easily been one of her clients. I don't know how you're going to get your hands on that little black book.'

Neither did I.

We emptied our mugs and thanked Judith for her time.

She walked us to the door and promised to keep in touch if she remembered anything that would help us with our investigation.

Frank and I walked back to the car.

'Want to come over to my place?' Frank asked, as we stepped inside the Ford Falcon. 'We can brainstorm everything we've got so far, look over the crime scene photos, re-watch the video, really get our minds wrapped around this investigation.'

I understood his excitement. When involved in a mind-boggling case, it was hard not to become obsessed. However, time and experience had taught me to pace myself. The best results were not always achieved under pressure. My private life still counted for something, even if I was just sitting in the backyard of my new home with a good book and a glass of Chardonnay.

And besides, Frank had picked the wrong night.

'I can't,' I said, while clicking in my seat belt, 'I'm booked for the evening.'

He nodded, half-turned the ignition key and revved up the engine. Without looking at me, he said, 'Who is he?'

'None of your goddamn business!' I snapped unintentionally.

'Hey, I'm sorry. I was just asking. No need to get so nasty.'

I straightened on my seat. 'No, no, I'm sorry. I'm just feeling edgy with this investigation. I still can't get over the fact that the victim was my friend.'

Frank did a u-turn and said, 'You can step down any time you want. I'm not going to stop you. I just want what's best for you.'

There was sincerity in his eyes.

'I'll hang in there,' I said. 'I need to find the bastard who killed her.'

'Yeah, well, just make sure you *do* hang in there for the right reasons.'

It was clear he was beginning to doubt my real motive in this investigation.

And so did I.

CHAPTER ELEVEN

When I got home, there was a message from Goosh on my answering machine. He wanted to know how the investigation was progressing. Instead of returning his call, I faxed him the preliminary report I typed that afternoon. I had concluded that at this stage we had no suspects and were unlikely to get one for at least another week. I also mentioned that if there were to be any suspects in the near future, they would most likely be some of Evelyn's clients. Other than that, I kept the report pretty formal and free of biased opinion. Unfortunately, Goosh's attitude towards unsworn contracted investigators limited my ability to reveal myself in a more candid manner. And he could only blame himself for that.

Michael was home, alone in the confinement of his bedroom. I saw little of him, and whenever I did, it was for a couple of minutes at the most. He usually rushed from one room to the other. Sometimes I caught glimpses of him when he left for school in the morning.

His form coordinator contacted me on my mobile phone a couple of weeks ago, expressing concern at the way Michael refused to participate in class activities or socialise with other students. His school work was borderline, and based on his current effort, I was told, it would be unlikely that he would pass year eight without having to repeat. Michael's teachers had been informed of what had happened to him the previous year, how he and I nearly lost our lives. The school principal recommended professional counselling, but Michael refused. The principal asked me to pressure Michael into attending the counselling sessions, and I replied it was ultimately his choice.

The right time would come when he would open up and realise life wasn't over yet, that we had been lucky to escape death on that particular occasion, and we should be thanking our lucky stars instead of dwelling on the trauma we had experienced.

Despite my self-assurance that Michael would eventually break-out of his cocoon, I often wondered if I was doing enough in helping him. If I said nothing and ignored his problem, I was a bad mother. If I nagged him, I was a bad mother. Was there any way to win this?

I shrugged while slicing capsicums and tomatoes on the chopping board to make a ratatouille for the following day. The fear of facing my own son was eating away my soul. But still I was acutely aware that I loved him too much to do nothing about it. After much internal debating with myself, I decided to bring dinner to his room. That would give me an excuse to confront him.

The ratatouille was ready within half an hour. I filled two plastic containers with it and stored them in the fridge. I hadn't asked Michael if he wanted any because he would have told me that wasn't hungry. I was certain he hadn't eaten anything all day, and although his loss of appetite was most probably genuine, it hurt me to see him fade away.

I filled his plate with two generous scoops of ratatouille, one serve of pasta and two slices of white bread. The plate balancing on my left hand, I grabbed a can of Coke from the fridge with my right one.

Without knocking on the door of his room, I pushed it open with my foot, maintaining balance with the plate and the can of Coke.

Michael was lying on his bed, staring at the ceiling, a pair of tiny earphones inserted in his ears. I could hear the bass and drum thumping from his portable CD-player.

He glanced towards me and twisted his mouth. Without removing his earphones, he yelled, 'I'm not hungry'. With the music blasting in his ears, he was probably not aware of how loud he sounded.

Ignoring his protest, I approached the bed and placed the plate on his side table. There, I noticed the plastic case of the CD he was listening to. I looked at the cover twice because I couldn't believe what I was reading. *Pussy Galore, Dial 'M' for*

Motherfucker. God, I didn't know it was legal to release such rubbish. And to think he paid for it with the pocket money I gave him made me sick.

I made a gesture with both my hands, asking him to remove his earphones.

He pulled an annoyed face and slipped off only one of the earphones.

'What?'

'Eat something.'

'I told you I'm not hungry.'

I should have kept it to myself, but I had to ask him the next question. 'What's this rubbish you're listening to?'

'It's not rubbish.'

'Pussy Galore? It's not rubbish?'

'It's a punk group.'

'Nineties trash.'

'They formed in 1985 in Washington DC with a rockabilly undertone pinched from The Cramps. Not what you would call nineties music.'

Whatever, I thought. He knew as much about music than I knew about crime-scene investigation. Every generation was pushing the boundaries of music one step further into vulgarity and decadence. The obscenities musicians got away with in the name of art and freedom of expression was unbelievable. Maybe I was too old fashioned. A few generations ago, parents said the same thing about The Beatles and The Rolling Stones. In twenty years from now, maybe Pussy Galore will be seen as a middle-of-the-road band, and dismembering fans on stage in the middle of screaming guitars would be the norm.

I went on, 'We need to talk, Michael. You can't go one living this way. It's unhealthy.'

'Yeah, well, I'm cut for it. I'm not complaining.'

'That's just it. Why aren't you complaining? Why aren't you saying what's on your mind?'

'Man, do you have to? I don't want to deal with this shit right now.'

I snapped. 'Watch your language, young man, I'm your mother. I only want to help you.'

He stared at me for ten seconds.

'If I eat this stuff,' he said, pointing at the ratatouille and Coke, 'will you split?'

I didn't answer straight away. 'Sure. You go ahead, eat your food and pretend I don't exist.' I was getting worked up, feeling heat on my cheeks. 'I don't mind, I don't have feelings, you're the only one who's hurting here. Go ahead and live your life the way you see it fit.'

Angry, I turned around and paced towards the door.

'Fuck you!' he whispered as I closed the door behind me.

I ignored him, letting hot tears cascade down my face.

Whether he believed me or not, he was the only person I truly loved.

When David arrived at my place, he knew I was upset straight away. I wasn't my usual chatty self. My eyes were still puffy and red from crying.

We were sitting at the kitchen table, drinking coffee before leaving for our restaurant outing. David tried hard to make me feel better, asking if there was anything he could do to help.

'I'm all right,' I said, not wanting to burden his conscious with my single-mother traumas. 'I'm just having trouble getting through to Michael. He hasn't been himself since an incident last year, and now, well, it's like talking to a brick.'

David sipped from his mug. 'Hey, that's normal. We were all the same at his age. Teenage years are the most difficult in life. You don't belong anywhere, you don't have any worth to anyone, everything you say comes out wrong, and mostly, you don't believe anyone could really love you for who you are. I don't remember my teenage years being much fun. Maybe Michael feels the same. Maybe he doesn't feel like he really belongs anywhere. Maybe he doesn't feel loved.'

'I love Michael, and he knows it.'

'Does he?'

'I give him everything he needs. The freedom he craves, I let him decide what to do with his life, and in return he treats me like if I'm the enemy.'

David took my hand in his. 'Ah, come on, Kristina. Don't you think you're over-reacting? Do you seriously think Michael doesn't care about you?'

I stood still for a few seconds, my stomach churning and

filled with highly-strung emotions. I pulled my hand away from his. 'I don't know what to believe any more. I brought up Michael by myself, thinking I had made the right choice. But now, I'm wondering if it wasn't a mistake. Without a father, Michael doesn't have a male figure he can look up to and respect. That's probably why he is confused. But whatever the reason, it makes me miserable to see him miserable. And I don't know how much longer I can live like this way.'

David said nothing for the next thirty seconds. He let me simmer in my own thoughts.

'You know, Kristina,' he finally said, 'I think you're the nicest person I've met in a very long time. Maybe you think Michael doesn't love you because you don't truly love yourself.'

I shoot him a defensive glare.

He went on, 'I'm not saying you can't accept yourself. At our age, if we haven't accepted ourselves, we're doomed. What I'm getting at is do you ever ask yourself, "Do I really love who I am?" Have you ever asked yourself that question, Kristina?'

No, I hadn't asked myself that question. I guess I was too busy wondering if Michael and the rest of the world loved me.

'You make it sound so simple,' I said. 'Life is not about loving yourself. It's about being part of society. It's about loving others and being loved in return.'

'Ah, but you see, that's where you become vulnerable. If your self-worth is build on someone else opinion or feelings, that you lose control of yourself.'

'Well, that's easy for you to say, you don't have kids.'

'So?'

'You wouldn't know what it's like to love someone unconditionally, to put your life at risk to save them, to give them everything you've got at the chance of loosing everything you want and everything you've got.'

'And because I don't have kids, that makes me incapable of understanding other people?'

I paused for a few seconds. Maybe he was right. Maybe it had nothing to do with it, and I was just trying to fight an argument I couldn't win.

'Okay,' I said, 'so what's your point?'

'If you want people to love you, to accept you for who your are, stop trying. Just embrace yourself and the world you're in, otherwise you'll let other people control your life. And that's how you become confused and lose direction.'

David was nice, but he probably read too many New Age books. He sounded like some guru who was trying to convert me into his religion. It was like watching Oprah.

'I know you mean well, David, but please don't try to lecture me about life. I'm a very independent woman. I fell to see how we're going to get anywhere if we start telling each other how to live our lives.'

His eyes went glassy, and I knew I hurt him.

'I'm sorry,' I went on, 'I don't mean to be rude. I just don't like being told what to do.'

'That's all right. I understand. I don't like people telling me what to do either. I'm fairly independent myself. Our independence is probably what attracted us to one another. I respect the choices you've made in your life, and I respect you as a person. That's why I'd like to get to know you better.'

I smiled and took his hand in mine.

Another man had just entered my life.

CHAPTER TWELVE

We ended up going to Jacques Reymond for dinner. I had never been to the French restaurant before, but David insisted that just the location in Prahran, and the way the grand old mansion and garden had been converted into a restaurant and reception room was worth the bother. He was right. We choose a private room with a fireplace.

'Jacques Reymond is the best chef in Melbourne,' David said as we read through our menu.

'Really?' I asked, a little taken back by the prices.

'Expensive, I know, but it's worth every dollar. Jacques is from the Burgundy regions, you know where they make great wines.'

'Yes, I know everything about wines.'

'Of course you do.'

I ended up ordering what he ordered because firstly I wasn't very hungry, and secondly I had never eaten anything on the menu anyway. We began with an entree of tart of scallop and baby octopus. I picked a bottle Auxey-Duresses, and on testing, its aroma was filled with the fragrance and freshness of raspberries and wild strawberries, as was often the case with reds of that region.

David was agreeably cheerful, but no matter how entertaining he tried to be, my mood remained low. Michael was on my mind, and all I felt was guilt of not having done enough as a mother to make him feel strong and confident against the challenges of life. I knew there was only so much I could do, but excuses never sat well with me. Maybe I was being too harsh on myself.

By the time we began consuming the breast of duck for our main course, David was elaborating on some renovation plans for his bookshop. But my thoughts were still scattered all over, and I found it hard to focus on our conversation. As much as I was glad to have some delightful company, the thought of rushing back home tempted me. Restaurants were not really my thing when it came to romancing. I liked the freedom of being at home, where I could act impulsively without having to worry about who's eyes were on us.

Finally, when the young waitress came and asked us if we were ready to order dessert, I said, 'Can we go home, David? I'm really not in the mood to stay up all night.'

'Sure,' he said, his voice surprisingly cheerful for someone who had just spent the whole evening with a grump like me.

When we got back to Craigieburn, Michael was asleep. At least, I thought he was. It was 10.32 p.m., and the light in his room was turned off. No music was blasting from his teenage sanctuary. I was tempted to go and see how he was, but resisted after concluding I had invaded his privacy once too many already today.

I invited David to stay for a nightcap but had another agenda trotting at the back of my mind.

'What have you got?' he asked. He slipped off his wool-blend sports jacket and carefully placed it across the arm of the floral couch in the living room.

'Brandy,' I said.

'Brandy is fine.'

'Cognac or Armagnac?'

'What's the difference?' He looked sightly embarrassed. 'I'm sorry, I'm not very familiar with fortified wines.'

'Cognac is more refined and elegant. Armagnac is earthier and more robust. Either way, the best brandy is always made from the worst wine.' My last boyfriend had an encyclopaedic knowledge of wines, and I was fortunate enough that some of it had rubbed off on me. 'But if that scares you,' I went on, 'I can always give you a glass of Fundador—it's a cheap and nasty Spanish brandy I keep behind the bar for people who don't appreciate the finer wines.'

'Okay, I think I'll just have what you're having.'

'Cognac it is then.'

We sat on the couch, sipping our brandy and getting used to being alone by ourselves. In the background Bill Cunliffe, one of America's best and busiest jazz pianists, was playing Bud Powell's Polka Dots and Moonbeams on my hi-fi system. The lights were low, thanks to the dimmer control I had installed, and the atmosphere was that of a Sunday bay-side cafe.

I was dying to make a move and kiss him, but I felt it better to wait and let him do the seducing. Still old-fashioned at heart, I didn't agree with the views of Gloria Steinem or any other radical feminists. I believed in my own power and my right to choose, but when it came to romance, I liked to be pampered. Also, if he made the first move, and later I changed my mind, I could always argue that he came on to me, that he didn't leave me a choice. And that I was drunk anyway, so I didn't know what I was doing.

'Any progress on the investigation?' he asked, breaking the awkward silence between us.

I hated discussing the Evelyn Carter case with him. It was bad enough I had invited him over when he was a key witness in the on-going investigation. But desperate for intimacy, and with the effect of the brandy clouding my judgement, I chose the path of least resistance.

'Nothing so far,' I said. 'We're looking for a little black book where Evelyn would have kept names and contacts of her clients. The killer would most certainly be in that book. I just don't understand where the book has gone to. Conveniently vanished the night she was killed.'

'Maybe the killer took it with him when he killed her. Since she was found naked, it's easy to assume that he took her personal belongings with him.'

Now that David mentioned it, it was true that we never recovered Evelyn's driver's license, credit cards and other personal items women usually took with them everywhere they went.

I took another sip from my brandy and continued on the same topic for lack of having anything else to say, 'So, you think the bastard got the book?'

'Seems like a logical conclusion.' He paused and then added, 'So, the lab's figured out who's semen it is they found inside her?'

'Nope. No idea at this stage.'

Nodding, I poured myself another brandy. Dizziness began taking over. I wasn't used to drinking so much, and I knew that when I drank it meant something in my life wasn't going right. And what the hell was he waiting for? I began to ponder on the possibility that he might be gay, and I never picked up the obvious signs.

I took a mouthful of brandy and swallowed it. It felt good.

And then, without warning, I tilted my head towards David's. The smell of his citrus aftershave filled my nostrils, sending my soul to a new level of ecstasy. So much for not making the first move. I had a serious need to review my stand on feminism and the art of seduction.

My head resting on his chest, I said, ' I always swore I'd never get involved like this... but you are so terribly attractive.'

He brushed my hair with his hand.

'I knew from the moment we met, you were meant for me,' he said.

I looked up to him smiling. 'Did you?' Half of me wanted to believe him, the other half assured me he was testing my gullibility.

'You have the most beautiful eyes,' he said. 'And that smile.'

I didn't answer, but stared at him instead. A warm sensation was taking over my body, and I knew it wasn't the brandy. The alcohol had gone to my head a while back. I wrapped my arms around his neck and gently moved my head closer.

We kissed slowly, like first-timers do, and then passionately. His kiss tasted sweet. It made me feel like I belonged somewhere. It reminded me of lollies I used to hide under my pillow as a little girl and ate at night when the lights were turned off, and everyone was asleep. I used to suck on the strawberry hard-boils, feeling secure and happy. David's kiss evoked those feelings.

After kissing, everything brushed past too fast for me to recall all the details. All I remember is I was drunk, and we were in my room, and we made love.

And it was good.

Damn good in fact.

I hadn't made passionate love to someone for a very long time. My heart and soul were bare for his taking.

David seemed to know what I wanted without asking. He explored every part of my body with such gentleness. It felt like the most natural thing in the world. I went to sleep in the haze of a drunken hour, feeling like I had just sucked on a kilo of strawberry hard-boils.

When I woke up the next morning, nausea forcing me to go to the bathroom and empty the contents of my stomach. My skin had turned yellow, bags hung under my eyes, and, basically, I felt like shit. The taste of expensive cognac was hanging at the back of my throat like cough medicine.

David was still in bed asleep when I returned to the bedroom, my auburn hair pulled back into a pony tail and my face refreshed from splashing it with tap water.

His hair was unkempt, and there was a smile on his face. I stood at the edge of the bed, watching him sleep. I was happy but at the same time confused. Was this really the man I had longed for all my life? How would I know, and how long would it take for us to trust each other beyond a shadow of a doubt? I wanted to get down on my knees and beg God to make him the one because I was sick and tired of searching for the right man. But I had enough dignity left in me to remain on my feet.

Trying not to dwell too much on my emotional despair, I paced to the kitchen and put some water on the boil for coffee.

While the water was heating up, I decided to sneak into Michael's room to see if he was still asleep. I had no idea what the time was, but daylight had already crept inside my home, and I could hear cows mooing outside. I left my watch by the side-table in the bedroom, and I've been putting off buying a wall clock for the kitchen forever. It felt like around eight thirty, but with a hangover, it was hard to tell for sure.

I pushed the door of Michael's room gently, in case he was asleep. But no one was in bed. The clock on his side table read 9:32 a.m. I miscalculated by an hour. Michael had already left for school and wouldn't be back until later this afternoon. Chances were I wouldn't be here when he got home.

When I returned to the kitchen, David was already up, scooping out coffee from a jar of Nescafé.

'How do you have yours?' he asked before I had time to greet him.

'Black, no sugar.'

'Mmmm...'

I moved behind him and wrapped my arms around his waist.

'Last night was good,' I said. 'Was it good for you?'

He turned around and kissed me. 'Nights are always good.'

'Do you still love them in the morning?' I asked.

'I love them to death,' he said and pressed his lips against mine.

CHAPTER THIRTEEN

Frank and I were on our way to the VFSC in Macleod. I was driving my Excell, while he was chain-smoking with the window open. The air was cold and went right through my blouse. Grey clouds hovered over the city, and I knew the day wouldn't end without another downpour. God, I hated Melbourne winters. All I really wanted to do was stay home with the heater on full blast and overdose on hot coffee all day long. Temptation was even stronger on that particular morning—I was still feeling the effect from drinking too much brandy with David the previous night.

'Do you have to?' I asked.

Frank knew I was talking about his smoking. Without arguing, he tossed the cigarette out the car, and wound up the window. He was clean-shaven and looked as if he had had his eight hours sleep. Even after a week, I hadn't gotten used to seeing him without his moustache, and my first impression still stood; he looked younger and almost attractive.

'So who was your hot date yesterday?' he asked, staring at the road ahead of him.

'Is that a trick question?'

He turned around and scrutinised me for a little while.

I choose to ignore him.

'Did you fuck him?' he finally said, all emotion drained from his voice.

I pressed hard on the brakes and pulled to the side of the road. I reached over his lap and opened the passenger door.

'Get out!' I ordered.

He stared at me as if I'd just knocked him over the head with a cricket bat.

I went on, 'I'm not joking, get out of the car now. You can catch a cab or hitch-hike'

The car was parked to the side of a busy highway, and there would be no way of him finding a cab unless he called one on his mobile. Frankly, I didn't give a damn. I was in no mood for his attitude, especially first thing in the morning.

'I'm sorry,' he said sheepishly. 'I didn't mean it like that. I was joking. I was out of line.'

'Get out.'

'Kristina...' His apology was turning into whimpering. 'Don't do this here. I was wrong, all right. What do you want me to say? If I'd known you were in such a pissy mood, I wouldn't have said anything. I swear. Give me a break.'

If I'd been a man, I would have punched him square in the jaw and let him collect his own teeth.

I slammed his door from the inside and said, 'Fine, but one more word out of you, and you can take a hike.'

'Sure, sure. I'm really sorry. I'm just not used to—'

'Not used to what? Not used to the idea that I'm my own person, and I've got the right to go out with whomever I choose, and that you're not the man I want to spend the rest of my life with?' I released the handbrake and merged back into the traffic. 'I can't believe you can be such a jerk at times. You think you know someone after spending so much time with them, and then you realise you don't know them at all.'

'Ah, come on. You make it sound like it's the end of the world.'

I said nothing more but clenched my teeth instead.

'You know it's not my fault,' he added. 'You know how I feel about you. I get jealous when I hear you've been out with another man. What do you want me to do? I haven't seen you for months. You haven't called. I mean, were we really friends to begin with or just work colleagues?'

'It makes no difference, Frank.'

'What do you mean it makes no difference? Don't you consider me your friend?'

'You're trying to hang on to things you can't hang on to.

Friendship is just friendship, and when it dies, you don't try to hang on to it. It's a mistake. Maybe we're just good work colleagues, you could be right. Maybe we were not designed to be good friends. I don't know. Let's not talk about this any more. It's driving me insane, and it really doesn't matter. Why can't you just take things as they come?'

He sulked in his seat during the rest of the trip.

At 2.34 p.m., Frank and I were in a laboratory, which was part of the biology department at the VFSC. John Darcy had finished conducting DNA testing on a vaginal swab from Evelyn Carter. John confirmed that the swab contained traces of semen.

John Darcy was a qualified forensic biologist and held the position of branch manager at the VFSC Forensic Biology Unit. Although he was fifty-four years old, blessed with blond locks, blue eyes and neatly trimmed beard, he could have easily passed for someone ten years younger. His lab coat was decorated with chemical and ink stains. A blue, a black, a green and a red pen were sticking out from his breast pocket, all having left a corresponding stain on his white lab coat.

John was comparing the polymeric sequences from the DNA autoradiograph from Evelyn's vaginal swab with those of another DNA test done from Peter Perezzia's blood sample. The cab driver had been reluctant to provide us a blood sample. I assured him that if he didn't commit the murder, he had nothing to fear. Then I threatened that if he refused to have a blood sample taken, he would be forced to give one. Initially, Perezzia was probably unaware that since he had previously been jailed for a minor offence, the police had the power to apply to the courts for a forensic sample, in most cases blood, to be used for testing and comparisons. The new legislation, which had kicked in only recently, had also prompted John Darcy to increase the number of samples taken from probable suspects from 2500 to 15,000 a year. After having discussed his case with his solicitor, Perezzia agreed to submit a blood sample.

Frank was standing by my side, lost in his own world. His hands inserted deeply in the pockets of his beige chinos, while now and then scratching somewhere awfully close to his private parts. I bet all he wanted to do was to go home and forget about me for a while. Frankly, it was his fault. If he couldn't accept that I wasn't interested in him, then he must have been blind. I'd made it clear in the past, and I was getting tired of having to repeat myself. For starters, he turned me on as much as a door knob. And then, even though he probably meant well, his obsession towards me was bordering on compulsive obsessive behaviour. Had I not known him better, I probably would have filed for sexual harassment.

'Any match?' I asked John, who was still pre-occupied with the analysis of the DNA testing.

'The HLA-DQA1, the D1S80 and the HUMTHO1 are all different; 2.3 to 2.5, 18/24 to 24/29 and 6/9 to 6/7. This is not the same guy.'

John was referring to the numerical values of a variety of DNA tests. He had conducted a variety of DNA tests to minimise the chances of error or misleading results. Every additional test which resulted in a mismatch indicating an increased level of reliability on the findings.

'Shit,' I said openly.

This was as bad as it gets since DNA typing is so specific that it can help identify one individual from a million others. Perezzia had been our only suspect to date. And now that the DNA tests from his blood and Evelyn's swab came unmatched, we were left with no concrete leads. At the back of my mind, I had hoped the killer would have been Perezzia. I wanted this investigation to be over and done with. It had only begun a week or so ago, but the pressure was affecting everyone involved.

I turned to Frank and said, 'Well, that's it, just as well we didn't keep Perezzia locked up.'

Frank didn't respond. He stared at a yellow biological container resting on a galvanised bench on the other side of the room. His eyes were glazed, and his face was drained from colour. I could smell his all-too-familiar body odour, a mixture of sweat and cheap after-shave. He seemed miserable, lost in his own twisted emotions.

'Hey,' I said, 'you're awake?'

He turned around as if I'd pulled him by the little hair he had left. 'Uh? What? What is it?' He looked at me and then at John. 'So, is it a match?'

John shook his head vigorously.

Frank went on, 'Oh, well, doesn't matter, we'll find the prick one way or another.'

When we returned to the car, Frank didn't comment on the results. Normally he had an opinion on every forensic test conducted. He enlightened me with his viewpoint, whether I wanted to hear it or not.

'You okay?' I asked, feeling somehow responsible for his down-spiralled moodiness.

'Yeah, yeah. You don't want to know anyway.'

'Frank—'

'Butt off, will you?' Anger infested his tone.

'What's wrong?'

'I made a mistake, okay? I should have left things the way they were.'

'What are you talking about?'

'I should have never asked you to join the investigation.'

I remained silent for a few seconds. Puzzled, I inserted the keys into the passenger door of my car. 'You don't have to get so personal about everything,' I finally said, sensing he was waiting for some form of reply.

'You're right, I'll keep that in mind in the future.'

We stepped in the car, not saying a word to one another. What now? I hated to be made to feel guilty and responsible for something I hadn't initiated. I hated it even more when I had so many worries on my mind, and Frank found nothing better to do than pick on the details of our friendship. Had this investigation been about anyone else than Evelyn Carter, I would have stepped aside.

As it was, my commitment to finding the killer was deeper than a professional endeavour. I would track the bastard down, and I would make sure justice would be served.

CHAPTER FOURTEEN

I left Frank at the St Kilda Road Police building complex and headed back home. The traffic was heavy out-bound on my way to Craigieburn. One hand on the steering wheel, I punched my home number on the mobile phone. The phone rang five times before the answering machine kicked in. I frowned as I pressed the end button. It was just on 4.30 p.m., and Michael should have been back from school by now. I was more than a little concerned, especially when taking into consideration the way he had been acting recently.

A bus on Mickleham Road slowed the caravan of cars down to fifty kilometres per hour, enough to annoy me and the driver of a 70's model Holden, who seemed to want to mount my car with its bumper. I had to keep one eye in front and one on the rear mirror. Had I been a cop, I would have pulled the bastard over and issued him a canary. Things being as they were, all I could do was grit my teeth and hope for the best.

Half an hour later, I parked in the driveway of my home, no Holden attached to my back fender. Through the fence, I could see the overgrown grass in the backyard. The last time it had seen a lawn mower was six months ago, and I hated to be the one who was going to get the task of cutting it next. The damn job would probably take three hours, not to mention endless trips to the tip.

Rubbing the back of my neck, I inserted the keys into the

front door lock, turned it clockwise, and pushed the door open.

'Michael?'

No reply.

'Michael? Are you home?'

I moved to the hallway and closed the door behind me.

Not a sound.

Maybe he had his head phones tightly strapped to his head and Pussy Galore busting his ear drums.

I paced to the kitchen, tossed my briefcase on the Formica bench and aimed for his room.

No one was there.

A chill rippled down my spine as I wondered why he hadn't made it back from school yet. I checked the time on my wrist watch: 5.23 p.m. He should have been back an hour and a half ago. I knew he didn't have any friends, so it wasn't like he stayed over at someone's place. And even if he did, he would have left a message on the answering machine or called me on the mobile.

I returned to the kitchen, panic settling in. My hands were shaking as I picked up the phone attached to the wall above the kitchen bench.

I had to call someone and share my despair. At the back of my mind, I knew I was probably over-dramatising the whole situation, but my nerves were raw from the emotional intensity of the working day.

I placed the receiver down and paced the kitchen up and down a few times. I really needed to talk to someone.

Without thinking, I sat on the floral couch in the living room, pulled David's business card from my hand bag and dialled his work number.

'David's Bookshop.' His voice was formal and friendly at the same time. It reminded me of a commercial jingle.

I was about to hang up, fearing I made a mistake calling him, but changed my mind.

'David, it's me, Kristina.'

'Oh, hi, Kristina. What's up?'

'I'm sorry to call you.' I explained how Michael had not come home and how I was worried.

'He's probably at a friend's place,' David said.

'He doesn't have friends. Not in this town. We've only moved in recently, and he has had a hard time adjusting.'

'Maybe he's got some homework and stayed behind at school to do them.'

'Michael hasn't touched his homework for at least two months. I don't think so.'

'Maybe he's got a detention.'

I shrugged. 'Well, that makes me feel better.'

'He's a boy you know. Boys do get into trouble.' He paused for a few seconds and added, 'Why don't you run up to the school and see if he's still there?'

I puzzled over his suggestion. 'Look, you're probably right, David. I'm sorry I've called you. I just needed to let the fear out of my system, and I didn't know who else to call. It's been a really long day—I'm probably a little stressed, you know with the investigation and everything.'

'You did the right thing calling me. It's not a problem at all.'

We talked shop for a while, and then he said, 'How are you going with the investigation?'

'No good. The cab driver is in the clear. We compared his DNA with that of seminal fluid found inside Evelyn Carter. No match.'

'Oh, well, at least you're one step ahead—you know he's innocent.'

'Yeah, I guess he his.'

There was an awkward silence, then he added, 'Why don't I come over for a while? You sound like you could do with the company.'

I hesitated and said, 'I want to find out where Michael is.'

'I can help you find him.'

Ten seconds of silence followed.

I twisted the telephone cord and said, 'I think it's better if I try to find him on my own.' I bit my lower lip as I hoped to God he wasn't going to take it the wrong way. I was attracted to him, and at this stage it was probably nothing more than lust, but still I hated the thought of hurting his feelings.

'Sure, that's fine.'

He took it well, and I was almost annoyed that he didn't try to argue with me. I could almost taste his kiss. I needed to feel him near me, hold me in his arms, tell me everything was going to be all right.

'Why don't you come around for breakfast tomorrow morning,' I suggested, not wanting to give in fully to my churning desires.

'I've got the bookshop to run during the day.' There was a slight edge of annoyance in his tone.

'Surely, you can keep it closed for one morning.'

He hesitated for a few second. 'Okay, sure, as you wish.'

We chatted a little more about a sale he was organising for the weekend, and I told him how I wanted this investigation to end so I could get on with my life.

'Quit now if it's taking too much out of you,' he said. 'You only took on this case because you're personally attached to it. You told me yourself that you stopped investigating homicides because it was affecting your personal life.'

'I can't quit, David. I owe it to Evelyn to find out who the murderer is.'

'Sure, I understand, but Evelyn is dead. And I'm not. You know as well as I do that we shouldn't even be talking to each other at this stage. The fact that we've started having a relationship is going to affect the outcomes of this investigation. You're seem to be forgetting that I'm a witness to this case. If the killer is ever found and the whole thing goes to court, the defence is going to have a field day between the two of us. I'll probably be dismissed as a witness, and the credibility of the investigation would be scrutinised every step of the way.'

Obviously, David had read a lot of crime books, and he knew what he was talking about. The last thing I needed right now was to make some mental juggling about the right thing to do and my need for emotional cocooning.

'David,' I said, 'don't think I haven't thought about all that. Don't think I haven't turned this whole thing over in my head hundred times over. For all I know you could have been the killer. In my line of work, everyone is a suspect. Do you remember Frank Moore, the detective I was with at the crime scene?'

'The one with the ugly mug and the bald head?'

'David!'

'What do you want me to say? I'm sorry, yes, I remember him.'

'A couple of years ago he got into a relationship with a witness in the course of an investigation, and he nearly got the both of us killed.'

'What are you implying?'

'I'm not implying anything. I'm just saying that I'm aware of the difficulty of the situation. I know where I'm standing, I know where you're standing, and that the investigation could fall apart because we're seeing each other.'

There was an awkward silence at the end of the line, and then he said, 'You don't want to end this, do you?'

'No, David, I don't want to end this,' I said, without the slightest hesitation. 'We have the genesis of a relationship, and right now I feel like I could do with someone like you. Your life seems so uncomplicated and settled. Believe me, I need that right now.'

'I'm glad to hear you say that. For a minute I thought you were going to suggest we should stop seeing one another.'

I took a deep breath and said, 'There's only one thing I can rely on it times of moral struggle; that's my instinct. In spite of your involvement in this case, I know I have to go on with what we've got so far. Maybe I'm running too fast, I don't know. I also believe in honesty in a relationship, so if I'm scaring you off, I'm sorry. But it's better that you know how I feel straight from the beginning.'

'You're doing the right thing. Honesty is so rare these days. Everybody is looking after themselves and forgetting there are other people out there.'

After I hung up, I stayed on the couch for a little while, thinking about the investigation. We still had no clue as to why Evelyn had been killed. All we found was blood in a cab and unidentified semen in her vagina. And we knew about a black book with names and addresses I couldn't get my hands on. I thought carefully about what my next move would be. I had to go back to Evelyn's apartment and search the place again. Maybe she hidden the address book somewhere no one could find it. It could have been lying under a floor board, hidden inside a coffee tin, buried in a packet of cereal, stuck under the top of the toilet cistern, buried in the backyard, planted inside the wall heater, or hidden in one of hundreds of places where people usually hid their secret possessions. At the worst, the killer might have taken the book with him.

I stood from the couch and walked to the kitchen, hoping Michael would make an appearance soon. From the fridge, I poured myself a glass of water and drank it in one go. I thought about Evelyn's friend in the US and wondered if there's was a way I could get in touch with her. According to Judith Kingman, the two kept in touch on a regular basis. I made a mental note about getting Evelyn's telephone record checked. If she rang overseas, the telephone company would still have details. In fact, if she rang any mobile phones, I still had the chance to be provided with fresh leads.

Suddenly the telephone rang, nearly giving me a heart attack. As I reached for the receiver, I expected to hear Michael at the end of the line. But my excitation was short-lived when I heard Goosh at the end of the line instead. He told me that he'd received my report, and that he found it rather incomplete.

'I've done the best I can,' I said, clearly upset by his bad-mannered approach.

'What you have done is an absolute waste of time. You're costing us an arm and a leg, and the type of reports you are producing stink of amateurism.'

That really hurt, even if it came from an arsehole like him. I had worked hard on that report, knowing he was going to try his best to shred me into pieces.

'You know,' I said, 'I don't know why you couldn't make this call during business hours instead of calling me at home. It's late, and if you don't mind, we can take this up tomorrow morning.'

There was a three-second pause, and then he said, 'I want you out of the case. Your past involvement with Evelyn Carter makes you unsuitable to investigate this crime. I'm going to ask you to step down now.'

'And if I don't?'

'Then it's only a matter of time. You count my words. In twenty-four hours, you'll have all the time in the world to teach yourself how to write professional investigative reports.'

Sonofabitch was really beginning to irritate me.

'I don't mean to be rude, Mr Goosh, but you're opinion really doesn't interest me. I've got better things to do that listening to your childish monologues. So, if you don't mind, we'll leave it at that.'

Before he could say another word, I hung up on him.

CHAPTER FIFTEEN

I cooked myself a frozen fish fillet with brown rice, and added a generous serving of ratatouille I made the previous day. Ratatouille tastes better the day after it's made, and I prefer eating it cold. It enhances its strong capsicum and black olive flavour.

I ate by myself at the kitchen table. The Los Angeles Jazz Quartet played at half-volume through the hi-fi in the lounge room. But I wasn't listening to the acoustic-based jazz group playing the classics of jazz greats, such as Wayne Shorter, Thelonius Monk, John Coltrane and Lennie Tristano. In spite of it being one of my favourite jazz groups, my mind was preoccupied with Michael. How long would I have to wait before reporting him missing? I knew he was old enough at hang around with his friends if he wanted to, and that was why I tried hard to carry on as if nothing had happened. But I knew he didn't have any friends, and that in itself was worrisome.

Finally, not able to stand it any longer, I called Frank at home.

We said hello, and then I asked him if he was okay after sensing tension in his voice. He was probably still worked up from the argument we had a few hours ago.

'Is that why you're calling me?' he asked.

'No, actually. I need your help.'

His tone softened, 'In what way?'

I explained how Michael hadn't turned up from school, and how I wasn't sure how to handle the situation.

'Why didn't you call me sooner? Jesus Christ, Kristina, I'm your friend.'

'I thought you hated me after this afternoon.'

'Kristina, no matter what a bitch you turn out to be, you'll always be my friend.'

His words nearly brought tears to my eyes. Frank had always been so nice to me, and I had always been such a cow. Even if suddenly he turned into a handsome man with a head full of thick dark hair and a well-toned body, I didn't deserve him.

I stayed silent for a few seconds, drowning in self-hatred.

'Why don't I come over and help you look for him?' he suggested.

'Okay,' I said.

I hung up the phone, placed my dirty dishes in the sink, squirted dish-washing liquid over them and began to sob.

Frank arrived forty-five minutes later.

Still no sign of Michael.

When I opened the front door to let Frank in, it was obvious he knew I'd been crying. His eyes dug straight into mine, and without warning he moved forward and hugged me. I noticed that he wore jeans and a white cotton T-shirt. It felt strange because I was so used to seeing him dressed in his shirt-and-black attire.

'Oh, Kristina, I'm so sorry about the way things have turned out. You know you'll always be my friend. You can always count on me. Don't hesitate to call next time if you have a problem. It makes me feel so inadequate that you've been bottling it up without calling me.'

I snuggled up to him, placing my arms around his chest, taking in the familiar and comforting smell of cigarette smoking and cheap aftershave. Thank God for you, I thought, realising that there was really no other man in my life who had genuinely cared for me for so long.

When the hugging lasted too long, and he began padding the back of my head, I stepped back and wiped my tears. As

110

much as I needed him, I didn't want our friendship to spin out of control and turn into one of these Beauty-And-The-Beast romantic scenarios.

'Thanks, Frank,' I said. 'You've been wonderful. After all that I've put you through time and time again.'

'You look drained,' he said, placing one hand my shoulder. 'You want something to drink?'

'No, I'm fine now.' I wiped the tears from cheeks. 'I just want to know where Michael is.'

'Let's go and find him.'

I grabbed my leather jacket from the couch, and we walked to his car. As soon as he got in the car, he lit a cigarette. I wasn't going to say anything since it was his car, and he'd been kind enough to turn up and comfort me in the first place.

'Do you want me to drive straight to Craigieburn Police Station?' he asked. 'Maybe we can ask them to have a look around town.'

'That would be good.'

He pulled the car out of the driveway, turned left, went around a bend, past a round about, turned right, and got out on Craigieburn West Road towards the police station.

'You're not still angry at me?' I asked.

He didn't answer immediately.

'Are you?'

'I'm okay,' he finally said. 'Nothing I can't handle. Let's not worry about me for the time being. You got me worried about Michael. I'm probably the closest thing he's got to a father right now.'

Even though Frank had been around us for a look time, I had never thought of him being some type of father figure to Michael. Men came and went in my life, but Frank had always been around. So, in a way, maybe Frank was right.

We were in a sixty-kilometre zone, but cars were flying past us as if it was the freeway. Frank could have pulled any of the drivers over, but he didn't care and neither did I. If people were stupid enough to kill themselves on the road just to get home and watch an additional five minutes of mind-numbing television, it was their problem.

In less than three minutes, we pulled into the car park of the Craigieburn Police Station. The blue-grey building was fairly new and had taken a lot of fighting and debating from André Haermeyer, Shadow Minister for Police and Emergencies, who also happened to be the State Member for Yan Yean, a large area in the far north region of Melbourne, which encompassed Craigieburn and a multitude of small suburban and rural towns. I had had the opportunity to meet Haemeyer once at a community public meeting, and he struck me as being one of the few politicians who genuinely believed in placing people before himself. Given that, politics was something I really had no interest in other than a mild awareness that people standing on the upper echelon of society decided everything on our behalf, from which roads would run through our town to whether we deserved a public hospital.

We walked inside the building through an automatic glass sliding door.

The reception area was that of a typical modern police station. A drink machine stood to the left. On my right was a community board with various information on drink driving, burglary, neighbourhood-watch programs, public meetings and other useless information which was supposed to entertain us while someone hidden behind a mirrored window decided whether we were worthy of attention.

Shadows lurked behind the fake mirror, which divided the reception and the rest of the building. In less than thirty seconds, a young male constable appeared from his not-so-secret hiding place. His name tag read John McLuhan. He had a permanent set of bags under his eyes, even though he seemed to be only in his mid-twenties.

Frank pulled his police ID out of his wallet and explained our situation.

'And how long has the boy being missing?' McLuhan asked.

'Well, actually,' I said, 'we don't know if he's missing yet. He just hasn't turned up from school.'

Constable McLuhan seemed slightly annoyed, but because Frank was a senior officer, he must have felt obliged to remain diplomatic. 'Well, why don't you go around and check at his school. He might still be there. In the meantime, I can send someone in the area to check the local Hungry Jack's, library and swimming pool.'

I was going to protest, insisting that Michael never visited those places. But then he was never late from school either. The fact was that he had to be somewhere, and searching the area was what we had intended to do in the first place.

Just when we were about to head back to the car, McLuhan asked, 'Did you ever fight with your son?'

His question took me by surprise.

I did a half turn and locked my eyes with his. 'What are you implying?'

He threw his hands in front of his body. 'Hey, I'm not implying anything, I'm just wondering. We've got a lot of teenagers in the area, and when they disappear it's usually because they've had an argument with their parents. I'm just asking the obvious.'

'No, I didn't have fights with him,' I said, matter-of-factly. I stood still for a few seconds before adding, 'but he did have problems adapting to this area. He had problems at school and was withdrawn after an incident last year.'

'What kind of incident?'

I didn't want to explain everything again. 'Let's just say that he could have been killed. He is still suffering from post-traumatic shock.'

'If he was depressed, maybe he took his own life.'

'I doubt it,' I said. That was all I needed to hear. I turned to Frank. 'Come on, let's go and see if he's still at school.'

When we arrived at Craigieburn Secondary College, everyone had left for the day.

We headed back to the town centre, a group of shops with a Shell petrol station and a Hungry Jack's attached to it.

A police car parked in the front of the Hungry Jack's took me by surprise. When Constable McLuhan said he would send someone around Craigieburn straight away, he hadn't been joking.

A bunch of teenagers, girls and boys, were hanging around the hamburger shop, dressed in Addidas gear, which had miraculously come back into fashion. BMXs were scattered around, as if they'd been abandoned. Two of the boys were smoking, looking unconcerned at the fact that there was a police car just parked there. At least the Hungry Jack's manager didn't tell them to go somewhere else. Grown-ups didn't understand that young people had to be somewhere.

They just couldn't stay home all day and watch television, although many of them did. But somehow, in spite of my empathy towards teenagers, what I was the most concerned about right at this minute was that Michael could be hanging around with a bunch of clowns like that.

Through the window of the burger restaurant, I could see a uniformed police officer talking to Michael at one of the tables. Michael didn't see me. There was half-eaten burger and a drink in front of him. The police officer seemed to be talking, while Michael was tight-lipped. My heart drilled out of my chest the moment I saw him. I didn't know if I was relieved or angry.

'There he is,' I said to Frank, pointing inside the burger restaurant.

'See,' he said, 'you worried about nothing. Just eating junk food with some friends.'

I rushed inside the petrol station, and aimed right straight for the table where the uniformed officer was talking to Michael.

'Michael,' I yelled.

Both the police officer and Michael turned to me, an expression of surprise on their faces.

'There's your mother,' I heard the police officer say. No one had told him who I was, but it would have been easy to guess.

I approached the table and said, 'Michael, what are you doing here? I've been worried sick!'

'Everything's cool, mum. Jeez, you're making a big deal out of nothing. What did you do? Call all the cops in the area?'

'Are you all right?' I asked. My motherly instinct had taken over, and no amount of logic was going to make me see things clearly. All I wanted to do was take him home and give him a good spanking. In my eyes he was still five years old, and I knew at that moment that even in twenty years time I would still see him as a child.

The police officer got to his feet. 'I better leave the two of you alone,' he said and aimed for the door. Who could blame him. I probably reminded him of his own mother.

I sat across from where Michael was sitting. The plastic seat was still warm from where the police officer's butt had been

114

resting.

'Mum, I'm fine, Why can't you just leave me alone? Why can't you just let me be myself?'

I looked at him as if he was speaking a foreign language. 'Michael? Why are you doing this?'

'Doing what? I'm just eating a burger. I'm ten minutes from home. What's the big deal? There's no serial killers in the area.'

Just then, Frank walked in on us.

'The big deal is,' he interrupted, 'that your mother has been worried about you.'

I turned to Frank and snapped. 'Bugger off, will you?'

Frank looked as if I'd just extracted all his front teeth with a set of pliers. 'Okay, fine, sort your own shit out. I'll be waiting outside. But don't make me wait forever.'

He aimed for the exit.

'What's this all about?' I asked Michael.

'What are you?' he said, 'Retarded? I need some space, you're all over me, Jesus. jeez. I can't breath, just leave me alone.'

A knot formed in my stomach. I was lost for words. I looked into his eyes, but all I got in return was an angry stare. I had never seen him like this before. People had warned me about teenagers becoming rebellious, but this was ridiculous. I just couldn't see what I had done wrong.

'Michael, I care about you. I just wanted to know you were, okay? Is that so wrong?'

He didn't answer. Instead, he jumped from his seat and aimed for the door.

I was left sitting by myself, feeling very anal. Hungry Jack's staff were looking at me from the other side of the counter and chitchatting amongst themselves.

I was going to say something, like 'all right, the show is over', but instead I swallowed my pride and left the restaurant.

CHAPTER SIXTEEN

Thirty minutes later, I was back home with Frank, pacing the living room. Michael had come back on foot from the Hungry Jack's and locked himself in his room. I didn't dare confront him a second time. It reminded me of when I was married years ago. Towards the end of our marriage, which only lasted six months, my husband and I couldn't even face each other without exchanging insults. Even now, I wonder if we had maintained some sort of respect for one another, maybe Michael was still have a father coming to visit him now and then. And maybe I wouldn't have to be the mother and the father all at once.

'I don't know what I'm going to do with him,' I said to Frank, crossing my arms over my chest. 'I try so hard to be a good mother. I try so hard to be here for him, to get his meals ready, to make sure he doesn't miss out on anything. And this is what I get in return.'

Frank crossed the room to the window and back to where I was sitting. 'Maybe that's what the problem is. You're looking too much over his shoulder. Wasn't that the point he was trying to make?'

'He's my son, for Christ's sake.'

'I know that, Kristina, but he's not a baby any more. He's growing up, and you don't seem to notice. I bet he's got his eye on some girl, and you're too blind to see. Did you ask him?'

'Ask him what? I'm going to ask him if he's lusting after a young woman? What are you? Nuts?'

Frank stopped pacing and came sitting next to me on the couch. 'You're his mother, and he doesn't have a father. So unless you talk to him about all these things, then he's got no one to talk to.'

'What about his friends?'

'You told me he didn't have any.'

'True.'

I puzzled over Frank's comment for a half a minute. Maybe he was right. But this single-mother business didn't exactly come with an instruction manual. Apart from having to worry about my own sanity, I also had to guess what was going on in my son's mind. Did life ever slow down? Couldn't I just flick my blinker to the left and pull over for a nap?

'I don't know, Frank,' I said. 'At times like these, I just want to give up everything. My best friend from school got killed, my son is turning his back on me, Goosh is barking up my tree again, and I feel so out of touch with the world, including myself.'

He took my hand in his. 'Hey, chill out, it's perfectly normal. Mid-life crisis. We all go through it. Just take it one day at the time. Everything is going to be all right.'

I liked to believe him, but somehow this mid-life crisis phase began to feel like Armageddon.

The next morning I was up at 6.00 a.m., but my head was heavy from insomnia. Until 4.00 a.m., I tossed and turned, worried about Michael and the case I was investigating. In the mist of my worries, I also thought about David, wondering if I had time to have him in my life. As much as I wanted his company, I was scared of using him for my own selfish purpose. Once the investigation would be over, I knew I would be more level-headed and capable of analysing the validity of our relationship. Over a cup of black coffee, I decided that Frank's advice was the best course of action to follow—I could only take things one day at time.

I went for an early morning jog, even though the cold wind was cutting through my flesh and bone. Since the move to Craigieburn, I'd stopped going to the gym or doing any form of physical activity. I missed Ken, my friend from Terry Bennet's gym in Prahran. The fifty-two-year-old librarian could pump iron for hours and looked as good if he'd just begun his training session. I met him at the State Library where he was working without his top during hot summer days, and subsequently ended up being referred to as the 'naked librarian' in one of Germaine Greer's books. Two years ago he saved my life at Terry Bennett's after someone tried to crush my ribcage with four hundred pounds of cast iron loaded on to a barbell. Since that day, I hadn't quite felt as enthusiastic about lifting weights. As a result, my thighs and buttocks softened as the months went by, so this morning, other than for the need to get away from worrying about Michael and life in general, I decided to do something about it.

The half-hour run up to the shops and back set my lungs on fire. It was still dark outside, but early risers were already making their way to work to avoid congested traffic that would take over Melbourne and its adjoining suburbs during the next three hours. The sky was clear, and it looked as if it was going to be a nice day, weather-wise, anyway.

My mind was too busy fighting the pain of exercising to think about anything else. My joints ached, and my muscles cried for mercy. I wanted to stop by the side of the road and throw up. But I imagined the fat melting away, and that gave me the willpower to go all the way. I sensed God watching me from somewhere above, and I could see myself, such a tiny person on a big planet, running towards my unknown destiny. And, there, for only a few seconds, the world seemed to make sense.

By the time I reached the front door of my home, my legs had turned to rubber, but my head was clear. The headache and grogginess I woke up with had vanished, and I felt as if I'd just been given a second chance at life.

Michael got up at 7.10 a.m., and I made sure I stayed out of his way. I didn't want the previous night's scenario to start all over, and frankly I was confused as to how I was supposed to handle him.

He ate his Coco-Pops-and-orange-juice breakfast, ignoring me as if I was part of the furniture. After that, he spent a good half hour in the bathroom doing god-knows-what, and then left for school without saying goodbye. My heart sank when he slammed the door, but somehow I was determined not to let his behaviour bring me down. Holding my tears back, I remembered David's wise words about all teenagers going through the same phase. His theory was more reassuring that Frank telling me I was stuck in a mid-life crisis.

Showered and dressed, I sat at my desk finalising some accounts for clients which I began working on before the Evelyn Carter investigation. I printed three invoices (two of them overdue), and finished typing a report for a customer who suspected her husband was having an affair. She'd almost been right because he was indeed seeing other women, but I'm not sure that you could call visiting brothels on a regular basis having an affair. With the report, I included a set of photographs showing in vivid details her husband entering and leaving various establishments with names like Tender Touch and First Ladies. Every picture was labelled with the appropriate date and time. At the back of my mind, I had doubts that ratting to someone's wife was an honest way to make a living. But marital problems were my main bread and butter, and I couldn't afford to turn the jobs down.

Peering through the window of my study, all I saw was blue sky and the sun draping itself on the green hills dotted with cows. At least there was something in my life which remained the same no matter what.

I was licking the envelope of an invoice addressed to a motor insurance company when David pulled up in my driveway. He stepped out of his red MX-5, a bunch of carnations in his hands. My heart skipped a beat as I rushed out of my study to welcome him.

When I opened the front door, he smiled and said, 'I hope I didn't turn up too early.'

I took the flowers and he kissed my on the lips.

I arranged the carnations in a vase half filled with water.

After a cup of coffee, I told him that I had some work to do, and so I wouldn't be able to spent the whole morning with him.

'Still wrapped up in this investigation?' he asked, his tone infested with disappointment. 'I wished you would have told me that before I drove all the way here.'

'Oh, I'm sorry. Am I being unreasonable?'

'No, no, I don't mean it that way. But what's the rush?'

'I have to go back to Evelyn Carter's apartment and look for that little black address book which her neighbour mentioned. There could be some serious leads in there.'

'I'll come with you. It's on my way.'

My mind did a double flip as I thought this over. 'Can't do that, it would be illegal.'

'I won't tell if you won't.'

'David, don't make it difficult for me. You know I can't take you to a crime scene or anything that comes close to it. If someone found out, I'd be in more trouble than I can imagine.'

'I'll wait in the car,' he said, giving me a cute grin, which I had found hard to resist.

I took one deep breath and said, 'Okay, but you definitely stay in the car. I don't even want to see you in the driveway of her apartment. Understood?'

'Loud and clear.'

We agreed that he would come back to my place and spend the night there, so we took my car.

The drive to Richmond took us forty-five minutes. In-bound traffic was running smoothly right up to Bell Street, after which congestion began to take place. Normally, I was quite aggressive on the road, but less than two months ago I coped a $165 fine for going at 110 km per hour in a 90 zone. I never noticed that the car which had been tagging me for the last ten minutes was an unmarked police car. Since the cops changed from Ford to Mitsubishi, I had problems spotting unmarked vehicles. Still, no matter at how angry I was for being booked, the speeding fine did tame my taste for speeding by a couple of notches.

During the entire trip, I had the radio going, so David and I said little in terms of fascinating conversation. Our subject matter revolved around the traffic, news reports broadcast every half hour, and the name of the artists whose songs were being played.

All in all, I felt good and relaxed and physically exhausted, thanks to this morning's solo marathon. I made the mental commitment to put physical exercise back into my regime. I knew it would also help me sleep at night.

I parked the Excell alongside the curb opposite Evelyn's apartment.

Before I stepped out of the car, I turned to David and said, 'You realise I might be a while? Maybe you want to take a walk or something.'

'I'll be right,' David answered, grabbing a James Patterson paperback from a soft travel bag he brought with him.

'Okay, it's your choice.'

I stepped out of the car and retrieved the PERK from the boot. I had no intention of collecting evidence other than Evelyn's little black book if I came across it, but still, I wanted to be prepared for the unexpected. When searching a place, I found it more efficient doing it by myself. Although having Frank around was company, too often he was more of a hindrance than a helping hand. At least if I disturbed anything at a crime scene, I knew I had done it.

I crossed the road, looking out for on-coming vehicles on both sides. Before entering the apartment block, I did a half turn and waved to David, who waved back in return.

From my jacket pocket, I retrieved the keys to the front gate of the apartment block and to Evelyn's home. I got the keys from the set Frank found not far from the SAAB before I arrived at the crime scene in Toorak on that dreadful morning which changed my life.

I paced the driveway and aimed straight for apartment number 2.

Anxiousness crept at the back of my skull.

I knew something was wrong, and I hadn't even entered the apartment yet.

CHAPTER SEVENTEEN

When I got to the front door, it had been left ajar. On close inspection, I noticed that the lock was damaged. Whoever entered the place didn't have the keys, nor a lock-picking kit like I did. The keyhole was badly damaged, as if someone had been inserting a tool, probably the size of a large screwdriver. I pushed the door fully open with my foot and peered inside.

No one was there.

I entered the apartment and left the front door wide open behind me in case I had to run out urgently. As soon as I made it to the entrance of the living room, my heart nearly jumped out of my chest. The couch had been slit open through its entire length; the drawers pulled out of the wall unit and their contents tossed on the salmon-coloured carpet; hard-cover books and paperbacks were scattered across the room; official-looking documents and magazines were torn to shreds; the coffee table and plants were overturned; the curtains ripped from their rods; and, all in all, the living room looked as if a tornado had passed through it.

As I circled the room, careful not to trip over any of the clutter, I half expected to find a body hidden in a corner.

Oscar, Evelyn's cat, was nowhere in site. I feared finding him nailed to the bedroom or bathroom door. I should have taken him home with me. What was I thinking when I left him behind the first time we searched the apartment? The poor thing had no one to look after him, and if he hadn't been killed, in all likeness, he'd probably ran away in search of a feed and a new owner to spoil him with love and a warm shelter.

Aware that the intruder might still be in the apartment, I retrieved my Mustang Plus .380 stainless frame, which I had tucked between my belt and the small of my back. Frank brought me the gun, featuring a blue slide and adjustable sight, two years prior when I nearly got killed during an investigation. The Mustang had become my best friend, and I could no longer imagine life without it. As much as I didn't believe in guns, I feared the possibility of coming face-to-face in my own home with a knife-crazed intruder and leave it to chance for my survival. The gun made me feel protected and in control. Although I am ashamed to admit it, I somehow felt sexy and sensual when handling the gun. Maybe I'd been watching to many cops shows or read too many books. Hollywood had eventually got to the core of my moral senses like the rest of the world. A gun was designed to kill, and yet I felt powerful and proud and sexy about owning one. Some say sex is power. Gun is power. Maybe there was a link.

Getting a license to own the piece had been a damn nightmare, especially when I wasn't even a sworn officer, and some of Goosh's friends had purposely misplaced my application to carry a concealed weapon. Recently I even joined a gun club to assure I would be capable of keeping the gun, even if my job no longer gave me the authorisation to do so.

I placed the PERK on the floor, next to an overturned magazine holder.

My senses on red alert, I released the security catch on the Mustang, checked the loading, and grasped it with both hands.

Plastered to the wall, I slid from the living room to the kitchen. I was scared and excited at the same time. My eyes flickered, feeding me flashes of my surroundings.

The fridge was fully opened, water dripping from the icebox. Rotten vegetables and fruits had been thrown on the grey linoleum, which was permanently discoloured in places as a result. A spilled carton of milk sat under the kitchen table. The bread-and-salami still life painting, which had once been hanging above the kitchen table, was now tossed on the floor, its backing slit open. Whoever had done this was definitely looking for something of importance to them, and whatever that thing was, it had to be small enough to be concealed under the backing of a painting.

'Anyone here?' I almost whispered, my throat tight.

No answer.

I tightened my grip around the Mustang.

If someone was still in the apartment, he wouldn't have heard me either way.

Chances were whoever broke in had already left.

Maybe it was the killer.

Or someone who was scared of being linked to the victim.

Since Evelyn had been a high-class prostitute, it wasn't hard to hypothesis on the type of clients she had. Her next door neighbour had already told me that—judges, CEOs, politicians, company directors, foreign diplomats, basically people in power who couldn't take a chance of having their names tarnished and watch their careers being destroyed. People who were *happily* married, who had children, who represented themselves as pillars of society. The same people who often imposed their moralistic judgements on others and lived a secret life which contradicted everything they stood for.

Then I heard a noise coming from the bedroom.

A cracking noise.

I froze for a few seconds.

I held the Mustang tightly, but my hands were still shaking.

Listening carefully, I could hear the sound of my own breathing.

It sounded like drawers being opened.

Without a word, I approached the bedroom door. *Should I go outside and call for backup?* If the intruder was armed, I could get hurt, maybe even killed. *Is it worth the risk?*

But adrenalin was pumping in my brain. I realised it might be Evelyn's killer who had come to her apartment to destroy evidence that would lead us to him. If he was armed and threatened me, at least he would give me the golden opportunity to blow his brains out and save taxpayers' money on a trial. The idea of avenging myself never appealed to me. But at that moment, I felt such intense rage at what had been done to Evelyn that I purposely let my judgement be clouded with hatred.

My right hand clinging to the Mustang, I was now resting against the bedroom door.

Another drawer was being opened.

There was definitely someone in there.

Slowly I pushed the door with my left foot.

A trickle of sweat dripped down my temple. I feared for my life. I thought about Michael. Why now, I wasn't sure. Maybe I was scared of turning him into an orphan. Would Frank take care of him if I was to go? I doubted it, especially the way Michael had been acting lately. Somehow, I just couldn't see Frank living with a teenage boy. Those two had nothing in common, and the day they'd become friends, I'd probably get a heart attack.

Suddenly, without warning, I kicked the rest of the door open and aimed the barrel of my Mustang at the person who was kneeling down in front of a chest of draws, hands sinking in Evelyn's lingerie.

We locked eyes, and she seemed as surprised to see me as I was to see her.

CHAPTER EIGHTEEN

Judith Kingman was still flushed. She'd screamed her head off when she turned around and saw me with the gun. I saw the fear of death in her eyes.

'God, you scared the shit out of me!' she said after I had just apologised for aiming the Mustang at her face.

I helped her back to her feet and said, 'What the hell are you doing here, anyway? Did you make all this mess?'

She pulled a face. 'Me? Are you crazy? I was just looking for that little black book. I thought I might be able to get my hands on it and hand it over to you before anyone else got hold of it.'

Curious, I stepped back two steps. 'So, what the hell happened here?'

'You tell me. It's your mob?'

'My mob?'

By the expression on my face, she must have known I was genuinely clueless.

'You mean, you didn't send them?' she asked.

'Send who?'

'Oh, God, now it all makes sense.'

I tucked the Mustang back between my belt and the small of my back. 'Yo, you're going to clarify yourself here. Do you know who broke into this apartment?'

'Two men came and identified themselves as police officers.

126

I asked for identification, which they produced. I'm not an expert, but the badges looked like Victoria Police genuine articles, and there was no reason for me not to let them in.'

'Did you get their names?'

'Are you serious? I'm going to stand there after they presented their IDs and take their names down? I asked them if you'd send them, and they said yes.'

Now I was confused.

'Believe me,' I said, 'I did not send anyone. These people were either crooks or cops with a bad agenda in mind.'

'Yeah, well, I sort of figured that out when I heard all the commotion going on in Evelyn's apartment. I didn't want to intrude, so I waited until they left. When I got to here, the door had been left open, so I walked in and found the place in a mess. That's when I realised something was wrong. And then, I remembered the black book, and how you said you hadn't found it yet. So, I thought I'd look for it myself, just in case the two cops decided to come back and look some more.'

'What if they'd already found it?'

'Just in case they hadn't.'

I stared at her for a few seconds, trying to figure out if she'd been lying to me. But her eyes expressed sincerity, and there was no reason why I shouldn't have believed her.

'Okay, at least you've seen who was in the apartment,' I said. 'But you shouldn't have touched anything. You should have called me.'

'I was going to do that.' She was now on her feet, inches from my face. I could smell her face moisturiser and some familiar perfume, which made me want to sneeze.

'Would you be able to recognise the cops who broke into her apartment if you ever saw them again?' I asked.

'I think so. I couldn't draw you a picture, but if came across them again, yes I would. One was tall, moustache, short hair and an expensive looking two-piece suite. He looked around thirty-five. The other was much younger, probably mid-twenties, maybe less. The senior one did all the talking. If he wasn't a cop, he certainly spoke like one.'

'Why did they come to you?'

'Rang my door bell. They couldn't get past the front gate. They identified themselves and that was it.'

Possible scenario since Frank and I had done the same thing when we first wanted to get into Evelyn's apartment.

All of a sudden, a male voice interrupted us. In less than half a second, my right hand had already landed on the Mustang tucked between my belt and the small of my back.

'Everything all right in here?' David asked, a look of concern on his face.

When David and I returned to the car, I was mad as hell. Back at Evelyn's apartment, I told Judith to not bother looking for the little black book. This was police business, and the more she got herself involve in it, the more complicated things would become. She seemed a little upset at first, but when she returned to her apartment she told us she understood, that we were only doing our job.

I crossed the road of the apartment block to where my car was parked. David was by my side, looking rather sheepish.

'Jesus, David, I told you not to come inside the apartment. What are you trying to do? Make me lose my job?'

'I'm sorry,' he said. 'I heard somebody scream. I thought it was you. I thought you were in trouble. What was I supposed to do? Stand there and pretend I heard nothing?'

As much as I was angry at him, if I'd found myself face-to-face with the killer in Evelyn's apartment, maybe I would have been glad to see David come to my rescue.

'Okay, okay, just forget about it,' I said. 'It's my fault. I shouldn't have brought you with me in the first place.'

Just when we stepped into the car, Frank's white Ford Falcon pulled in front of us.

'Oh, shit,' I said. 'Why the hell is he doing here?'

Frank looked as surprised as I was.

'Stay put,' I ordered David as I stepped out of the car at the same time as Frank was walking towards me. His eyes shifted to David and back to me.

'What's going on?' he asked before I had time to say a word.

'Long story. I was looking for evidence. Someone broke into her apartment.'

He pointed at David. 'What's he doing here?'

My lips remained sealed. I couldn't find the right answer.

'Did he go in the apartment with you?' Frank asked, red colouring his face.

'I told him to wait in the car.'

'But he went inside the apartment with you?'

'Yes, but that's only because he thought I was in danger.'

I didn't know how I was going to talk my way out of that one. Ops, sorry Frank, I'm screwing one of the witnesses. You would understand. You did the same two years ago.

'It's not what you think,' I went on.

He threw his hands in front of his body. 'I don't want to know. All I know is this guy is a key witness, and unless you have a damn good reason to take him with you on an investigation, then I'm going to demand a written report explaining this incident.'

Shit, that was all I needed. Frank turning bureaucratically ethical on me.

'Come on, Frank, give me a break. Instead of wasting time playing politics, why don't you help me find out what's been going on in Evelyn's apartment.'

He threw me an inquisitive glare.

'Someone broke into her apartment,' I continued. I explained what Judith Kingman told me when I caught her in Evelyn's place.

Frank now seemed genuinely intrigued. 'And she's certain they were cops?'

'To the best of her knowledge. They showed her police badges.'

'I've got to see this for myself,' he said, aiming for the other side of the street.

With a hand signal, I ordered David to stay in the car.

Slightly embarrassed, I followed Frank, hoping he would forget about David.

'And what are you doing here, anyway?' I asked, changing the focus to him instead of me.

He gave me a non-committal look and said, 'Just checking her apartment was secured properly. I was on my way to the VFSC and thought I'd drop by for another look at the place, just in case we missed something.'

When we got inside Evelyn's apartment, everything was the same as I left it.

Frank's eyes circled the living room while he let out a long whistle. 'Whatever they were looking for,' he said, 'it must have been important.'

I recalled to his attention the little black address book.

'Now, that's a damn good possibility,' he acknowledged. 'If there was one thing I would want to get my hands on after screwing Evelyn, that would be that little book, especially if my name was in there.'

I didn't like the language he used in regards to my friend, but I was in no position to argue.

'My view too,' I said. 'What's intriguing is that if the intruders were in fact the police, then we can easily assume that some of her customers were police officers.'

He chewed on my comment while continuing to look around the room. 'Let's not jump to conclusions. You start spreading rumours like that, and you're going to have the whole police community on your back. Maybe the intruders were not police officers. It's not that hard to get a fake ID, believe me, I've seen a lot of them over they years.'

'I'm just stating the obvious, Frank. You're the one who keeps telling me everything is black and white in an investigation, and how I shouldn't look for shades of grey.'

He twisted his lips. 'Have you conducted a crime scene examination?' he asked.

'Well, no, that's not why I came here in the first place. But now that you mention it, since the place had been disturbed, a search will have to be conducted. I'll put down the reason as suspected robbery and wilful damage to property.'

'Unfortunately, I don't have the three hours to help you with collecting evidence. You're going to have to do it by yourself.'

'Sure, not a problem. I've just put the PERK back in the car. I'll go and retrieve it.'

Frank checked his watch and added, 'Time for me to go.'

I walked him to the Ford and noticed David was no longer sitting in my car.

'Where's your boyfriends gone to?' Frank asked, sarcasm infesting his tone. He still couldn't digest the fact that even though I'd known him for years, I kept on seeing other men, even if I'd only met them a few days ago. He obviously had his own misconception about what sexual attraction was. Just because he was a man, and I was a woman, and he was hanging around me all the time, didn't mean I was going to jump in bed with him, not in his wildest dreams.

'He's not my boyfriend,' I protested.

'Yeah, right.' He dismissed me with a wave of the hand. 'And my middle name is not dickhead. I can smell hormones in a five-kilometre radius.'

I froze, jaw dropped, while he calmly slid into the driver's seat.

'And don't forget to explain in your report what David was doing in Evelyn's apartment,' he said through the unwound window on the driver's side. 'Oh, and you can speculate on why you're fucking a key witness.'

Heat crept up my face.

CHAPTER NINETEEN

I scanned up and down the street for David. He was no where in sight.

Frank took off without saying goodbye.

Were men really worth all that trouble? I swore out loud that one day they were going to drive me insane, if they hadn't done so already.

I removed the PERK from the car and left a note on the windscreen for David. I scribbled that I had returned to Evelyn's apartment, and if he wanted to see me, he'd have to press the buzzer outside the front gate. Somehow, I no longer cared whether he entered the apartment or not. Frank, Judith, David and I had already been in and out of the place, not to mention those two crooked cops, so how much more contaminated could a crime scene really get?

Back inside Evelyn's apartment, I opened the PERK and glanced around me. When I realised the full extent of the damage done to Evelyn's belongings, and the amount of work I had to undertake to process the place for collection of evidence, I began to doubt the value of my existence on this planet. After all, processing of a crime scene was really nothing more than cleaning a place up, not that there was anything wrong with cleaning as long as it was your life ambition.

I began with a sketch of the premises, followed by photography. It took five 24-exposure rolls to cover the whole area, including lounge, kitchen, bathroom and study. By the time I was done with the photography, I had a sore arm from holding the Minolta up to my face. Imagine taking pictures for a living. For a spilt second I was joking to myself about suing the police and the VFSC for repetition strain injury. How much was a damaged wrist worth these days?

It took me four hours to collect, bag and label everything in the place. By the time I was done, I had assembled trace evidence of all sorts—fibres, mud, dead insects, clipped finger nails, food residues and a ton of cat hair. I rang the Forensic Centre for a van to come and collect the larger pieces of evidence, such as the slashed couch, the smashed television and the painting in the kitchen.

Throughout the entire process of collecting evidence, I'd hoped to find Oscar sleeping somewhere in a corner of the house.

No such luck.

And then, there was David.

Where the hell is he?

After lunch, I became seriously concerned about David's disappearance. Back in the car, I punched the number of his bookshop on my mobile phone.

'David's Bookshop,' the familiar voice sang out like a television jingle.

'David, I've been looking for you everywhere! Why did you run out on me?'

'I had some work to catch up on. I'm sorry, it's just that you looked so busy, maybe you were right. I shouldn't have come with you after all.'

'How did you get back to work?'

'Hailed a cab.'

I was mildly upset. 'You could have told me you were leaving. For Christ's sake David, that's not asking for much.'

'I'm really sorry. I heard you guys argue outside, and your cop friend gave me that foul look, so I thought it'd be better if I leave. You know, I'm not much for physical confrontation.'

'He's not that type,' I said. 'He yells a lot, but he doesn't hit people unless he has to.'

'Yes, I didn't really want to hang around and find out if he *had* to. Maybe there's more to him that meets the eye.'

David was right, of course, but I wasn't the kiss-and-tale type. The only people who knew about Frank's crush on me was Frank and myself. I didn't want to make life more complicated than it already was, so I changed the topic.

'You're still staying over tonight?' I asked.

'Sure. Look forward to it.'

As soon as he hung up, the mobile phone went off.

'Dr Melina,' I announced.

'Kristina, it's Charles from the mortuary. You've got to get over here as soon as possible.'

'Why? What's wrong?'

His tone was filled with anxiety. 'Oh, God, you wouldn't believe me if I told you over the phone.'

'Try me. What? The place's gone up in flames?'

'Evelyn Carter's body has disappeared.'

Within half an hour, I parked in the car park of the VIFM. I stepped out of the Excell and rushed to the blue-grey building, past glass sliding doors, cleared myself at the front desk and rushed to Dr Main's office.

I stormed in the room without knocking. 'What do you mean her body has disappeared?'

Dr Main wore the expression of an out-patient. He was seated behind his desk filling up details of what looked like an official government form of one sort or another.

'I can assure you that whoever did this knew what they were doing,' he said as if cued.

'How can that be possible? How can someone just walk into a morgue and snatch a body? We're not talking about a sandwich here, but a full-size body!' I was doing a waving thing with my arms as if I was controlling traffic at a congested intersection.

He stood up from his chair. 'I know, I know, and I understand why you're upset. Please sit down,' he said, offering me a chair opposite his desk. 'This has never happened before, and if you think you're upset, just imagine how I feel. The press is going to come down on me like a ton of bricks, and I bet you there will be an independent inquiry on this breach of security. I'm hope I'm not going to lose my job over this.'

I caught back my breath, letting empathy take over, and said, 'All right, so what happened?'

'I finished the autopsy, and the body was ready to be shipped to the funeral home. When the mortuary assistant went to get it from the cold room, it was gone.'

My mind was jumping all over the place. I thought about the cops who broke into Evelyn's apartment. And now her body had gone missing. Just as well Dr Main had finished the autopsy before Evelyn disappeared.

'Okay,' I said, 'did you get me a copy of the autopsy report?'

More colour drained from his face. At least he wouldn't have to travel too far if he died from a heart attack. 'Well, that's the other thing I needed to talk to you about.'

The way he said that, I knew he was not about to retrieve ten certified copies of the autopsy report from his top drawer and hand them over to me.

'Someone got into the system and wiped out her file.'

I placed one hand on my chest. 'You are joking!'

'Would this be a good time to be joking?'

'What about a hard copy? Didn't you print one out?'

'I don't bother until it's finished.'

And that's why I hated computers. Not because computers made mistakes—everybody knows computer never make mistakes—but because whoever uses them is so goddamn lazy. How difficult was it to click the print button every time new information was added to a report?

'What about a backup file?' I asked, desperately hoping there was something left for me to work from.

'They stole the backing tape as well.'

I threw my head back in amazement and laughed.

Dr Main looked at me as if I'd suddenly grown a gigantic zit at the end of my nose.

I regained my composure and said, 'The body is gone, the autopsy report is gone. Have we got anything left? Do I still have a case here?'

Dr Main shrugged embarrassingly. And who could blame him. Two years ago, I had already made a fool of him by stealing files from his office, and now someone snatched a corpse, complete with the autopsy report. I didn't know who was going to get into more trouble. Ironically, even thought the disappearance of Evelyn Carter's had nothing to do with me, it would still give Goosh some formal reason to kick me out of the investigation. He'd argue that without a body and no autopsy report, we'd have little to work from. And, as much as I hated to admit it, he'd be more than justified.

'What about the samples and the toxicology results? I asked, clutching at straws.

'They've ransacked the fridge as well. We've got nothing.'

Biological samples to be tested were usually kept in a fridge, labelled with the case number. Someone obviously knew that, and helped themselves as if the mortuary was a 7-Eleven.

I heard enough. Twisted minds were playing a dirty game, and the way events were unfolding, it had to be people connected to Evelyn's murder.

Or someone who was scared to have his name linked to her death.

'Who else knows about the disappearance of the body?' I asked.

'Well, you're the first person I talked to,' he said, playing nervously with his hands. 'Since you're in charge of the investigation, I thought it normal to let you know before making it official.'

'What about the Deputy Commissioner of Police?'

'Goosh doesn't know anything at this stage, and I'm sure you can understand why I'm not exactly looking forward to having him informed on the matter.'

Yes, I understood perfectly well. Goosh was a real-life vampire who was after everybody's blood.

'I'm going to get my partner on this,' I said. 'You don't mind if I have a look at the cold room where the body was kept?'

'Sure, I can get someone to take you there.'

'It's okay, I know the way.'

I left his office, forcing a smile to cheer him up a bit. I'd never seen Dr Main looking so miserable, and I thanked God on my way to the cold room that I wasn't in his shoes.

CHAPTER TWENTY

On my way to the cold room, I dialled Frank on his mobile and told him to drop whatever he was doing and to get his arse over here on the double.

'We got what?' he yelled into the mouth-piece, causing temporary deafness in my right ear.

'A body snatcher,' I said. 'Evelyn Carter has vanished. Someone's fucking around with us, and whoever they are, they're doing a good job.'

'Give me twenty minutes.'

Knowing him, he'd roll up in forty minutes.

To end the call, I pressed the NO key on my banana-coloured, toy-sized Ericsson.

The cold room was kept at ten degrees Celsius to preserve the state of the bodies for as long as possible and to minimise the breaking down of complex proteins and fats into simpler constituents—or in layman terms, to slow down decomposition and putrefaction.

Galvanised trolleys were lined up against the right wall like soldiers ready for an inspection. Four of the trolleys were empty. There were only three bodies in the room. The bodies were that of two men, who'd probably died of old age, and of a woman in her early twenties, complete with extensive bruising on her face and neck. All the bodies were stripped naked and ready for the obligatory autopsy. Other than for law enforcement, autopsies were performed to collect accurate medical records in order to gather meaningful statistics for use in health care, preventive medicine, and, in particular, medical education. Even in death, we still served a purpose. Just as well this was the end of the road—I shivered just thinking about the recycling process pushing the boundaries of moral dignity one step further, and, as a result, we'd all end up in a can of dog food.

I checked the door and it looked secure enough, even though it wasn't fitted with any kind of locking device. This was no surprise since no one would expect an intruder to steal a corpse. It certainly was the first time I'd ever come across body snatching since I'd been investigating homicides. I just hope it wasn't someone who was into necrophilia, the act of having sexual intercourse with the dead for those who don't know.

I stood alone in the cold room, lost in thoughts, wishing Frank would hurry up.

Who in the world would have taken the body of Evelyn Carter? Most likely someone who had access to the premises, or someone with power and money who could talk himself into anything. I considered having a chat to the forensic technicians who worked on the premises. I'd be able to test my ability to detect those who weren't as skilful as they thought themselves to be at the art of lying. How much was a dead body worth these days. Fifty bucks? Hundred bucks? A thousand?

I aimed for the door, bewildered at how someone could just come unnoticed into a mortuary and snatch a body in broad daylight.

I left the cold room and steered for the staff cafeteria, where I ordered a black coffee, no sugar. Feeling a headache coming on, I swallowed half my brew in one go and waited for Frank to turn up.

Another twenty minutes, and two cups of coffee later, Frank walked into the canteen, a panic-stricken expression painted on his face.

'Has she turned up?' he asked, before he even reached the table where I was sitting.

I shook my head and said, 'Her body hasn't gone walk-about. Someone stole it.'

He sat at the table, hands crossed nervously. 'Are you sure?'

'Am I sure what? Am I sure she's missing? I've spent fifteen minutes grilling Dr Main, I inspected the cold room myself and found no one matching the description of Evelyn Carter. So, yes, I'm sure, as sure as one can be.'

I was surprised at how angry I was. Unresolved emotions were still zigzagging within the four corners of my mind.

Frank stood there for half a minute, simmering in his own thoughts. 'Shit, and you have no idea who might have done that?' he finally said.

'Well, after two cops raided Evelyn's apartment this morning, it's beginning to look like a conspiracy of one sort or another.'

Frank tilted his head. 'A conspiracy of what? We're talking about the death of one prostitute, and you think it's a conspiracy. I find that quite extraordinary.'

I puzzled on his comment and said, 'What I find extraordinary is that you believe Evelyn Carter's disappearance is just another incident after this morning's break-in. It's obvious someone is trying to hide something, someone who's got a lot at stake and is willing to take a high degree of risk to eliminate or find whatever he's after.'

'Okay, so what kind of people are we talking about? Organ collectors? I heard there was a good market in China and some Eastern European countries.' He chuckled, thinking himself clever and amusing all at once.

'I don't think this is funny, not even for a minute. My friend's been killed, and people are trying hard to hide what really happened to her. And all you can do is stand there and laugh at my suggestions. Since you're so fuckin' intelligent, what have you got to say? What's your theory?'

Seeing I was hurting, Frank mellowed his tone. 'I'm sorry, I didn't mean to be offensive. It's just that this idea of a conspiracy sounds a bit far-fetched. What kind of people are we talking about? If the two men who broke into Evelyn's apartment this morning are indeed cops, then you're implying the police are involved in an obstruction of justice.' He shook his head right to left as if an insect had crawled inside his ear canal. 'You're not even a sworn police member, Kristina. Making this kind of accusation without any solid foundation is going to get you in trouble. Why don't you just let it go?'

I didn't answer his question. 'You heard what Judith

Kingman said. She said Evelyn's clients included politicians, television personalities and the police. Why is it so hard for you to believe that some of these major players have joined forces to keep their names and reputations intact? If you think about it, it would have to be people in power who would be able to throw this investigation off course. You don't seriously believe that by chance someone walked off the street and broke into Evelyn's apartment, in spite of it being fenced off with crime-scene tape? What kind of an idiot would do that?

'I don't know—'

'And you don't seriously believe, also by chance, someone walked into the mortuary and snatched a body for god-knows-what-reason, and it just happened to be Evelyn's body, and it happened to be on the same day.

'Life is stranger than fic—'

'And then,' I went on like a runaway train, 'a computer hacker pulled files at random from the VIFM database and happened to erase Evelyn's autopsy report. And some bum walked off the street, aimed straight for the pathology fridge and snatched her biological samples. You're going to tell me there is no logical connection between all these events? Come on, Frank, give me a break.' I rolled my eyes to the top of my eyelids.

Frank didn't answer straight away. He looked at me as if he was trying to figure out where I was coming from. Forget the fact that we had worked hundreds of investigations together, and that by now he must have known exactly which side I liked my toast buttered on.

He played with the tip of his orange tie, twisted his mouth like a shoelace, and said, 'I don't know, Kristina, maybe you're right, and if you are, this murder investigation is getting way above our heads. If you think we're being jerked with by our own people, maybe we should let the CIB take over'. Frank was referring to the Criminal Investigation Branch.

'I'm not one to disagree for additional manpower. But if you're asking me to drop the investigation, you know damn well that I can't do that. I've invested too much time, effort and sanity into this case.'

'I'm not asking anything. I just think that the way the investigation is going, maybe it would be better if we get other experts on the case. If you're right, and if this whole situation is in fact a conspiracy, then God knows, we're going to need the extra help. I'm not willing to follow this case through if people with a lot of string-pulling power are going to try their best to destroy the little evidence we have accumulated so far. I say wash your hands and get on with your life. Your friend is dead either way, and nothing you do is going to bring her back to life. Someone will be able to put things right in due time.'

In a way, I wasn't exactly surprised by what I was hearing. Frank had always seemed like the type of person who would choose the easy way out. And that's why after all those years, despite the fact that I considered him a good friend, I couldn't find anything admirable in him. In my heart, I respected people who were fighters, people who didn't take no for an answer, warriors who fought against the odds no matter what the enemies thought or did, especially when the fighting was a battle for truth and justice.

'You're just scared, aren't you?' I said, placing the palm of my right hand on the table top.

'Me?' He looked around as if I was talking to someone else.

'Yes, you're scared that whoever is in on this is going to get to you next. You're scared, so you think the best thing to do is walk away. You don't have the balls to follow this through like a man.'

'Hey, come on, Kristina, now you're really starting to piss me off!'

'Well, that's not exactly news to me. Somehow, I seem to be pissing off a lot of people lately. It's all part of my job, it's how I get things done. And believe me, I'm not phased by it yet. Ninety-five percent of people are full of shit, and no matter what you're going to say, I'm not jumping into the bandwagon like you. I belong with the other five percent. I got enough dignity to stand up for what I believe.'

Frank stood from his chair, redness covering his face. He looked as if he was going to jump over the table and beat me to a pulp.

I swallowed, realising I did go a bit far with my personal judgemental attack. But I felt cornered like a kitten in a dog pound, and it came out in one go without me thinking things over.

'You're really something, you know?' he said. 'You want the damn investigation, you've got it. You think I'm a wimp

141

because I'm walking away? Well, maybe you're right. But that won't matter next week when someone's going to find a floater in the Yarra, and it'll happen to be you. I'll be alive and breathing, and I'll still give a damn about the people around me. Evelyn's dead, and I'm not going to risk my neck for her. Firstly, I didn't know her like you did, so I know when to stop. And secondly she was a whore, so as far as I'm concerned, my life is worth more than a bonk-bag.'

Frank was furious, and he probably hadn't meant every word he said, but it hurt nonetheless. His attitude towards women came unveiled during difficult arguments. I knew not all men were the same, but somehow I'd seemed to have been cursed spending a great part of my life with a disproportionate ratio of imbeciles.

I looked at him, unable to utter a single syllable. What could I have replied to this verbal cascade of chauvinistic monologue? I hated to repeat myself over and over since Frank knew exactly what my viewpoint was on most issues, especially women, prostitutes and arseholes like him. God, sometimes I wondered why I liked men in the first place. But I guessed it was their emotionless differences which made them interesting, no matter how repulsive I found their beliefs at times.

He threw me one final glare and left the cafeteria without looking back.

CHAPTER TWENTY-ONE

When I got back home, I was nearly in tears. The headache, which had begun at the cafeteria, had now taken the entire under-surface of my cranium. It felt as if someone had removed my brain, kicked it to a bruise, and threw it back in there. I knew I wasn't dealing well with all the contradictions in my life. I couldn't believe Frank had pulled me into this investigation just to walk out on me. Now I was left to my own resources and contacts to find Evelyn Carter's killer. All in all, this wasn't an entirely unfamiliar scenario. In the past, I had found myself fighting alone and always managed to pull through. People referred to me as enterprising and independent; others said I was arrogant, especially when arguing with authoritative figures. It was written in my stars— I was a Virgo, and lived by the characteristics which had been assigned to me since birth. It wasn't something I was proud of, nor ashamed of. By the time you reach forty, you more or less come to accept your true self, for better or worse. It's other people who become increasingly intolerable to live with.

I considered going back on Prozac for a little while, just to give me the moral boost I needed to keep me level-headed. It would help me to remain faithful to my own instinct, another birth right, a balanced blend of logic and sensitivity referred to by experts as 'woman intuition'.

There was one message on the answering machine, indicated by a single, repetitive, flashing red light. When I pushed the play button, David's voice came on:

'Didn't forget about tonight, did you? Give me a call at the

143

bookshop.' He paused for a few seconds. 'Oh, and, Kristina, I'm sorry about this morning. I shouldn't have just disappeared. It won't happen again, promise.'

Standing still, I listened to his voice echo in my ears.

I liked the reassuring tone of his voice, the way he came across as sincere.

And, yes, I did want to spend the evening with him, forget about all my troubles and let myself be pampered. At least, I was offered the opportunity.

Rubbing the back of my neck, I returned his call immediately. He asked me about the rest of my day, and I told him the truth. He said he would be over soon and would give me a nice neck massage to get rid of my headache. I said I was looking forward to seeing him.

Not two minutes after I hung up, I heard the front door of the house being opened. I was in the kitchen tossing two Aspro Clear in a half glass of water in the hope of getting rid of my headache by the time David got here.

Michael walked past me without saying a word. He headed straight for the fridge and grabbed a Coke from the door compartment.

'Hi,' I said, trying hard to sound cheerful.

'Hi,' he replied without looking at me and pulled the ring from his Coke. I was about to say something else, but he headed straight for his room.

Although I tried to ignore it, I had this urge to follow him and ask him why he was treating me like this. But I knew better. Perhaps our relationships would improve if left untouched at this stage. With time, he might realise I wasn't such a bad mother, a half-truth I was trying hard to believe. If there was anything I could have done to help him out of his pain, I would have done it. Instead I felt helpless and had to wait for fate to take care of us.

I emptied my glass of Aspro Clear, and ten minutes later I was sitting on the living room couch, my headache gradually vaporising into nothingness.

As I pulled *N is for Noose*, the latest Sue Grafton novel out of my bag, I prayed to God that Michael would find his happiness in this world. I'd liked to be naive and believe that everything in life would eventually turn out for the best, but

144

this was not a Hollywood movie. A clear-cut resolution might never manifest itself, no matter how good my intentions were.

I read for a good hour then David turned up. For a few seconds, I had almost forgotten he was coming over because I was so enjoyably engrossed in my novel. I had just begun Chapter Twelve, where Kinsey Millhone, the protagonist in my book, was up to her neck in trouble as usual by sticking her nose into what was clearly none of her business.

The knock on the door jolted me out of my seat. I tossed the novel on the coffee table and looked out the window facing me.

As usual, David bought carnations with him.

Excited like an love-struck teenager, I raced to the front door. There was still a hint of headache bugging me, but I chose to ignore it.

'You want me to open a flower shop,' I joked, as I took the bunch of carnations from him and kissed him tenderly on the lips. I surprised both of us with my affection. I knew I'd been thirsty for good company, but it wasn't until I was face to face with David that I'd realised how desperate I really was.

He smiled, his blue eyes sparkling with excitement. This was the same man who ran away on me that morning and now had just driven over an hour in peak hour to be with me. Love did strange things to people.

We moved to the lounge room, where I opened a bottle of Chardonnay and poured the contents into two glass from behind the bar.

'Any progress on the investigation?' David asked casually as he sipped from his glass.

I had already given him a run down when he rang up earlier, but he was obviously more then just merely curious. In a way, I could understand. If someone had been killed behind my fence, I would have wanted to know what the hell happened.

'No one knows where the body has disappeared to,' I said, realising at the same time that I shouldn't be sharing everything about the investigation with him. But Frank had just turned his back on me, and I needed someone to listen to my problems. David was charming and seemed genuinely interested in what I had to say. And I also sensed that he truly cared, which was more than Frank or other people I had been working with had done lately.

'What about your partner? Why did he seem so cross when he saw me this morning?'

'Guess?'

'Because I'm a witness in this investigation?'

'Exactly.' I paused for a few seconds. 'Mind you, Frank went out with someone two years ago, who happened to have been a key witness in a homicide. And that was in spite of him knowing it was wrong to be involved with the wife of a murdered victim.'

David nodded thoughtfully and sipped more wine from his glass.

'And what has he got to say about the disappearance of Evelyn Carter?'

'Nothing much. After I told him this whole case begins to feel like a conspiracy, he said he wanted out.'

I replayed the conversation I had with Frank earlier on that afternoon.

'Well,' David said, 'for what it's worth, I believe you.'

'Which part?'

'The one about the cops being involved. When you think about it, it reeks with logic. Two cops ransack her place. Someone takes her body from the morgue. Hell, you've got to know what you're doing to get away with something like that.'

Enchanted, I stared into his eyes and smiled. 'You're just agreeing with me because you want to spend the night here,' I said.

'Well,' he said, smiling back, 'yes, I would like to spend the night with you, but no, this is not the reason why I agree with your theory. I think there is some merit in what you've suggested.'

I moved closer and kissed him passionately.

He kissed me back in return, his hands on my shoulders, moving down along my arms and then to my waist.

Gently, I pushed him back. 'We shouldn't be doing this here,' I said. 'Michael could be coming into the room any second. What kind of impression would it make on him?'

'He would learn that his mother is a hell of a sexy woman, and that she's got good taste in men.'

I stared at him for a few seconds, feelings churning in my stomach. 'Okay, Romeo, follow me.'

I led him to my bedroom, where we undressed and made love like two young lovers losing their innocence for the first time.

When we finished, my headache had completely vanished.

CHAPTER TWENTY-TWO

Early the next morning, David left for work. I went back to bed after waving him goodbye at the door. My head lying on the side of the bed where he had slept, I breathed in deeply the smell of his masculinity. The musky odour triggered memories of our lovemaking we made the previous night. Slowly I closed my eyes and visualised his naked body arched over mine, while warm filtered sunlight from outside draped itself over my bed. I knew I would find it hard to focus on work that morning. Closeness made me feel secure but incapable of functioning like a whole human being. Once I had a taste of intimacy, I longed for more.

I lay still, enjoying the quietness of non-urban living. I wanted David to love me more than anyone he had ever loved before. I wanted him to hold me in his arms forever and tell me I was the one and only woman for him. I wanted to feel his breathing down my neck, down my breasts, throughout my entire body.

As those thoughts crossed my mind, I opened my eyes and felt heat on my face. I blushed to the four walls which surrounded me, not from lustful shame but as a result of tinkly emotions.

After a shower and light breakfast of cereal, black coffee and vitamins, I sat at the desk of my home office and checked my e-mail. Even thought I had already concluded that it would be difficult for me to get any work done because my mind would be preoccupied with thoughts of David, I was resigned to make an effort and not let the day go by without having made any progress on the investigation.

While I was logging into my e-mail provider, an exciting thought crossed my mind. Evelyn Carter had a friend in the USA whom she kept in touch with on regular basis. She probably didn't do it by phone because it was too expensive. Letters took too long to get from one place to another. But I hadn't thought about e-mail. I don't know why considering she had a computer at her place. Now, all I had to do was to enter Evelyn's full name into an address search engine and see if her name came up.

The idea excited me, not only because I would be able to read Evelyn's mail if I did manage to login into her email provider, but also because they'd be a very good chance that she'd kept an address book with all her regular email contacts in it.

I logged into the search facility of my address book and entered EVELYN CARTER, after which I hit the SEARCH button with the icon and a click of the mouse.

The search took a while to process. I sat there for a full two minutes, playing with the tips of my hair, hoping to God I was on the right track.

I thought about Michael, wondering if he ever was going to talk to me again. Since he disappeared into his room last night, I hadn't seen a glimpse of him. Today was Wednesday, and he should have been at school. But I was in no mood to harass him and get insulted in the process. I had already decided to let it be and trust fate to take care of everything.

Suddenly the video display unit spilled the result of my search. There were ten people by the name of Evelyn Carter who had an email address. I run down each name with my index finger:

Evelyn Carter
Evelyn Carter
Evelyn M. Carter   evelyn.carter@mailplus.com
Evelyn Carter
Evelyn Carter

Evelyn Carter
Evelyn Carter
Evelyn Carter
Evelyn Carter
Evelyn Carter

The third listing seemed to be a match. The middle name of the listing was an M, in fact the only M in the list of ten names. I knew Evelyn's middle name was Maree, so there was a good chance this way her. There was also the chance that this was just a coincidence and that I would be hitting a blank.

Now that I had found her email address, I had to have access to it. I recognised the extension of her e-mail, mailplus.com, as one of the man free email services for people who used the Internet.

I logged into the Internet using Netscape Explorer 4.0 and typed mailplus.com at the URL section. In no time I was faced with a screen which asked me for my name and password. I typed in *Evelyn. Carter* at the name box, and racked my brain for the password. I hadn't seen Evelyn for a very long time and trying to figure out what she was using as a password seemed like an impossible task. I tried all the obvious things, like her birth date, her middle name, the brand name of her car, her street number, her phone number, but none of those were successful.

Frustrated, I kept returning to the sign-on screen, wondering what in the world she could have used as a password.

After another half hour of trying prospective passwords, I gave up.

Standing from my office chair, I headed for the kitchen where I made myself a cup of coffee to let the frustration out of my system. There had to be some word, something which was easy for her to remember, something which I could figure out. But there was also twenty years of life separating us—now even death—and maybe she choose a word which had nothing to do with my life.

Over my cup of black coffee, I tried hard to remember the things which were important to Evelyn when we were still friends. But nothing came to mind. We didn't share little secret words or expressions that other girls did when we were young. And even if we did, I remembered none. This was another time, another place, another world.

Back behind my desk. I was about to give up when Evelyn's cat came to mind. I wondered if it had returned home, only to find an empty, ransacked house. I still felt a tinge of guilt for not having taken it with me on that day when we first entered Evelyn's apartment.

I typed O-S-C-A-R and pressed the enter button.

Bingo!

Evelyn's missing cat was the access code to her email.

There were only two new messages waiting to be read. Both were from Celia Pressly, Evelyn's friend in the USA.

I opened the most recent:

Dear Evelyn,

What's happening? Have you received my last e-mail? Haven't heard from you yet. Send us a message, okay? You're getting me worried.

Chao,
Celia.

I checked the message prior that one.

Dear Evelyn,

Got your e-mail. I'm glad you found a boyfriend. What does he think of your job? You know, if he's not happy, then just remember it's your life You don't have to put up with anyone's bullshit. But why am I telling you that, I know you wouldn't.

Okay, let me know the dates for when you get to the States. I can't wait to see you again.

Chao,
Celia.

The last e-mail was dated two days after we found Evelyn's body. All I learned was that Evelyn hadn't answered her last e-mails, let alone read them, and that she was supposedly on her way to the USA in the not-to-distant future. Fact one: she never answered her email because she was dead. Fact two: because she was dead, she would never make a trip to the USA.

I wondered who the boyfriend was. The cab driver did mention something about a boyfriend, and at first, we didn't want to believe him, but now that Celia had mentioned the mysterious boyfriend again, it was something I had to look into seriously. I wondered if Evelyn had worked for an escort agency prior to setting herself up. She probably had to at the beginning, to just ensure a constant flow of work. But since an escort agency was taking fifty percent of her earnings, she only had to work half the time if she worked for her self to make the same money. I had no idea what kind of money we were talking about, but based on the car she was driving and the furniture in her house, I knew it was a serious income. Also, if she did work for an escort agency, it could have been years ago. I wasn't sure what I would learn from people who worked with her that far back, but I nonetheless made a mental note about checking her past employers. It that type of industry, I assumed, friends probably lasted a lifetime.

I scanned down the other messages. Most of them were from Celia. Nothing serious, just mindless chit-chats about every day life, which no one would give a damn about. It didn't look as if Evelyn was using her e-mail for business correspondence. This was a bit of blow given that I had hoped for a major breakthrough by illegally accessing her email.

But all was not over yet. I decided to check her address book. When the address screen came up, it gave me a choice of three folders to chose from—'friends', 'customers' and 'black book'.

I nearly flipped backwards in my chair.

And all this time I had been looking for a three-dimensional address book, not a digital book. Judith Kingman had even described the size of the address book, as if she had seen it. Maybe she did, and maybe this was only a cyberspace back-up copy of the real thing. Whatever the case, I was glad I'd finally found the goddamn thing. I pat myself on the back. Ingenuity always wins in the end.

There were quite a few email numbers in the folders, most of them too secretive to figure out who they belonged to. What was I supposed to do? Send an e-mail to all these people asking them their names, address and contact number and hope they would reply back?

Many people chose nicknames for their e-mail address for privacy. I could more or less understand why. I didn't trust the internet or anything associated with it. As recently as last week, one of the largest free e-mail providers through the internet had been broken into by a hacker. If I was considering becoming a career criminal, the first thing I would do would be to get myself a solid education in computer programming, preferably to a higher degree level. After all, it was safer to break into a major bank database and transfer a few millions dollars to a secret account in the Cayman Islands than storming into a bank at gunpoint and watching yourself in full action on Australia's Most Wanted the following week.

I sipped from my mug, scanning the e-mail addresses.

One of them almost jumped out of the screen and slapped me in the face:

sg@vicpolice.au.gov.

I checked my wallet for a business card from Goosh, which I kept in a clear plastic holder among tens of others. I found it between a business card from David's Bookshop and one from Cee Bee Cleaning. The e-mail address read:

fmoore@vicpolice.au.gov.

I looked at the screen and back at the card. Judith Kingman mentioned that some of Evelyn's clients worked for the Police.

Two police officers broke into Evelyn's apartment.

Her body had vanished from the morgue.

My brain was kicking into high gear.

I checked the screen and Frank's business card again.

The extension on both email addresses was the same.

@vicpolice.au.gov.

There was no doubt in my mind.
I knew who the bastard was.

CHAPTER TWENTY-THREE

Two hours later I was at the Victoria Police St Kilda Road building complex in the conference room with Frank. My body was tensed, filled with panic and anger all at once. Every time I thought about the e-mail address I found in Evelyn's address book and its owner, I wanted to throw up. It all began to make sense. All the answers were not there yet, but it would only be a matter of time.

'Are you sure?' Frank asked for the second time. He wore heavy bags under his eyes, and his shirt could have done with ironing. If his mind was ticking like mine, he would have had little sleep since the beginning of this investigation. Even though today was clearly not the case, Frank had this amazing way of looking as if nothing was getting to him, but on the inside he was no different from me. I knew he woke up in the early hours of the morning and worried about the case he was working on, worried about where his life was heading, worried whether the work we did ever really made any difference at all. I knew what he was going through because that's exactly how I and thousands of other law enforcement people felt. Unlike other jobs where you could just switch off at the end of the day, we were taking our work home with us. The mental strain of working on a homicide was beyond what anyone out there could imagine. No matter how many times I'd gone through it, it never ceased to amaze me what humans did to one another. And even on days when I was preoccupied doing something else, the back of my mind was always itching with details of the homicide I was working on.

'Of course, I'm sure,' I said, pushing a printed page of Evelyn's e-mail address book under Frank's nose, 'There, I've even made a copy for you.' I had highlighted the suspicious e-mail address with a yellow marker.

Frank stared at the printed page and shook his head. 'Oh, boy, and you've come to ask me for advice? What can I tell you? Maybe you were right after all. This is... this is...'

'Go on, say it.'

'This is a fuckin' nightmare.'

The *fg* in *fg@vicpolice.au.gov* stood for Goosh. Frank pulled a business card from his wallet and threw it on the desk. The e-mail number on the print-out matched that of Goosh's business card.

'That probably explains why he sent police officers to Evelyn's place,' I said. 'That sonofabitch was probably using Evelyn's services, and when he realised she'd been killed, he knew his name would be linked to her murder.'

Frank seemed at a loss as to what to say. He waited half a minute before commenting. 'I don't know, Kristina. Maybe this has nothing to do with nothing.'

'You don't really believe that?'

'No, but, I think we should take it one tiny step at a time. Like, I wouldn't exactly go and burst into Goosh's office and start pointing a finger. We don't know how much he knows, and the last thing we need is to be on someone's hit list.'

I took back the printed copy of Goosh's e-mail number.

'You already told me you wanted out of the investigation,' I said. 'What about now? Now that you know your boss could be involved in the tampering of an on-going murder investigation, do you still think you can just walk away?'

'I say let's keep it quiet for a little while. You don't want to get yourself into more trouble than you already are. Especially with Goosh. He's already working hard on getting you off the investigation. If you snap at him and start making wild accusations, that might just be what he needs to have you suspended indefinitely.'

'Or that might just be what I need to get him to tell the truth. He'd know that if I go to the press with this, it'd be the end of his career.'

'True. It could also be the end of life as you know it.'

'I'm certainly not going to stand here and pretend I found nothing. Jesus, Frank, I can't believe you're taking all this with a grain of salt.'

Frank played with a button on his shirt sleeve. 'Do you think he has something to do with the body gone missing at the mortuary?'

'More likely than not,' I said, certain Goosh was capable of anything just to cover his own arse. 'You know how this thing is going to go down with the media. And Judith Kingman's already told us how other people in power were using Evelyn's services. We still don't know who killed her. It could have been anyone of her clients. It could even have been Goosh. It could have been Goosh and other dick heads with fat cheques and too much free time on their hands.'

'You don't seriously believe he could have killed her?'

'No, but he seemed eager to get his name cleared before we even linked it to Evelyn's murder. The way these people see it is that she was only a prostitute, so there's no point in a thorough investigation. Why do you think Goosh wants me off the case so fast? I was Evelyn's friend, so he knows I will do everything in my power to find the killer. He's seen me working in the past. He knows I never fail. What does that tell you?'

'It doesn't tell me he killed her.'

'I never said that. He probably didn't. He's just looking after his own back. No one knows who killed Evelyn and why. I certainly don't, but I am as hell going to find out.'

Frank shifted uncomfortably in his chair.

'Let it go for the time being,' he said. 'Let's find out who are the other people in Evelyn's address book. Maybe they'd be easier to front up to than Goosh. Maybe he has nothing to do with it, and it just happened that he was using Evelyn's services.'

Suddenly I realised that no matter how much I was going to say, it would make no difference to Frank. He had already decided to back off and take the easy approach. It looks as if I was going to have to take the part of the lone ranger once more.

'Okay, we'll wait,' I said, not wanting to disagree and ending up strangling him.

But another idea crossed my mind.

When I got back home, there was one of those red-on-white cards from the post office telling me to pick some registered mail. I wasn't expecting anything, so it kind of took me by surprise. Registered mail only meant two things—bad news or legal matters, or something in the form of both. As reluctant as I was to go and pick up the registered mail, curiosity got the better of me. Before the engine in my car got a chance to cool off, I backed up from the driveway and headed for the Craigieburn shopping centre.

When I signed for the registered item at the post office, the woman at the counter gave me an envelope with the name of a solicitor on the top right corner. I knew now it meant trouble.

On my way back to the car, I grabbed a copy of the p.m. edition of *Herald-Sun* and an Aero chocolate bar from the local newsagent. There was something on the front page about a gas explosion which was to deprive Victorians from gas supply for a least two weeks. No hot shower, no stove cooking, no central heating. Welcome to the twentieth century. With all that was happening in my life, that was the last thing I needed.

Back in the car, I slit the envelope to remove an official looking document which looked like a court summons. Peter Perezzia, the cab driver who took Evelyn Carter on her last drive to destiny, was suing me from battering and abuse of power. Someone said once that bad news comes in three. I was now scared to go home and find out what the third deed of the day would be.

Back home, I studied the summons where the alleged victim claimed he had been not only battered, but forced into custody when we had nothing against him. He claimed I tried to make him sign a confession and tricked him into answering questions which would make him look guilty. He also claimed that I never told him he was legally entitled to speak to a lawyer.

I felt rage building up. That sonofabitch was lying through his teeth. I remembered clearly asking him if he wanted a lawyer. And since the interview had been videotaped, it would be easy to prove.

Immediately, I rang Frank on his mobile and told him the news.

'I know,' he said. 'We've just received two summons on this side. He's also got me and the Victoria Police. This guy's after money. He must be working on his retirement fund.'

'We don't deserve this, Frank. Why are people such arseholes when you're trying to do the right thing?'

'Hey, I don't know. Everyone tries to get something for themselves these days. Greed is the way of the world.'

'Well, the way of the world sucks.'

After I hung up, I felt like I just swallowed a bucket of sand.

I snatched my car keys from the table and headed back to my car.

I needed to know I wasn't alone on this.

CHAPTER TWENTY-FOUR

David was writing in an A4 pad when I walked into his bookshop. The air outside was cold, and the heating from inside the bookshop was most welcome. The warning bell at the entrance got his attention.

He looked up and said, 'Kristina? What a surprise. I didn't expect you.'

'I wanted it to be a surprise.'

'Well, it's a surprise, all right.' He moved from behind the counter. 'Hold on a sec.'

He locked the door of the bookshop and turned around. 'What's up?'

'What do you mean?'

'Ah, come on, Kristina, you look like you've seen someone being amputated.'

Reluctant, but too weak to fight it back, I told him what I found out about Goosh.

'Oh, boy,' he said, stepping back behind his counter. 'Yes, I can see why you're worried now. This is starting to sound like a John Cleary novel. But you know you have to do what's right. It doesn't matter who these people are, they can't get away with murder.'

'Easy to say, but I'm fighting this alone.'

'What about your partner? What has he got to say?'

'He wants to lay low for the time being. He thinks that if we get involved, we might be next on somebody's death list.'

David stared at me for a moment and said, 'I haven't known you for long, Kristina, but I know you want to catch this killer more than anything in the world. If she'd been my friend who'd been killed, I'd want to catch the killer as well. You do what you think is right. Don't let them water down this investigation. You have to remain strong and level-headed. You know as well as I do that the odds can only make you stronger. You've got to do this not just because she was your friend, but because of everything you believe. That's why you took on this case in the first place.'

'I know, David, And I know you're right. But sometimes, I wonder what's it all about. Can one person really make a difference? At the end of the day is anyone going to notice? Does it really matter?' I had no idea where all this negativity was coming from.

'It only matters if you want it to matter,' David went on. 'That's what life is all about. Caring about something. The moment you give up, you might as well not be living.'

I puzzled over his comment for a few seconds. Was life really just a battle of will against fate and other people's misdeeds?

I spent another half hour with David, only to end up feeling guilty about sucking up his time just to make me feel better about my own existence. Although I would have loved to stay longer, I knew it wouldn't be fair on him. He seemed to enjoy working in the bookshop, and if I'd stayed, he probably would have felt obligated to close for the day and entertain me.

'You don't have to go, really,' David insisted, and I knew he meant every world of it.

'I know I don't,' I said, 'but I've got a lot of work to do. This investigation has taken most of my time, and I've got clients jumping up and down in regards to some work I was supposed to have finished weeks ago. I really need to clear up my schedule and my mind.'

On my way back home, I was wondering how I was going to face Goosh. I knew I had to tell him what I had discovered because the only way I was going to find out what had happened to Evelyn Carter was to explore every avenue possible. I didn't agree with Frank about putting Goosh on the back-burner. To me, it felt like it was easier to deal with things

161

straight away rather then letting them simmer and increasing the chances of another disaster. And if it was indeed Goosh who was trying to jeopardise this investigation, then I knew he wouldn't stop until he got what he wanted.

The federal elections were only two weeks away, with both major parties promising GST or no GST, and some minor parties promising a white Australia or more lenient gun laws. I had had no time to put my thoughts around any of the issues being offered by the political parties. I would make up my mind at the last minute when it came to voting. Frankly, it all seemed like waste of time to me since I wondered how well-balanced a person could be by thinking him or herself capable of running an entire country.

When I arrived home, Frank and Michael were waiting for me at the door steps. The sight of them nearly caused me a heart attack. Although I wasn't exactly surprised to see Michael, I hadn't expected to see the two of them together. It was almost as if they had conspired some evil plan, the way men seem to be doing when they get together.

I parked the Excell in the driveway, just behind Frank's Ford. I stepped out of the car and forced a smile. Anxiously, I paced towards the front door, my fingers tightly gripping my briefcase.

'What up now?' I asked in a tone which probably didn't sound too friendly, which in a way seemed justified because of the way they were staring at me.

'We need to talk,' Frank began, giving me the impression that this was going to be a me-against-them type of situation. I wasn't ready for it, and, for a spilt second, I considered telling them to buzz off and to leave me alone.

But the look on Michael's face seemed so desperate that all I said was, 'Why don't we go inside if we're going to talk?'

They both looked at each other and stood on their feet.

I opened the door and feared the worse. What had I done this time? Had I turned into a worst mother than I already had been by not spending enough time with my son? Or maybe I was too harsh on him? Maybe he'd grown-up much more than I had noticed, and I wasn't giving him enough room to move? Thoughts were running at a hundred miles an hour in my head. I had tried to keep my distance with Michael in the last few days, not only because he had asked me too, but because I wouldn't have known what to do anyway. And every time I opened my mouth, the wrong words seemed to be coming out of it.

'You guys want something to drink?' I asked when we reached the kitchen. I wasn't thirsty, and I gathered they weren't either, but that was my way of getting ready for a joint verbal assault.

'This is serious,' Frank said as he took a seat at the kitchen table.

'What?' I said, looking at Michael instead. 'Have I done something?'

Michael rolled his eyes to the ceiling.

'It's nothing like that,' Frank said. 'Michael rang me up, and he was all worked up about you and him, and I drove over here, and he told me what was on his mind.'

I opened my mouth, but nothing came out for a few seconds. Frankly, I thought Michael never liked Frank, so it did take me by surprise.

'Why didn't you call me on my mobile?' I asked Michael. 'If something is wrong, you should know better than calling Frank at work.'

'See what I mean,' Michael said to Frank. 'She's talking like that all the time. What chance have I got?'

'All right, all right,' Frank said to Michael. Then to me: 'You're going to have to back off a bit. You're driving him insane. I don't think you've realised that he's done a lot of growing up since last year, and he feels that you're still treating him like a child.'

An iron fist was stuck in my throat. How in the world did I end up in my own kitchen with these two clowns, and Frank telling me how to be a mother when he had no idea what it was like to have a child?

And yes, as far as I was concerned Michael was still a child. He didn't have a driver's license, the right to vote, the ability to generate his own income, and the maturity to face issues head on.

'Are you serious?' I asked.

'Kristina, this is not a you-against-us situation,' Frank said.

'No, so what is it? Why does my son need someone else to speak for him? I mean why you? Why not just get a lawyer and make it official? Why not take me to court and sue me for being a bitch?'

'Kristina, you're twisting everything around. Michael called me because he didn't know how to handle you. He knows you act irrationally when it comes to you and him, so he spoke to me, hoping I would be able to mediate between the two of you.'

I shook my head in disbelief. 'Mediate? What? We're going through a divorce or something? Jesus, Frank, why don't you mind your own goddamn business?'

He twisted his lips, obviously hurt. 'Hey, I'm only trying to help here. Your son comes to me and asks me for help, what did you want me to do? Turn him down? Call you on the mobile and betray him? If you guys are having a problem, you should get it resolved as soon as possible. I'm fuckin' tired of your bullshit!' His tone of voice had gone up by a couple of notches.

'Michael!' I snapped, glaring at him straight in the eyes. 'What in the world is wrong with you? I've done everything I can to make you happy. I've given you the freedom you wanted. I've stayed clear when you asked me to. What in the world do you want from me?'

He stood there, not saying a word. There was pain in my voice, and he must have sensed it.

'Mum, I don't think you understand.'

'Well, try me, you might be surprised.'

And then he started to cry.

Frank crossed his fingers in embarrassment.

I moved behind Michael and hugged him from behind while he was still sitting in his chair.

'I love you, Michael,' I said. 'You know I love you, and I want to make things better for the two of us. You tell me what you want, and I'll do my best to give it to you. All I want is for you to be happy,.'

'I know...' he sobbed. 'I don't know, mum. It hurts so much inside. I'm scared all the time.'

'You can see someone if you want. The school principal has already told you that. You don't have to keep it all inside. Talking to someone will help you to overcome your fears.'

'I'm not a freak, I don't want to see a psycho head. The

other kids at school are going to make fun of me.'

I wiped the tears from his eyes. 'No one has to know, Michael. This is just between you and me.' I glanced at Frank from the corner of my eye. 'And Frank.'

'I don't know,' Michael said.

'And people who go to see psychiatrists are not nut cases. They're just having problems dealing with every day situations for one reason or another. As far as I'm concerned, I don't know how the hell you can deal with all this by yourself. I think that's the insane bit. You nearly got killed last year. You're still suffering from post-traumatic shock. It's not going to go away all by itself. I promise you will feel a lot better if you talk to someone.'

'I don't know.'

I turned around and faced him head on. 'Why don't you do this for the two of us. Try it for a couple of weeks, and if you don't like it, then you don't have to go any more.'

'Okay,' he said, hesitating.

'And remember,' I added. 'You don't have to do anything you don't want to. I'm not making you do anything you don't want to. Do we understand each other?' I tickled him in the ribs.

A small laugh came out while he was still crying. 'Okay. I love you, mum.'

'I love you too, Michael.'

Frank looked outside the kitchen window, one hand covering his face from embarrassment.

CHAPTER TWENTY-FIVE

I was on my way to the St Kilda Road Police Complex, fear taking over me as if I was someone having my last meal on death row. I drove over the West Gate Bridge, from which I had a vintage point of the entire city of Melbourne and its surrounding docks. The famous Crown Casino and the newly developed tourist-enticing Southbank river-side walk stood to my left, attracting thousands of Melburnians on weekdays as well as weekends. Five years ago, the city was dead. With a change in government, Melbourne had become one of Australia's premium cities with the hosting of the Australian Grand Prix, the Australian Open and the forthcoming Paramount Film studios in the docklands.

I exited the freeway at Princes Highway, drove straight up for a couple of kilometres, took a left turn, and slipped into St Kilda Road.

After speaking at length with Frank the previous night, we concluded that if I wanted to confront Goosh, then it was up to me. He advised me against it at this stage. In spite of his well-intended recommendation, I knew I had no choice in the matter. After all I was in charge of the investigation, and so the finally decision rested on my shoulders. It wasn't as if I could just walk away and feign ignorance. Either way, he would back me up, he said, but I shouldn't be expecting him to get too involved. When it came to solving cases, he was willing to do anything, but inside politics and internal investigations were not in his line of expertise. Did he actually believe that they were in mine?

All night, the apprehension of what I was about to do engulfed my nerves and paralysed my sense of reality. Tossing and turning, my mind and body were in a state of almost non-existence, as if I was floating on clouds. In spite of being aware that apprehension was nothing more than a state of mind, I couldn't detach myself from the claustrophobic chains which made me doubt my own logic.

But the next morning, as I drove down the West Ring Road and towards the city centre, my fear was being taken over by anger. *Why do people always fear the bad guys? Why is it that evil has such a power over us?* The dark forces in our lives always seemed to be dominating righteousness in spite of our moral sense of truth and justice. I hadn't done anything wrong. I was following a logical chain of events based on the evidence I had found during the course of my investigation. I hadn't pulled Goosh's name out of the computer at random and tried to frame him. It just happened that he was involved in this case, and he's left me no choice but to proceed in a manner which I believed to be diligent and virtuous. And if he was in fact responsible for the disappearance of Evelyn's body, then I had every right to be angry.

I parked the car in front of the St Kilda Road Police Complex, ignoring the red-and-white no-parking sign. Angry and anxious all at once, I stepped out of the car and slammed the door without locking it.

As I made my way up the steps of the building, I took a deep breath, gathering in vain the nerve and courage I needed to confront the man who was the moving force and the spokesperson for the entire police community in the state of Victoria. Although I should have been used to face-to-face confrontations with Goosh, this time the stakes were higher. I was going to accuse him point blank that he was directly involved in a murder. Being a reasonably logical person, I would normally be able to anticipate the result of any confrontation. This time, however, I had no idea the depth of complication I was getting myself into. If this case did involve corruption at a high level, I knew my life would be in danger. But that was a chance I was willing to take, if not for myself, at

167

least for Evelyn Carter who would never be able to fight for justice.

After clearing myself with security, I passed the metal detector and headed for the elevator.

One minute later, I was on the ninth floor of the St Kilda Road Police Complex.

'Is he in?' I asked Goosh's secretary, a young strawberry-blond bimbo who seemed to be at his service for other things than administrative duties.

'Have you got an appointment?' she asked, pursing her lips as if I'd just swore at her. The contrast between her and me was like fire and water. I wore plain make-up and choose my clothes for comfort and appropriateness of a given situation. A business meeting required me to dress in the obligatory blouse, skirt or trousers, and matching jacket. Everything Goosh's secretary wore was a come-on sign, from the ash-blond peroxided hair and the bright cherry lipstick, to the almost-see-through, flower patterned cotton dress and little white socks. Even though she looked in her mid-twenties, she dressed like a sixteen-year old who was wrestling with an overwhelming newly-found sexuality. She knew I thought she was cheap, even though I had never said a word to her. Call it women's instinct if you wish.

'It won't take a minute,' I said and aimed for his office door.

'You'll have to make an appointment,' she protested.

'Well, I'm afraid this is kind of urgent.'

Not looking back, I knocked twice and, not waiting for an invitation, walked in.

Goosh lifted his eyes up from some documents he was reading. His face was flushed, and his eyes expressed surprise.

'Dr Melina?'

'I need to talk to you right away.'

He glanced at his diary and said, 'Have we got a meeting of some sort?'

'No, we haven't, but this is rather important.'

'Well, have you ever heard of the phone?'

'It's about the Evelyn Carter investigation.'

'Include it in your progressive report.'

I moved closer to his desk. 'I think you'd might like to hear what I have to say before I include it in the report. This matter actually concerns you.'

He shifted uncomfortably in his chair. 'Are you threatening me?'

I wasn't sure where this was coming from. How in the world had I threatened him just by telling him I had important news for him regarding the Evelyn Carter investigation?

'A beg your pardon?' I said.

'What do you want from me?'

The defensive attitude seemed ridiculous. Maybe he'd guessed what I was here for. If he was in fact involved with the breaking in of Evelyn Carter's apartment, then he knew there would have always been the chance that I was going to connect her death with him. The fact that he seemed to have been a client of hers told me that he knew this conversation was going to take place sooner or later.

'Okay, so I know about you and Evelyn Carter, and that's why I'm here.'

'You know what?'

'Ah, come on, do you want me to spell it out for you?'

He silently glared into my eyes for a few seconds, and followed this by a full minute of silence. I waited patiently for him to compose himself. He did a half turn and stared blankly out of his office window, overlooking St Kilda beach and the endless blue sea, which became one with the sky as far as the eye could see. I looked as well and realised that life was so simple—it was only humans who made it so complicated.

Finally, he turned his attention back to me. 'So what do you want?'

'What do I want? Surely you have had enough time to anticipate this moment was going to take place. You're going to tell me why your name was found in Evelyn Carter's address book.'

'What address book?'

'You know what I'm talking about.'

'I thought you couldn't find *that* address book.'

'Let's just say I have for the time being. My point is still valid. Why was your name in her address book?'

He stared at me for a few more seconds and picked up the telephone handset. 'Take messages for the next half hour,' he said into the receiver, 'and cancel my four-thirty appointment with the Shadow Minister for Police and Emergencies, whatever the hell his name is.' He slammed the receiver and turned back to me. 'I have nothing to do with her death.'

'I'm sure you don't,' I said matter-of-factly. 'And I've never implied that you had. My main concern is that her apartment has been ransacked. Someone has been trying to get access to something they can't find. My guess is that whomever that person was, he wanted to get his hands on the address book.'

Goosh didn't reply.

I went on, 'And I was wondering if you might know who that person could be?'

He stood from his chair, circled his desk and paced up and down the length of his office. 'Look, Kristina, we've had our differences in the past.' So now I was *Kristina* and not *Dr Melina*. 'But at the end of the day, we're on the same team. You have to understand that I want to get the person who killed your friend as badly as you do. I didn't even know she was your friend. Believe me, there was never any mention of your name. You even said yourself that you hadn't seen her for twenty years. I'm talking on a professional level here.'

I decided to cut the chase. 'Did you use her services?'

'Why do you need to know that?'

'Because I need to establish why your name was in her address book.'

More silence.

He knew he was trapped, and any lie he would say would be obvious to the both of us.

'You're going to include that in your report, are you?' he said.

'Not unless I have to. Not unless it's relevant to the investigation. But if you've done nothing, like you claim you have, then what are you worried about?'

He puzzled over my comment for a few seconds. If I'd been in his shoes, and if I indeed had nothing to do with the murder of Evelyn, I would lay all my cards on the table. He knew me well enough by now that I wasn't there to trap people into a corner and to avenge myself for no reason. Sure, I didn't like Goosh, and that was more because of his hatred for me. But that didn't mean that I would frame him for something he hadn't done. He must have realised that when he finally decided to give in.

'Okay,' he said, 'I did see her, but you wouldn't understand all that. It's not what you think it was.'

'Oh, I know you were not having an affair with her. Don't you worry. She was a call-girl. You paid her for the time you spent together.'

'I wasn't the only person using her services. Why don't you hassle everyone else? I'm only—'

'Hey, I'm not judging you of how you spend your pay-packet. I want to know if you've got anything to do with her missing body at the mortuary.'

'How could you ever think that I've got anything to do with that?'

'Well, the way I see it, it's pretty straight forward. Being a highly ranked police official and having you're name tied up to a murdered high-class prostitute isn't exactly a notch on your resume. So, I say, yes, you, and others within your circles, would have had a pretty good reason to get rid of the body. Why, I don't know. I can only guess that further forensic tests would have shown something that you don't want the investigative team to know.'

'This is absolutely ridiculous. I would never do such a thing. Okay, so I was seeing her, but so was half of who's who in Melbourne. That doesn't make me a killer. I wouldn't go and steal a body from a morgue. Hell, I've got enough to do here as it is. Do you have any idea who you're talking to? I resent your accusations. It's just ludicrous. I can't believe you can just be standing there and talking to me the way you are. What in the world is wrong with you? We're on the same side, Kristina, the same goddamn side. Can't you understand that?'

After working for years as an investigator, I liked to believe I could tell more or less when a person lied. Sure, in the past, I'd made some catastrophic judgemental errors, but right at that moment, it all seemed black-and-white. He was fidgeting with his fingers. He avoided eye contact. His knees were locked together. There was sweat on his upper lip. His tone was unreasonably defensive.

Goosh was a fuckin' liar.

And a bad one at that.

171

'Look, Mr Goosh, either you tell exactly what you know, or I'm going to push for an independent inquiry. You know that all I have to do is make one phone call to the media, and your face will be spread all over the front page of every newspaper in this country.'

'Kristina, you don't seriously—'

'And stop calling me Kristina, nothing's changed between us. I'm still Dr Melina to you.'

He raised his hands in protest. 'Why are you doing this? I told you I had nothing to do with the disappearance of her body?'

'What about ransacking her apartment?'

'I know nothing about that.'

'Not according to Evelyn's neighbour. She claims men who identified themselves as the police broke into her apartment. Care to explain how that could have happened?'

'I didn't even know someone broke into her apartment.'

He blinked in quick successions.

'I'm sure you didn't,' I said.

'Why don't you believe me?'

'Give me a good reason why I should. Since the beginning of my contract with the VFSC, you've tried every cunning trick in the book to get rid of me. You lied time and time again just to make my life hell. You wanted me out, and I don't see how it's different now. I don't trust you, Mr Goosh, I never have and never will.'

A few seconds of silence.

I had no idea as to what he was thinking about. Maybe he was going to pull out a gun from his top drawer and shot me right there on the spot. And then he would arrange for the disposal of my body. No autopsy, no forensic evidence. Dr Kristina Melina vanishes into thin air.

His eyes fell upon me, scrutinising every square inch on my face, as if he was trying to figure out which part didn't belong to me.

My heart raced.

Finally, he moved his head closer to mine.

'Maybe we can work something out,' he said almost in a whisper. 'Maybe everything can work out for everyone. I can be good for you, Kristina. I can give you what you want.'

There was sweat on his upper lips.

'Like what?' I asked. 'You're going to pay me so I can shut my mouth?'

'You know I have a lot of influence as to what comes and goes in here. I can have your contract extended indefinitely. I can review the terms of your payments. Name your price.'

I didn't reply straight away. Not for a second was I considering his offer, but I wanted to make him believe I was. Let him sweat it out a little. His eyes glistened with hope. His future was in my hands, and he damn well knew it. I could break him, or I could get anything I desired from him. Anything but the truth. And unfortunately for him, the truth was all I really wanted.

'No deal. You give me the names of the people who took Evelyn's body from the mortuary, the names of the people who broke into her apartment, and maybe even the name of the person who killed her. That's the only negotiating I'm going to be doing with you. I don't do deals with arseholes.'

His face went red. 'I'm not admitting that I'm involved in anything. I just want you off my back, that's all. We can work this out. We can be friends, and everyone can go home. What's it going to take to make you come to your senses? Come on, you're being unreasonable.'

'I'm being unreasonable? My friend's dead; her body has vanished from the morgue; I'm sitting in the Police Commissioner's office, and he's trying to bribe me so we can all go home and pretend nothing's happened. Well, guess what? I'm way past being unreasonable.'

I jumped from my chair, sending it flying half way across the room behind me.

I went on, a menacing finger pointing at his face, 'Give me what you've got, or I'm going to bury you.'

He jumped from his seat and slammed both hands on the table top, tipping his coffee all over his paperwork. 'Okay, look, that's it! I want you out of this investigation now. I want you out of this fuckin' building. I don't need authorisation from the VFSC to do this. You're trespassing as of this very second.' He punched the intercom button on the phone. 'Get me security. I'd like someone to escort Dr Melina out of the building immediately.'

'Don't bother,' I said, 'I can find my own way out. You're making a big mistake. A serious one for that matter.'

I paced towards the exit.

'Don't you come back here with your wild accusations, *Ms* Melina. I'm going to keep tabs on you. One wrong move, and I'll have you charged with obstruction of justice. Do you hear me? One *fuckin'* wrong move!'

'What are you going to do? Get rid of me like you got rid of Evelyn Carter? You're going to hire crooked cops to do your dirty work? You think you're above the law or something? You think the rules don't apply to you?'

He stared at me for a few seconds, obviously puzzling over a reply.

Before he had time to say another word, I stepped out of the room and slammed the door.

Just then, a uniformed officer paced towards me, a serious look etched on his face.

'I'm on my way out,' I said, and let him escort me out of the building.

As I took the steps down the front of the St Kilda Road Complex, I felt rage pumping in my veins.

There would be no stopping me this time.

CHAPTER TWENTY-SIX

I spent the next few days at home in a post-traumatic stage. I refused to see anyone or do have anything to do with the investigation.

When I left the St Kilda Road Police Complex, I thought I would be strong enough, all the anger and the rage pumping into my veins, giving me the adrenalin rush I needed to get myself going. And it did for a little while. On my way home, I pushed my car to 150 km/h on the West Ring Road, risking my life as well as that of other motorists. I hated pathetic drivers, and now I hated the fact that I'd just turned into one of them.

By the time I got home, I was in tears, unable to insert the keys into the front door lock. I went down to my knees and began to sob like a child. The whole world was crumbling around me. Everywhere I turned, evil seemed to be winning. Where had God disappeared to? Wasn't He supposed to be here in times of despair. Well, I was desperate enough now, on my knees, crying like a newborn, slamming my first into the wooden panel of the door. And all I could think about was Evelyn. Her face was right in front of my eyes, begging for justice, but my hands were tied. The clues I had were few and not very convincing. The people I was working with were too busy worried about their own little lives to care about someone who was dead. And I was still buried deep into my own grieving for Evelyn to be able to function on a logical level. And yet, I knew I would have to find the strength within me to fight on, no matter how alone I felt in this world. Since my parents had died in a car accident when I was a young child, I never felt like I truly belonged anywhere, always looking for love, for an excuse to exist, for a reason to wake up every morning and look up to the sky and tell myself that everything was going to be all right. But that was a damn lie, and I knew it. I was incapable of loving another person without hurting myself or other people. Even my own son felt I was suffocating him with my presence. My life was halfway over, and yet I felt as if it had not even begun.

After what felt like an infinite amount of time, I managed to get back on my feet and open the front door of my home. Michael wasn't there, and it was just as well, because the last thing I needed was to explain why I looked as if I'd just stepped out of the shower.

My nerves were raw, and I spent a good deal of time in the confinement of my bedroom. I wasn't doing anything in particular, other than staring at the white ceiling above my bed, letting thoughts drift endlessly from one corner of my mind to the other. I was too close to the investigation for me to be able to see everything from a detached viewpoint. Maybe Goosh had been right from the beginning. I was too close to this case to be able to do a good job. But then, who the hell was he to tell me what to do? After all, he was half the reason why I was plastered in bed.

During the next forty-eight hours, Frank rang five times, but I let the answering machine take the calls. Michael was in-and-out of the house, and although he didn't say anything, he knew something was wrong. Since we had spoken the other day, we had build a mutual code of respect for each other's existence. We were not going to completely ignore one another, but we were also not going to get on each other's case. It wasn't a commitment we made verbally, just a psychological understanding between two human beings.

David called, but I also let the answering machine take it. The third time he called, I was almost going to pick up the phone. When I heard his voice coming through the speaker of the answering machine, I could almost smell the scent of his flesh, the taste of his kiss, the warmth of his body so close to mine. I longed to be with him, and yet I didn't want to trouble him with my problems. Showing weakness had never been my forte, no matter what.

On the third day, I refused to get out of bed. I tried to read my Sue Grafton novel, but my mind was too pre-occupied with the injustices of this world. Goosh was involved in this up to his neck, and he knew that I knew. What I needed was time to figure out what I was going to do next. Frank didn't want any part of what was happening, and I didn't know anyone else who'd be able to help me. I hadn't heard anything about me working on the investigation, and whether I had been officially dismissed or not. And frankly, I couldn't care less. Whatever their decision, I would end up doing whatever I pleased. Other people's opinions and orders never stopped me in the past to get what I wanted, and it wasn't going to happen now.

I tossed my Grafton on the side table and headed for the bathroom where I ran myself a long hot shower. It was 2.30 p.m., and I realised it was time for me to make a decision one way or another. I couldn't go on sitting on the fence, fearing whatever evil force was hovering above my head. Anger and the need for justice was fuelling my mind, but I had no idea which direction to take.

I stepped out of the shower, dried my hair with a clean towel, and noticed the bags under my eyes. It didn't matter that I'd spent all night and all morning in bed, I hadn't managed to get the sleep I so badly needed. The tiredness, of course, hindered my ability to find a solution.

Maybe I would interrogate a few of the Evelyn's neighbours.

Or maybe track down other people who were down on her address book. Goosh was one of them, but they were many others. Someone had to know something. I didn't believe that the killer was just someone she had met by accident on that fatal night. She was very careful with who she went out with. That was what high-class escort girls did, to my understanding, anyway. Of course, I really had no concrete idea of how the industry worked, what kind of scrutiny potential clients went through, and how the psychopaths of this world were filtered out of the system. Whatever the case, Evelyn's system had a hole in it, and some big shark managed to squeeze itself through the net.

'How long have you known Evelyn for?' I asked the woman

who was sitting across the table from me.

We were eating lunch at Cafe Max in the city. The buffet food for lunch was excellent and well priced. I ordered a Cajun chicken salad and Paulina a serving of vegetarian gonococci We could have sat outside and watched the crowd on Hardware Street, but the temperature was not all that hot. I'd been here before, and there was always a real sense of community between the cafe and the surrounding shop, providing the perfect atmosphere for special events and interesting music.

Paulina had been in the escort business for as long as Evelyn. Although they began working together during the early stages of their career, they both ended up working for themselves. They've known each other for twenty years now, which was far longer than I ever managed to keep a friend.

'I told her the money was much better,' Paulina said. 'Those bastards take fifty percent of your earnings, and for what? They don't do anything apart from making phone calls and advertise. Really, you've got to ask yourself, what kind of fool would give away fifty percent of their wages? This is the worst kind of deal I've ever heard of. I mean, do you know any other business where you have to give fifty percent of your earnings?'

'Cab driving,' I said matter-of-factly.

'Really?' She seemed genuinely surprised. 'I didn't know that.'

'Yes, and the money is probably not half as good as what you're making.'

Paulina was extremely attractive, and I never expected her to be any less given that she was working as a high-class escort. She had long hair the colour of winter wheat and green sparkling eyes. She was tall, and the way she handled her cutlery, you could have been forgiven for thinking she'd been born and bred in high society. Her yellow jacket was the expensive designer type made of material that winkled easily if not careful. She could have been a model if she never bothered with prostitution. Or an actress given she had some form of talent to begin with, or a game-show host, or any job which required someone to look like the cover girl of the latest issue of Vogue.

I tracked Paulina down from the email number listed in

Evelyn's address book. Two days prior, I sent unsolicited emails to all the addresses in Evelyn's book and asked everyone to contact me in regards to the investigation I was conducting. No one replied to my request other than Paulina. She had heard that Evelyn had been killed through the media, but didn't want to get involved, that is until I got in touch with her.

'It's a revolting profession,' Paulina said as she sipped from her cappuccino. 'I hate what I'm doing, and I hate myself for doing it. But I've been working this job for so long, I'm not experienced at doing anything else. I keep telling myself that one day I'll quit, but it doesn't look as if it's ever going to happen. You really get used to the money, and there would be no way that I could go back and live on the breadline. I mean, what's the point? At the end of the day, you only live once, so at least I get what I want.'

'What did Evelyn think of the work?'

'She didn't. She was too interested in the money. And believe me, that's all it is. Unless you're an nymphomaniac, it's nothing but the money. And we're talking a lot of money.'

'What kind of money?'

Paulina looked at me suspiciously. 'You're not a cop, are you?'

'No, I'm not. I couldn't care less whether you've paid your taxes or not. I'm just trying to figure out what happened to Evelyn.'

'Okay, then.' She paused for a few seconds as if she was adding figures up in her head. 'On a good week, I can make up to $10,000 easy.'

I nearly fell backwards. 'Jesus! What do you charge by the hour?'

'I'm going for top clientele. They can afford it. It depends on what they're after, but you're looking at $500 to $1000 per hour.'

'Why would anyone want to pay that kind of money?'

'There's really three main reasons why men come and see us. Their wives won't give them a head job, they want to try something different, and they simply like the idea of paying someone to fuck them. That's really all there is. There's no great mystery. You lose faith in men after you've being doing this for too long. I mean, at the end of the day, they're all pigs. And I'm not scared of saying that.'

I was completely astounded. I never heard of anyone making so much money in real life. Sure, I'd heard of Forbes top five hundred rich list, but to me that was just fiction. They were just numbers and names in a magazine. But no one I knew made that kind of money. No wonder some of these women couldn't kick off the habit.

Paulina must have sensed my shock from the expression on my face.

'It's great having all the money,' she said. 'You never have to worry about buying anything. I mean, I just go down Chapel Street, and see all these dresses, and I don't have to compromise between one or the other. I just take the lot. And it's such a good feeling, you know having all this money. Money is power, there is no doubt. If you have enough money, you can buy yourself just about anything. But fucking for a living is a bitch of a way to make your money. I wish I made the same type of money some other way, but I started when I was sixteen, so I guess I never got the chance. Sure, with my looks, I could have found a rich man and married him. But that wouldn't have given me the freedom to do what I want. I couldn't live with someone who'd tell me what to do all day long, who'd expect a cooked dinner every night, and who'd want his shirts pressed every morning by six. I've seen what family life does to women. It's degrading. No matter how advanced we think we are, women are still slaves to men and to society.'

I didn't totally agree with her viewpoint, but I was in no mood to have a moralistic debate on women's place in the world.

'Was Evelyn making as much money as you are?' I asked.

'I never asked her for exact figures, but I did help her to get herself started on her own. I don't see why she wouldn't have. She drove a SAAB, that I knew. She bought it cash straight from the dealer. I was with her when she did, and you should have seen the face of the car dealer when she gave him $70,000 cash. I thought his eyes were going come out of his sockets. He almost jerked himself off when she told him what she did for a living, like just because she bought a car from him, he thought he was entitled to a freebie. I mean, really, this bastard had a picture of his wife and kids on his desk.'

'Really?'

'Yeah, and you know what really make me sick?'

'What?'

'When one of them tells you this story on how his wife went into labour the previous day, and she's still in hospital. And I ask him, well, shouldn't you be with your wife, and he says that she hasn't fucked him during the whole time she was pregnant. I mean, what was he thinking when he got married? There's more to life than getting fucked all the time. You meet someone like that, and I swear, you just want to throw up all over him.'

'I can imagine,' I said and emptied my cup of coffee. 'Do you know if Evelyn was seeing anyone?'

'As in boyfriend-girlfriend?'

'Boyfriend, yes.'

'There was this one guy she mentioned a few times. It seemed quite serious, but she didn't really want to talk about it.'

'What did she say about him? Did she tell you his name?'

'No, she was quite secretive about the whole thing. She'd only been going out with him for a couple of months, so in a way I can't blame her. Until you're certain something is going to work, you don't want to start bragging on about it to everyone. That's one way to fall flat on your face, if you know what I mean.'

I certainly did. I done that enough times in my life, and I never seemed to learn my lesson.

'So, there's absolutely nothing you can tell me about her boyfriend?'

She puzzled for a few seconds.

'Now that you're asking, she did mention something about him wanting her to stop working as a call girl. He was getting a little possessive apparently. Not that she minded too much. The only men she met in her life to date were those who'd been paying her. She felt it was nice to have someone caring about her because of who she was rather than what sexual services she provided. You know, this guy was concerned that something bad might be happening to her, which, unfortunately, it did.'

181

'So, she was in love with this guy?'

'I don't know about love. When you've been in the escort business for as long as she and I have, I don't know if you can still believe in love. It's seems that there is only lust out there. You know what I mean?'

I nodded but didn't pass on any comments. Maybe she was right. Maybe love was nothing more than an acceptable explanation as to why people who lusted have one another so relentlessly. To date I hadn't experienced my understanding of true love in my life, and passing judgement on what lovers felt towards one another was not in my field of expertise.

'That's all you can tell me about this guy?' I asked.

'He made enough money to support himself, and obviously felt that he made enough money to support her as well, otherwise he would have never asked her to give up her job. He must have been in upper management, maybe a company director or someone who owned a successful business.'

'So, there's a possibility that he killed her because she refused to give up her job?'

Paulina stared at me as if I'd just called her a four-letter word.

'Now, that's not something I'm going to comment on,' she said. 'I don't know the guy, and I have no idea what he's capable of. I wouldn't go as far as to confirm that her boyfriend killed her. How did you come to that conclusion?'

'I was only trying to get an opinion based on what Evelyn said about him. Did she mention anything about him being violent?'

'Nope. Not that she would have told me anyway. We were not best friends. We just worked together for a while, and after that, our relationship remained strictly business. You know, whenever she had problems with one of her clients or with her taxes, she rang me and asked me for advice. Really, that's all I can tell you. I wish I knew who did that to her, because right now I want to kill the bastard as much as you do. Fuckin' men. They're all the same. Pigs. I'm telling you, there is no love in this world. It's all bullshit. One day I'm going to buy this huge scissors and cut all their dicks off.'

Her tone was filled with bitterness, and her vocabulary had dropped by a couple of notches on the scale of social graciousness.

I checked my watch. It was just on 4.20 p.m., and I had promised David to join him at the bookshop so that we could spend the night together.

'Well, you've been really helpful,' I said. 'It's a shame that nothing's come out of this.'

'You're welcome.' She touched up her left eyebrow with one finger and glanced around her, as if someone might have been spying on us.

I went on, 'But if you do remember something, please do not hesitate to contact me.'

I handed her a business card with my contact details.

'Sure thing,' she said and threw the card in her handbag.

I was just about to leave my seat when she added, 'Hey, you know, you're pretty good looking, you'd do really well in this business. I bet you don't make a thousand buck an hour doing what you're doing now.'

CHAPTER TWENTY-SEVEN

David was in the bookshop when I parked my car alongside the front of his shop window, hitting the front left wheel a little too hard against the kerbside.

There was a man in his mid-fifties with an overhanging belly talking to him over the counter. He wore a blue jumper and had a walking stick by his side. A pile of paperback and hard cover books stood between them. David was patiently transferring the books to white plastic carry bags, the kind which were given freely at my local supermarket when purchasing groceries. The overweight man was obviously a ferocious reader, maybe a retiree with nothing better to do with his time.

David wore his tortoise shell glasses halfway down on the bridge of his nose. He looked like an academic with his tweed jacket and concentrated frown. A shiver ran up and down my spine. Every time I saw him again, I was always surprised at how attractive he was. As I stepped out of the car, I wondered why David bothered with someone like me. Hidden behind my so-called good looks, I was a neurotic mess on the edge of a nervous breakdown. To desire to be in a relationship with me bordered on sheer lunacy. But who was I to criticise the opposite sex's blind appetite for intimacy?

It wasn't raining, but the side walk was wet as if someone

had just doused it with buckets of water. The sky was painted white, and I could smell waste decay from sewerage below the city level. The Yarra river was often overflowing at that time of the year, creating an over-abundance of water, and losing itself into rainwater drains. A downpour followed by hot weather caused the putrid odour to rise above ground level and into the city business district.

I pushed the wooden door of the shop open. The little silver bell announced my presence throughout the shop. The comforting odour of old paper and ink filled my nostrils. David had turned the heater on. The inside of the shop was warm and inviting, and at that very moment I understood why he resolved to spend a good deal of his life in this room. He had created a sanctuary for himself, a comfortable place where no one told him how to behave or to charter his daily routine. A tinge of jealousy unexpectedly crept inside my heart. His life seemed so simple and mine so complicated. I had once read that we found ourselves at a specific point in our lives because we had chosen to be there, not by accident, but as a result of all the decisions we had made over the years. Had I known that earlier on in my career, maybe I would have steered my malleable destiny towards a path of greener pastures.

David was still talking to his customer when he glanced in my direction. He made eye contact to acknowledge my presence and raised one finger, indicating he would be with me in a minute or so.

I vanished between two rows of books, while David and the customer hastily resumed their whispered conversation.

To my right was a hard cover collection of Agatha Christie novels, all in reasonably good condition, given that they must have been printed over twenty years ago according to the font type used on the spine. Pink on white was also an uncommon combination of colours found on crime books dust jackets nowadays. As much as I was an avid fan of crime fiction, I shamefully realised that I'd never read an Agatha Christie novel.

I was flicking through an Aaron Marc Stein's paperback when I heard the silver bell from the front door.

Someone leaving or coming.

I listened for voices.

'He's gone,' David shouted from the other side of the shop.

I returned the Stein's paperback to its shelf and emerged from my hiding. There was no one else in the shop but David and me.

'Oh, David, you don't know how good it is to see you.'

We both seemed surprised by my emotional, verbal out pour. I felt a tear rolling down my right cheek. Even though I'd been hibernating for three days in my room, I was still highly strung. And that conversation I had with Paulina, the high-class prostitute, got me even more depressed. I was losing faith in humanity, and I hadn't figured out how to get it back. But unlike Paulina, I didn't hate men, and I never could. Life with them seemed impractical, but life without them was impossible. Their self-assurance and carefree confidence, their assertiveness on other people's lives, and the way they were shamelessly driven by an endless hunger for lust and power-control was as much admirable as repugnant. I couldn't figure out which of the two sexes was the master and the other the servant.

David circled the counter and paced towards me.

'Are you okay?' he asked. Before I had time to reply, he gave me a bear hug.

I kissed him passionately in return.

We looked into each other eyes for a few seconds.

'It's been a difficult week,' I said, 'everything seems to be going against me. But, I know, I should be used to it by now. Been there, done that. I just have to be strong and move on.'

He stepped back a little and held my head between the palm of his hands.

'Hey, you don't have to be strong all the time, it's okay to be attuned to your inner-self.'

The New-Age guru inside David was alive and preaching.

'I know, David, but sometimes you just want to let go of everything, and it's usually exactly when you need to detach yourself from life's commitments that you find yourself chained up to them by the neck.'

He puzzled on my comment and said, 'Well, maybe you should break the chain before you break your neck.'

Ah, ha, very funny, I thought. But at least he had a sense of humour.

He went on, 'You don't have to do this any more if you

186

don't enjoy it. Sure, I understand why you want to find the killer of your friend, but look what it's doing to you.'

'I'll be okay.' I straightened up, trying hard to get a grip on myself. 'Why don't you make me a coffee, get some energy pumping back in my veins? I loath self-pity. It makes me think of all these people who keep blaming others for their misfortunes. Really, it's not all that bad.'

He tilted his head slightly, his blue eyes digging into mine. 'You should really give up if it's bringing you down.'

'Like I said, it's not that bad, nothing a caffeine injection won't cure.'

I followed him to the kitchenette. I didn't want to give my game away. If I told him that I'd been hibernating in my room for three days, he might have felt that he was right. And I hated the idea of someone knowing me too well, digging into every corner of my mind, pulling out every secret from every cupboard, dragging every ghost from the past. The only thing I still had full control of was my dignity, and I intended to hold on to it for as long as I possibly could. I functioned with the fear that everyone one I knew would eventually let me down. Maybe I hung on too much on past experiences and gave little room for new friendships to develop. Either way, no matter how much control I wanted to have over my life, fate had a way of pulling people back to reality.

David put some water on the boil in a white electric jug and filled two mugs with instant coffee.

'You know,' he said, 'if it's a money problem, I can help you. The bookshop is doing quite well, and I don't have a family to support.'

'What are you saying?'

'Well, you're obviously struggling with your job, and I'm wondering, maybe you're just keeping up with it because of the money. If that's the case, just quit. I make enough money for two.'

His generosity took me by surprise. I didn't think the depth of our relationship was strong enough for him to make me such an offer. In fact, I never considered that we were really in a relationship. We only slept together a couple of times, and that was hardly a reason for him to offer me access to his private funds.

'I don't think so, David, I'm pretty independent. Even if I did force myself to work just to make a living, I would never expect you or anyone else to bail me out. And it's not the case, anyway, so there's no point trying to convince me. You have to understand that no matter how difficult my job is at times, it's my vocation. I'm sorry if I complain about it too much, but deep down I love what I'm doing, and I wouldn't have it any other way.'

The water in the electric jug began to rumble.

'I know you're just saying that,' he said. 'I know you're proud of who you are and how far you've come, but don't let your pride be your downfall. It's okay to get help from someone else now and then. I'm not talking about a permanent thing here. All I'm saying is that if you're job is bringing you, and you can't do without the income, I'm here for you.'

The electric jug clicked off, and the rumbling sound of the boiling water settled.

I watched him pour the water into the mugs.

David's proposition was an attractive one, but one I would never consider.

'I really appreciate your concern,' I said, 'but everything is fine.'

He handed me over my mug of coffee.

'Okay, okay, sure, you know best, but like I said, don't get swallowed by your own pride.'

I sipped from my mug and snapped unexpectedly, 'For God's sake, I'm hardly what you call a proud person. I'm just living my life the best way I can. And for you to stand there and tell me I need to be rescued, well, that's almost an insult. I know you mean well, really, but listen to yourself, it's almost as if you're trying to take control of me. I'm not for sale, David, forget it.'

'I'm sorry, I didn't mean to offend you. I'm only trying to help,'

'I know you are, but I don't need a rescue package. All I need is to be loved like everyone else. Can't you understand that? I'm not some homeless puppy you found on the street. I can take care of myself.'

He stepped back to the curtain which separated the

bookshop from the kitchenette. As he sipped from his mug, a frown appeared on his face.

Fifteen seconds went by without a word. I felt redness on my face as I realised I might have gone overboard.

Suddenly, he half-circled the room and said, 'Hey, look, you don't have to be such a nasty bitch about it, I'm sorry if I offended you, but no harm was intended. I just wanted to help.'

Without hesitating, I emptied the rest of my coffee in the sink.

'Well, thank you, David. Like I've said, I really appreciate your concern, but I think the *nasty bitch* is old enough to look after herself.'

Without saying another word, I crossed the room, pulled the curtain aside and stepped into the bookshop.

'Hey, hold on a sec,' David said behind my back, 'I didn't mean it that way.'

I ignored him and headed for the exit.

'Wait a minute,' he went on, 'don't be like that.'

I pulled the door towards me, and suddenly felt myself being dragged backwards. His right hand was gripping my left arm.

'Don't go like that,' he said.

I jerked my arm. 'Let go of me, David, you're hurting me.'

Immediately he let his grip loose. 'I'm sorry, I didn't mean to...'

'It's okay, let's just leave it at that for the time being. Just let me go home.'

His eyes expressed sadness. 'Sure, but you know I didn't mean to offend you. It's just that, well...you look so miserable.'

I stepped outside the shop. 'Thanks, David, I'll call you.'

Before he had time to reply, I paced across the street.

CHAPTER TWENTY-EIGHT

I was half way back home when my mobile phone went off. One hand on the steering wheel, I was still worked up about the argument I had with David in his bookshop. Had I been unreasonable? Even if I had, did he have the right to call me a nasty bitch? I knew the answer and I didn't have to ask myself why. The last person I went out with who called me a bitch was my ex-husband, and I hadn't seen him since the mid-eighties.

I pressed the YES key on my mobile and brought the phone to my ear while keeping an eye on the road for any cop cars. I wasn't keen on paying a $135 fine for the privilege of talking to someone on the mobile.

Grey clouds blanketed the blue from the sky, and with my window half way down, I could smell rain in the distance. A shiver ran up and down my spine because of the cold wind, but I resigned myself to leave the window open because I wanted to breath fresh air.

'Dr Melina,' I said matter-of-factly into the mouthpiece.

'It's Dr Main here.' He paused for an answer.

'Ah, yes, what's up?'

'I need you to get here straight away, if you can. I've got some test results that might interest you.'

My brain did a somersault. 'Is that in relationship to the Evelyn Carter murder?'

'Certainly is.'

'I thought someone stole all the samples from the fridge?'

'Yes, they did, but I had some sent away for independent testing. I completely forgot until the samples came back today. I knew you'd want me to call you straight away. It might be very significant to your investigation.'

'Okay, give me half an hour.'

I left the West Ring Road at the Pascoe Vale exit and jumped back on it from the other side. A tinge of excitement got a hold of me. Just when it seemed that there was nothing to go on with, luck had finally come my way.

I changed to the right lane and pushed the car to 150 km/h, guilt-free of any wrong-doing.

Twenty minutes later I was parked at the VIFM. I jumped out of my car and hurried to the front entrance of the bluish-grey building, my heart racing with anticipation.

I cleared myself at the front desk and was informed that Dr Main was waiting for me in the biological lab on the second floor.

When I walked into the lab, Dr Main was sitting on a high chair, his back turned on me, flicking through what looked like an official report of one sort or another.

'Dr Main,' I said almost in a whisper as if I was scared to have distracted him.

He turned around, and I saw the glittering excitement in his eyes.

'Oh, yes,' he said, 'I'm glad you came so quickly.' He stood from his high chair and paced towards me. 'Do you remember the foreign substance I found under Evelyn's fingernails during the autopsy?'

He flicked through his report.

'Not really,' I said in all honesty.

'Yes, yes, you must remember,' he said. He turned to a specific page, pointed at a section and passed the report on to me. 'Look here.'

I read the paragraph he indicated, an edited transcription based on the recording he made during Evelyn Carter's preliminary autopsy, which I had attended weeks ago: 'Unidentified black sticky tissue was recovered from under the nails of the subject. The substance seemed organic in nature at during initial observation, but it was impossible to determine whether it was of an animal or vegetable origin.'

'Okay, so?' I said.

He pushed his glasses up the bridge of his nose and said, 'Well, I've sent the stuff for independent testing and one thing has been clarified. Whatever was under her nails is not human tissue.'

'Animal?'

'No, I did examine the gooey substance myself, but came to no hard conclusion, which is why I sent it away. And that was just as well since we've got nothing else left from the autopsy. If I had stored the sample in the fridge with the others, no doubt it would have vanished as well.'

'When you say you examined the sample yourself, what exactly did you do?'

'I soaked the sample in glycerine to give it more flexibility and to extract the oxygen, which would have accelerated the state of decomposition. It took a few days for the sample to become malleable enough to be placed between two microscope slides and viewed under favourable conditions.'

All right, he now had my full attention. As much as I wasn't into all the technical details, his delivery had the right amount of tension and pace to stop me from interrupting him.

'Naturally,' he went on, 'I tried to make some type of reasonable scientific deduction, and by the time I had thoroughly analysed the sample, I had no idea what I was dealing with, so I decided to send whatever was left to histology.'

He was referring to the Department of Histology, which dealt with the study and analysis of the minute structure of tissues and organs.

'So what was the conclusion?' I asked.

Dr Main grabbed a file sitting on the laboratory bench behind him, one which I hadn't noticed when I first entered the room. He pulled out several sheets of paper from it.

He scanned through the front page and said, 'The sample was viewed by short-wave light under magnification—times eight to be exact. According to the lab report they've sent me, the sample had a system of veins and capillaries. A high-intensity light was passed through, showing the presence of a red tint among the decomposition. So far, there was not a clue as to what the substance was, that is until microscopic pollen molecules were found resting in the fibres. This was definitely some sort of vegetable substance.' He offered me the lab report. 'Want to have a look?'

'No thanks,' I said, 'I believe you.' I puzzled for a few seconds. 'What vegetable substance are we talking about?'

'Well, my guess is as good as yours at this stage. I've forwarded the sample to John Darcy yesterday—he's a biologist working at the VFSC—hopefully he'll be able to tell us exactly what we're dealing with. Might take a few days to get a result. He's inundated with work at the moment.'

Obviously Dr Main wasn't aware that I knew John Darcy quite well, and that John had been more than helpful in previous investigations when I needed the test results yesterday. But since I had stopped working for the VFSC centre for six month prior to taking on the Evelyn Carter case, I hadn't seen John or communicated with him in any way.

'Can't we speed up the process?' I asked, not wanting to be the one making the call and having John thinking that the only reason why I called him was because I wanted something from him. Of course, that was the truth, but since I had Dr Main right here in front of me, and he had sent the sample to John, then it only seemed appropriate that they dealt directly with one another.

'I can make a call and apply some pressure if you insist.' He smiled and locked his eyes into mine.

'You do that, Dr Main, and I'll owe you one.'

He continued staring and said, 'Oh, you owe me more than one by now.' Gently, he rested his hand on my left arm. 'How about dinner tonight?'

His forwardness took me by surprise. I should have known this was going to happen one day. There had always been a sexual tension between the two of us, and if it hadn't been him who'd asked, it would have ended up being me. Too bad he asked me at the wrong time in my life.

'I don't think so, and I don't mean to be offensive. While I do appreciate the offer, I'm kind of busy with this investigation at the moment. I wouldn't make very pleasant company.'

'And when the investigation is over?'

I considered his offer for an instant. When I first met him three years ago, I found him rather handsome with his straight nose, greyish temples and small creases under his eyes. The fact that he cut up bodies for a living did put me off, but he was still as appealing to my eyes as he had been during that first encounter. If I had not being seeing David, I would have taken up his offer without the slightest hesitation. I had been at the morgue enough times to watch autopsies and had seen enough people butchered in my line of work to come to term with Dr Main's occupation. If it wasn't for people like him, ninety percent of homicides would remain unsolved, not to mention that his direct involvement in the collection of medical statistics sourced from post-mortem autopsies and made available for scientific research arguably saved thousands of lives.

'I'm sorry,' I finally said, 'but I don't think it's a good idea.'

'You don't find me attractive.'

'It's not that at all.'

'Then what?'

'I'm actually seeing someone at the moment, so, it would a little inappropriate.'

'Is it serious?'

I coughed awkwardly. 'Well, this is kind of private, if you don't mind. Believe me when I say that you shouldn't take it personally.'

The creases under his eyes deepened. 'All right then, I guess you must know what you're doing.'

I shrugged.

'Of course,' he added, 'this doesn't mean that I won't be making that phone call to John Darcy for you.'

I should think not, I thought as I retreated towards the exit of the laboratory.

'Well, thanks for everything,' I said. 'I do appreciate you calling me so quickly.'

'You're more than welcome.' He smiled broadly. 'I'll call you as soon as the results become available. Or I can get John to call you. Whatever you prefer.'

'Thanks,' I said and headed straight for the exit.

CHAPTER TWENTY-NINE

The moment I pulled into the driveway, I knew something was wrong. It's was only a few seconds later when I stepped out of the car that I realised I'd been right. The front door was left ajar, and I knew I closed it before I left. Even though I lived in a low-crime area, dealing with criminals and wrong-doers on daily basis, I had developed a justified level of paranoia and, as a result, always assured that my home was carefully locked before I left for anywhere.

My heart pounding, I made my way to the front of the house, hoping it was only Michael who'd forgotten to lock the door. He's been absent-minded lately, I told myself, and maybe he forgot to lock behind him.

I stood in front of the door, listening for anything coming from inside the house. Even though it was cold, perspiration was forming at the back of my neck. My stomach churned in anticipation. I listened hard.

Silence.

Two steps forward, one hand holding the door frame.

More silence.

I pushed the door with my left hand.

Expecting the worse, I retrieved my Mustang Plus .380 from the small of my back with my right hand. I'd never used the gun before to shoot or kill anyone, but it had caused death in a previous investigation when a friend used it to spray someone's brain into a three-metre radius and saving my life in the process. I had had plenty of chance to hone my shooting skills with the stainless-frame semi-automatic at the Police Academy in Mt Waverley whenever I pleased. One of the many perks for working in association with the Victoria Police. I just never found the need, nor the desire to do so, a choice I greatly regretted right at that moment. Nevertheless, the fact that the gun was designed to eject one cartridge and chamber a new one without manual intervention from the shooter after each shot was fired made me feel protected and in control.

I took one deep breath and pushed the front door open.

I listened.

Only traffic travelling up and down Craigieburn West Road.

Nothing coming from inside the house.

Acutely aware of my surrounding, I stepped inside the house, my back glued to the wall adjacent to the entrance, and my gun pointing at the ceiling.

'Michael?' I almost whispered.

Three steps forward, and I could see the entrance of the living room through the corner of my eye. The first thing I noticed was the contents of one of the bookshelves emptied on the floor. Okay, I hadn't been over cautious after all. Someone had been in the house, and it sure as hell didn't look as if it had been Michael. We had our differences, but he'd never been the violent or destructive type, certainly not when it came to my belongings. I hoped to God he hadn't come home yet.

Slowly, I lowered the gun and held it closer to my chest. If someone was still in the house, I'd have to be extremely cautious. I hated the idea of been bludgeoned at the back of the head like a baby seal in my own home. If the intruder was your common variety burglar, he probably wouldn't have a choice weapon like I did, so he'll take whatever he can grab to do me good.

I counted to three, held the gun tightly in my hand and did a half circle, aiming the weapon directly in front of me.

My eyes circled the room, looking out for anything that resembled a person.

No one was there.

I paused for a few seconds and lowered the gun.

I checked the room again, this time in slow motion. Every

single book from the three bookshelves in the room were on the floor, some torn apart, others thrown around. The floral sofa was slit open, its stuffing coming out like a gutted animal. The bastard even took the liberty to smash the tube of my new television set. This was not a common burglary. Nothing seemed to be missing, but whoever broke into my house took great pleasure in destroying as much as possible. I could feel the hatred hanging in the air like a toxic fume.

Pausing for a few seconds, I let the shock settle in. Just as well I had taken out a contents insurance when I moved in the place. Replacing everything out of my own pocket would have drained out all my savings.

Carefully, I crossed the room, stepping over Naomi Wolf's *Promiscuity* in trade paperback and Sue Grafton's *G is for Gumshoe* in hard cover Both books were severely damaged— pages pulled out, spines broken, covers ripped and crumbled. It broke my heart. Money would never replace the love and dedication I had put into building my own home library. Other than my collection of jazz and classical CDs, my home library was the jewel of my life, a sanctuary where I could escape from the daily lunacy of making a living, or whenever I felt the need to hear somebody's thoughts other than my own.

I ground my teeth. Whoever did this was going to pay dearly. Revenge would be swift and severe. Let there be no doubt. No one touches my books and gets away with it.

I recalled that there were no strange cars parked in front of my home or nearby. I peaked through the living room window to double-check. No other car in sight other than my Hyundai. The intruder must have already left. This fact was confirmed when I stepped into the kitchen. The white-rimmed plastic clock, which had been hanging on the wall when I left home that morning, was smashed and lay on the kitchen bench. The time read 2.32. It was just on 6.30 p.m. according to my watch.

Full broad daylight breaking-and-entering and no one notices.

So much for neighbourhood watch.

I stared emptily at the damage in the kitchen. The contents of every drawer was emptied on the floor. My plates, mugs, cups and saucers were smashed into a thousand pieces. The curtains had been pulled down and slashed with some kind of large knife, maybe the one I kept in the second drawer to chop lettuces in half. The coffee machine had been pulled apart as if someone had tried to extract its internal organs. The microwave oven, its door badly battered and barely hanging by a screw, would cost more to repair than to replace. The freezer compartment of the fridge was wide open, ice melting and dripping all over the kitchen floor. I stepped on a soggy forty-piece fish finger cardboard box which had once occupied a small corner of the ice box. The smell of fish rose straight to my nostrils.

Now I regretted not having had much to do with the neighbours. We glanced over each others backyard now and then, waved at one another whenever we picked up our mail, and nodded and said hello if we met at the local supermarket. They were a married couple with four kids, three girls and one boy, all under the age of ten. He must have worked rotating shifts because his car, an old battered thing which would end up at the wreckers within the next five years, was parked in front of the house or in the driveway at odd times. She seemed to be taking care of the kids full time, expect on Fridays were her red Ford Falcon disappeared early in the morning and re-appeared late at night. He took great care of his front yard, unlike myself, whom Frank loved to tease by naming my overgrown nature strip the Craigieburn National Park.

All in all, they were quiet and good neighbours, the kind I had nothing to complain about, but still, I was angry at them for not noticing anything. If they had, the police would have been all over my place by now.

It's not their fault, it's not their fault, I told myself as I finished crossing the kitchen and walking down the hallway.

Some dickhead had squeezed Toilet Duck all over the salmon-carpet and the walls. The pink-coloured disinfectant had stained the carpet, and I knew just by looking at it that I would have to have it replaced. Now I began to wonder if the house contents insurance would be enough to cover the cost of the all the damage.

Just when I thought I'd seen everything, I stepped into my bedroom and felt a tightness in my chest. I smelled the chocking fumes before I stepped inside the room. The bed was covered in cow manure, no doubt from the big, black, gentle creatures who resided in the paddock across the road from my home. The manure had also been used to write me a larger-than-life message on the white wall above the bed. The animal who did this forgot his marker.

LEAVE IT ALONE BITCH!

Now, this was getting rather nasty and personal. I'd been called 'bitch' twice in one day, and I began to wonder if there was some truth in the accusations. My ego was bruised.

The methane gases escaping from the cartload of manure spread on my bed was eating up my lungs, entering every single one of my pores, sending a shock-wave throughout my body. I had smelled cow shit before but not in concentrated amounts and in the confined space of my bedroom. Not to mention that the visual aspect was not exactly enthralling.

I stepped into the en suite attached to the bedroom and emptied the contents of my stomach and all my fear into the toilet bowl.

I pulled my head back and came to the inevitable conclusion.

This day was turning into shit, and there was no doubt about it.

CHAPTER THIRTY

The local police came within five minutes of my phone call. When they saw the condition I was in, they called an ambulance immediately. By the time the ambulance arrived, I was sitting on the front steps of the house and felt a little better, certainly not sick enough to justify being whisked away to a hospital.

It started to rain again, but only lightly. I didn't mind. What I had seen inside my own home had made me sick enough to never want to set foot in there again. The rain was refreshing, like taking a shower. I let the water run down my face and licked my lips. I was thirsty but didn't have the energy to stand up and get a glass of water. I could have asked for one, but I didn't want to talk to anyone. I knew I would have to eventually.

My mind was numb, and I wondered why I bothered with all this work in the first place. I had given up homicides for that very reason—because of the way a murder case can infiltrate your life so easily, and before you know it everything and everyone around was affected. Crime was a disease that ate at the very fabric of society, and the closer you were to it, the more difficult it was to deal with. I was soaking in that poison called crime, and I wondered if it wasn't too late to find an antidote.

The uniformed officer who looked through the house while I was waiting outside said that he had never seen anything like it in his life. Neither had I. The break-in of Evelyn's apartment was nothing compared to what I had experienced in my own home. Thoughts of selling the house were running in my mind. I had only moved there six months prior, but knowing that some psychopathic arsehole knew where I lived made me want to jump in the first available plane to Perth, some 3500 kilometres, away from the lunatics who were cramping my lifestyle.

The paramedics requested that I came with them, but I said that I was fine. But when they persisted, I told them in a less-than-polite manner that I was old enough to make my own decisions, and if that if I didn't want to go, I wouldn't, and that was that.

It didn't take long for the news of my break-in to go around. A Channel Ten and a Channel Seven news crew had already pulled up in front of my house. Microphones were shoved in front of my face as if I were requested to consume them.

'Do you think this has anything to do with the investigation into the murder of Evelyn Carter?'

'Do you think this was a warning from the killer?'

'What did the writing on the wall say? Did it say the world *bitch*?'

'No comments,' I said, hearing irritation creeping into my voice.

'Is it true that you suspect some members of the police to be involved in the disappearance of Evelyn Carter's body at the mortuary?'

'Is it true that the Deputy Commissioner of Police is involved in the murder?'

'Did Goosh know Evelyn Carter? Was he using her services?'

'Why did the intruder write the word *bitch* on the wall? Was he referring to you?'

I had no idea what sources journalists used, but it was certainly mind-boggling how fast confidential information travelled. Some cop somewhere was swimming in tax-free money feeding the sharks anything which could be turned into best-selling, front-page news. I had spoken only to a few people about Goosh and how I found his name in Evelyn's email address book, and already it seemed that the whole world knew about it. Someone would pay dearly for this leak of information, and I had little doubt that this someone was more likely to be me.

Finally, much to my delight, two uniformed officers ordered the journalists back to their vehicles. The journalists did what they were told, but not without a protest about how people had the right to know what was going on. But the police wouldn't have any of it. The news crews ended up taking their footage from a distance and interviewing nosy neighbours, who seemed to have come from all over Craigieburn and its adjoining suburbs.

When Michael finally arrived from God-knows-where, he was welcomed by a circus of police cars and media vehicles. Journalists tried to talk to him, but he pushed his way past them. He was used to dealing with the media because of the high-profile cases I had been involved with in the past. He'd often seen my face splattered all over the papers, or watched me playing the mute in the evening news. He was still dressed in his school uniform. I guessed he must have been at a friend's place, although the last time I spoke to him, he didn't seem to have any friends.

'What's going on?' he asked as I walked towards him.

'The house's been ransacked,' I said matter-of-factly, 'you can't go in there.'

He tried to make his way past me. 'I've got all my things there. What's happened to all my stuff?'

I grabbed his arm. 'Michael, forget it, you're not going in there. They've destroyed everything.'

'Who?'

'I don't know. The police are working on it.'

'But where am I going to go?'

'I've called Frank. He's be here in half an hour. We're going to stay at his place until we figure out what the hell is going on.'

Michael puzzled on my suggestion and said, 'Does this mean I don't have to go to school?'

'Not for the next few days, that's for sure.'

'Okay, cool, maybe it's not so bad, after all.'

'Oh, it's bad, Michael, It's really bad.'

Before Frank got here, the area was sealed off with crime-scene tape. I had never had my own place sealed off as a crime-scene area, and it was a hell of a thing to take. Looking around me, I was seeing the world from the perspective of a victim. And it wasn't a nice world. Chaos all around. People trying to make money from other people's misery. Curious minds hanging around just to have something to say to their work colleagues the next day. Vultures who had nothing better to do but dwell on other people's suffering. Right at that very minute, I was angry at everyone and at everything around me. The world wasn't a nice place to be in any more. Had it ever been?

I sat back on the steps with Michael next to me.

'Are we're going to be on TV?' he asked.

'I don't think we've got much choice,' I said.

'Do you know who did this?'

'I have a fair idea. But, no, I don't know what their names are.'

He nodded and preoccupied himself with the commotion that was taking place all around us.

Another twenty minutes went by before Frank made an appearance.

He parked his car on the empty block of land opposite my home. Journalists tried to approach him, but I heard him say, 'Get the hell out of my face. Haven't you got a family to go home to?'

By the time he reached me, Michael and I were on our feet.

Before I had time to utter a word, Frank gave me a bear hug so tight I thought he was going to crush my ribs.

'Oh, thank God you're alive,' he said. 'Are you okay?'

He pulled back.

'I'm fine,' I said, 'I came home when it was all over.'

'What the hell happened in there?'

I told him the state the house was in when I entered it.

'Jesus Christ!' he said. 'This is serious shit. You can't stay here.'

'I know, Frank, that's why I called you. Is it all right if we stay at your place for a few days, just so that we can find ourselves again? I probably won't come back here, anyway, not after something like this has happened.'

'Sure, sure, you can stay as long as you like.' He paused for effect. 'But we need to have a serious talk about your involvement in the Evelyn Carter investigation.'

I sort of expected something of that nature was going to crop up eventually, especially when Goosh had warned me that he was going to do everything in his power to make sure I would have nothing to do with the investigation again.

'What is it you want to talk about?' I asked.

'Not here.' He stepped back. 'Hey, you're all wet. You're gonna catch a cold. Why don't we get back to my place, and you can have a hot shower? Have you got anything to wear?'

'In the bedroom, in my cupboard. There are probably a few items of clothes which haven't been destroyed.'

'You want to get them?'

'Are you crazy? I'm not going back in there.'

Frank looked over my shoulder and towards the entrance of the house. 'You want me to get them for you?'

'Suit yourself.'

He then turned to Michael and said, 'Hey, buddy, do you want anything from your bedroom?'

'Yeah, can you see if the PlayStation is okay?'

'Will do.'

Frank vanished inside the house.

I was left alone with Michael, the uniformed cops, the noisy neighbours and the news crews. My head hurt, as if my brain was trying to squeeze out between the cracks of my cranium.

My once-peaceful life had reached a point of no return.

Life was never going to be the same again after today.

Never.

CHAPTER THIRTY-ONE

I stayed a good half hour under the shower, draining all of Frank's hot water supply. The water cascading on my head relieved the pain inside. I had swallowed two headache tablets an hour ago, and the effect was wonderful. Other than images of cow shit all over my bed spread back home, my mind was cleared-up.

I shampooed my hair into a thick lather, finger-massaging my cranium, letting myself drift away into the peacefulness of steaming water and apple-scented body-wash lotion. I was thinking myself lucky to have someone like Frank in my life. If it hadn't been for him, I'd probably would have had to move to a hotel room to accommodate Michael and myself until I'd be level-headed enough to decide the next course of action. As it was, nothing was rushing me, and as long as I could stay with Frank, I'd feel a little more secure.

On our way to Frank's home in Richmond, I asked him what it was he wanted to talk to me about. Back at my place, he had mentioned it had something to do with the Evelyn Carter investigation, and according to the tonality he used, it had to be bad news. Given the way the investigation had been heading, what else could actually go wrong?

'Why don't we get you home first? I'll tell you later' he said, one hand on the steering wheel, the other on my knee.

Under normal circumstances, I would have taken his hand off my knee and told him where to stick it. But given the state I was in, and the fact that he was going to let me stay at his place for as long as I wanted, I hated to break the moonlighting effect. I knew he was sexually attracted to me, but he was also aware that I wanted nothing to do with him other than friendship. And as long as we upheld that understanding, we could have remained friends until the end of time.

'I can take it,' I said, stretching my legs as far as the confinement of the car would let me. Outside it was still raining, but this time it was a downpour. Michael seemed mesmerised just watching the rain from the back seat. I glanced at him from the vanity mirror, hoping he was coping. Our relationship had suffered greatly, and after this incident, I had no idea how things were going to turn out between the two of us.

'I think it's better if we talk about this tomorrow morning,' Frank insisted.

I was in no mood for an argument, so I let it slide. No one said another word until we got to Richmond, and then I headed straight for the shower.

When I came out of the bathroom, my wet hair brushed back and my naked body wrapped in a giant white bathrobe, Frank was standing by the bar with a glass of amber liquid in his hand. Michael was in front of the television, taking advantage of the fact that Frank had managed to rescue his precious PlayStation and half his games. At first I thought he was watching some car race on one of the commercial channels, but as it turned out, he was playing a car racing simulation game. The digital imaging was so crisp, it was hard to believe that what I was seeing was a game.

'Do you want something?' Frank asked when he saw me glancing back in his direction.

I hesitated for a few seconds. With everything that had been happening, drinking might not have been a good idea.

He went on, 'I got brandy, rum, bourbon, Bailey's, vodka... you name it, it's behind the bar. You look as if you could do with a shot.'

I gave in. He was probably right.

On my command, he poured me a brandy, which I gulped in one take.

'Okay, Frank,' I said, 'you might as well tell me what's on your mind because we both know I'm not going to sleep well tonight either way. So why don't we just get it out of the way?'

'Tomorrow morning.'

'You're being silly.'

'Haven't you had enough for one day?'

'You're being silly, I'm grown up, Frank, stop treating me like a child.'

'I just don't want you to get upset.'

'I'm way past being upset. I've got homicidal thoughts running through my head.'

He sighed and refilled my glass.

I didn't protest.

'Fine,' he said, 'there's been some heavy shit coming from the top.'

'What are you talking about?'

'What am I talking about? Well, you're no longer working on the Evelyn Carter case.'

'Uh?' I wasn't exactly shocked, but I pretended to be.

'You knew that was eventually going to happen after you busted into Goosh's office and accused him point blank that he killed the girl.'

'I never said he killed her.'

'Whatever, point is it's over.'

I emptied the contents of my second glass. On an empty stomach, the brandy went straight to my head, and it felt good.

Confident, I placed the empty glass on the bar and said, 'You know I can't do that. You know I'm going to seek justice, no matter what you or anyone else says. It's always been that way, and that's why the VFSC has been using me. They know I don't give up until the case is solved.'

'I know, Kristina, and that's why you and Michael are going away for a while. I want you as far as possible from Melbourne. The furthest you are, the safest you and Michael will be, and the better I'll feel. I'll make all the necessary arrangements. Don't worry about a thing.'

'Have you concocted all this by yourself?'

'Well, after tonight, it's pretty clear you're not going to hang around Craigieburn. In fact, I'd suggest you go interstate on the double. Where do you want to go? I can arrange some kind of protection program. All re-allocation costs covered by the State Government. Think of it as a holiday you won. The perks of being a victim of crime. I wished someone had broken into my home.'

It was hard to know if I had to take him seriously. Everything he said came out like a half-joke, and even thought I knew he did it on purpose to loosen up the tension resulting from the break-in, it kind of annoyed me. I wish he'd be more direct, more dramatic in a way.

I paced the room from the bar to the coffee table and back to the bar. I could have done with a holiday, getting away from the madness of it all. But was that really a solution? Would running away achieve anything at all other than making me feel like a coward? In the first couple of weeks, I'd probably appreciate that the huge weight I'd been carrying on my shoulders had finally vanished, but soon enough doubt, emptiness and disgust would take over. Letting other people down was one thing, but letting yourself down was unforgivable. The wounds of self-betrayal would linger on for as long as my heart would go on beating. And as the years would go by, I would pass on my frustration to everyone around me, including Michael who had already suffered enough from the neglected childhood I had laboured upon him.

'And what are you going to do?' I asked, intentionally changing the focus of the conversation to Frank's intent.

'Same as you,' he said. 'I'm dropping out of the investigation. This thing is too big for the both of us. If we're dealing with police corruption at the top level, you don't want to be involved. This is a job for the Federal Police.'

'I don't now, Frank, it's like we're just giving up—'

'Don't think of it as giving up, think of it as being smart. You know, get the hell out before the ship sinks. Didn't you watch *Titanic*?'

'Oh, for God's sake, Frank, we're not in the movies, this is real life. My school friend's dead, my house's been destroyed, my life's been threatened, and you're telling me that I should just run away. Do you really think that whoever did this is going to give up on me so easily? What am I going to be doing for the rest of my life? Play hide and seek?'

Frank twisted his lips and took a sip from his amber liquid. He looked as if he was seriously considering what I was saying, but I knew he was just putting on an act. Once his mind had been made up, it was impossible to make him see things differently. His stubbornness was the only personal trait he shared with me.

'Orders from above,' he said as if he'd just laid on me some new information, 'nothing I can do about it, and frankly nothing I want to do about it.'

'Goosh gave you the order?'

'Actually it wasn't Goosh, it wasn't one man's decision, trust me.'

'And what did Goosh say?'

'Don't know, haven't seen him. In fact no one knows where he is.'

I puzzled on this for a few seconds. 'Is that so?'

'Hasn't turned up to work for the last three days. His secretary tried to contact him at home, but all she keeps getting is the answering machine.'

The sonofabitch had probably runaway after he realised I was on the right track. He must have known it would be only a matter of time before everything would fall back on his head. I had no doubt that Goosh's involvement in the murder of Evelyn was far more significant than what I had figured out so far. This whole case was like a time bomb waiting to blow up in everyone's face.

'So who's taking over the case?' I asked.

'I don't know at this stage,' he said, 'no one's telling me shit. Internal investigation procedures. Everyone is a suspect until cleared.'

'I see.'

'You know your life is in danger, Kristina. Whoever broke into your apartment wasn't a juvenile delinquent. This is serious shit. If these people are the same ones who killed Evelyn Carter, they're not going to hesitate taking you out.'

I shrugged. Frank could beat me over the head with a baseball bat before I was going to quit, especially when I wasn't the one who started the ball rolling.

He went on, 'You don't want to go any further, and I won't have it anyway. This is an order, and anything you do from here on will be considered as interfering with an on-going investigation. You could be charged, you understand that? You listen to me, Kristina, this is no longer a game.' He was jabbing his finger in front of my face while saying this. I felt as if I was back at prep school.

'Sure, whatever you say, big man.'

We left it at that. He was overbearing, but I was gratified that he cared enough to argue about my well being. Maybe in another world we could have been more than just friends.

I finished my drink and retired to the spare room. Nothing spectacular. A single bunk with a second-hand wardrobe and a small wooden side-table. The small window was overlooking a large courtyard which had been neglected, but not as badly as mine back home. Raindrops were glistening like thousands of stars under the moonlight. In the darkness, the effect was haunting and mesmerising all at once.

I sat on the edge of the bunk. My room smelled like mothballs and floorboards. There was no carpet, and the walls were bare and painted white. Not much of a guest room, but if I was going to stay here for a week or so, I might be able to do something about the decor, just as a thank-you gesture. I pictured in my mind's eyes new curtains and pictures on the wall, and maybe even a vase with flowers.

Then I thought about Michael. He would sleep on the sofa bed tonight. I felt sorry for him. I wished I could have provided him a home and a childhood where he could have lived a normal life. But now it was too late for regrets and wishful thinking. The fact was that we had no home to go to, and God only knew what the next day would bring.

I pulled my legs up and lay on the bed. I had so much on my mind that I didn't know where to begin. Frank was right about my life being in danger, and not just mine, but that of Michael as well. If Michael had been home when the intruders broke in, they might have killed him. For a little while, I tried to figure out who would have the nerve to destroy my home in broad daylight. It had to be someone who was confident enough to go in and out of a home without looking suspicious.

And then I thought of who broke into Evelyn Carter's apartment. Two cops. Maybe it was also the cops who broke into my home. After all, it was the cops who told us to drop the investigation, no matter how high on the ladder they were positioned.

As I switched off the side-table lamp, I decided that I had

to have another chat to Judith Kingman, Evelyn Carter's neighbour. She saw the two cops who broke into Evelyn's apartment. If I probed her, she might remember a detail she forgot earlier on. That and the substance found under Evelyn Carter's nails were the only leads I could follow immediately.

I closed my eyes and hoped for a good sleep, even though I knew it wouldn't come easily. A small inconsistent detail was nagging me at the back of my skull, like someone jabbing a finger every now and then. It was something that someone wasn't suppose to know, and yet they did. I wondered if my recollection of events failed me. It had never done so in the past, so why would it this time around?

I knew what I had to do the following day.

CHAPTER THIRTY-TWO

The next morning I woke up refreshed in spite of not having had as much sleep as I had hoped for. With all these ideas running in my head, I decided to take control of my life. The fact remained that I wouldn't back away no matter what, not even if Frank handcuffed me to the bathroom sink. Given that much, I was going to do the utmost to find the bastard (or bastards) who broke into my home, and I was going to find who the hell killed Evelyn Carter. And whoever was going to stand in my way had better watch out.

I dressed in jeans and my black leather jacket. Street wear was the safest way to go when one's decided to play it rough. I polished my Mustang Plus .380 to a shine and loaded it with 9mm Luger, the most famous and frequently used handgun cartridge in the world, so I was told by the guy who sold me the full-metal case bullets in a fifty-per-box pack. I had no idea what I was going to do with the handgun, but I didn't want to feel scared shitless and look over my shoulder for the rest of my life. This was clearly becoming a case of me verses 'them', whoever they might be. And it wasn't even a matter of becoming a tough cookie—I was now on defensive mode and decided to let my instinct take over.

Michael was still asleep on the sofa bed when I sneaked into the kitchen for a cup of coffee. He looked like an angel, his sweet face peacefully resting on the blue pillow. I wanted to walk over and hug him, and tell him how much I loved him, and how everything was going to be all right, but I didn't want to wake him up. He'd probably had as much trouble getting to sleep last night than I did.

I sipped from my coffee mug and looked around. It was

just on 6.30 a.m., and the sun had yet to materialise. Outside I could hear traffic, people on their way to another working day, struggling to just exist.

It was cold in the apartment, and I considered turning the central heating on so that Frank and Michael would wake up in the comfort of its warmth. Half an hour earlier I had stepped out of the shower on to cold tiles, and it was an experience I didn't wish on anyone else. I hated Melbourne winters. In fact I hated winters altogether. There was nothing nostalgic and comfortable about freezing to death and being subjected to constant downpours. The winter-romantics could take it all away from me, and I wouldn't miss it one bit.

As I emptied my mug, I considered the possibility of moving to a warmer state after this whole case would be over. Maybe WA or Queensland. If I'd live through the ordeal, that was. I wouldn't move back to Craigieburn, no matter what, so if I was going to make a dramatic change, the time to do it would as soon as the investigation would be over.

As I was about to refill my mug, Frank appeared at the door unexpectedly.

'Christ,' I said, 'you scared the shit out of me.'

He wore blue underpants and white Bond T-shirt. His morning erection was showing, but I avoided staring. His legs were skinny and hairy, and his hair unkempt from the night's sleep. He looked as if he could have done with another eight hours sleep.

'What you're doing up so early?' he asked and yawned all at once while scratching the back of his head.

'Business to take care of.'

'What business? I thought we made an agreement yesterday?'

'What agreement? I didn't promise you shit.'

'Oh, great!'

He stepped into the kitchen, grabbed a mug and filled it up with black coffee. Then, from the bench, he grabbed his cigarettes, pulled one from the pack and lit it up. I hated passing smoking, but it was his house, and I'd just have to put up with it.

He did a half turn and noticed the bulge of the Mustang tucked between my belt and the small of my back.

'And what the fuck are you doing carrying this thing around?' he asked one decibel too loud.

'Keep you voice down,' I ordered. 'Michael is still asleep.'

'All right, all right. But what the fuck are you doing? What's with the gun and the leather jacket? You're going to play wise guy or something?'

'I do what I have to do, which is more than I can say about you.'

'And what the fuck's that supposed to mean?'

'It means some of us seek truth and justice even if it means putting our lives at risk. Others find it easier to just duck away. And watch the f-word. It's still considered vulgarity where I come from.'

He sucked obsessively on his cigarette. 'You're a real fuck, you know. Is that how you thank me for sheltering you and your kid?'

'For God's sake, Frank, why don't you mind you own business, let me do my job and get on with yours.'

'Ah, yeah, and what's my job supposed to be?'

'Look after Michael, make sure he eats his cereals and drive him to school.'

As I stepped out of the kitchen, I heard him say, 'You've got to be kidding. What the hell is wrong with you?'

Before I got to Judith's apartment, I decided to take a detour via David's Bookshop. I hadn't bothered ringing him the previous night because I didn't want to alarm him. But I knew I had better tell him what was going on because if he tried to ring my place or if he turned up just to say hello, he would get a heart attack. Of course I hadn't forgotten our little clash the previous day, but this was a man I had made love to, and in spite of me, I still felt obligated to tell him something. Our connection was not severed yet, no matter how damaged it seemed. One always hopes that things are going to turn out for the better, and that was the burden that came by being driven by emotions. I was still a romantic at heart, no matter how pathetic my love life had been so far. And then there was this other thing I needed to get done. Of course I hadn't told anyone yet because I had only figured it out last night while trying to fall asleep.

The sun had just appeared on the horizon, and David's Bookshop was still locked. It's was 7.38 a.m., and it wouldn't be open for another hour and a half or so. Nevertheless, I wasn't going to wait around.

Outside, it was freezing, and even though I already swallowed two cups of coffee, I was dying for another hot brew.

I pressed David's doorbell and stepped back onto the walkway. I looked two floors up from the street. His curtain moved and a head appeared. I waved, but he seemed puzzled. It felt like an eternity before he got to the door.

'Yo, what's happening,' he said as soon as he opened the door. He was in his jeans and T-shirt. 'Shit, I didn't recognise you with the jeans and jacket.'

'No time to explain. Mind if I come in?'

Before he had time to answer, I pushed my way past him.

'Hey,' he said, 'I'm really sorry about yesterday. I didn't mean to call you a bitch. It's just that I was worried, you know, and things just got messed up in my head.'

'Save it for later. I've got something to tell you.'

He flicked the light of the bookshop on and said, 'Yeah, sure, what's going on? Are you okay.'

I gave him a condensed version of the breaking-and-entering of my home.

'Oh, my God,' he said, a genuine look of panic on his face. 'You didn't get hurt, I hope.'

'I got there after the ordeal.'

'Jesus, why didn't you call me?'

'What do you expect?'

'I'm sorry, if I would have know—'

'If you would have known that I was going to get broken into, you wouldn't have called me a bitch.'

'No, but—'

'Okay, I get it. Like I said, we'll sort this out later. I'm going to follow some leads. I need to know who's screwing with my life.'

He shook his head and scratched the back of his neck. 'I don't know, Kristina, maybe you should just let this one go. Is it really worth it? Look what's happened to Evelyn?'

'Don't bother, David. I didn't come here for a lecture. I got enough of that from Frank yesterday and this morning. You guys are obsessed with this idea that a woman can't take care of herself. What is it with you? Where did you get the idea that somehow God has made you wiser?'

I could tell he wanted to reply, but he choose to remain silent instead. A sensible decision.

There was an awkward silence hanging in the air for the next ten seconds.

I moved forward and kissed him on the cheek.

'You're forgiven,' I said, 'we can try again. Let's just not argue, okay?'

If anyone else had called me a bitch, I would have erased them out of my life immediately, no looking back. But I had a hidden agenda, and he had no idea what was coming.

He looked at me sheepishly and said, 'Yeah, sure, I'd like that very much. I thought I'd never see you again after yesterday.' And suddenly, as if he'd just realised we were standing inside the bookshop freezing to death, he added, 'Hey, you want a cup of coffee or something? It'll only take a minute.'

'I'd love one.'

As I moved away from him, I pulled a strand of his hair.

He jerked back and yelped, 'Hey, what'd you do that for?'

I held the few strands of hair between my thumb and my forefinger and sniffed them. 'Souvenir,' I said, 'I like to remember what you smell like when I'm feeling lonesome.'

He stared at me suspiciously for a few seconds and said, 'Okay, whatever turns you on.'

Ten minutes later I was back in the car, my stomach full of coffee and my brain pumping with excitement and anticipation. I bagged the hair sample and labelled the bag with an identification sticker from the VFSC.

It was time to move into high gear.

CHAPTER THIRTY-FOUR

'If I was you, I would butt out,' Judith said, her eyes digging into mine. She looked as if she had put on more weight since I'd last seen her. It must have been the green cardigan she was wearing, which looked two sizes too small. The fact that I caught her off-guard didn't help either. She hadn't showered yet and wore no make-up whatsoever. Women looked so different without their face-paint that it's always a shock to see one stripped bare faced. What Evelyn had in style, her friend Judith certainly lacked in.

We were sitting to one side of her kitchen table over a cup of coffee. We had been going over and over the day when she saw the two cops going into Evelyn's apartment. Yet, there was nothing new she could tell me that filled me in on the missing details. And when I told her what someone had done to my home, she became convinced, like everyone else I had spoken to so far, that it was time to get the hell out and save my own skin.

'Yeah, well,' I said, 'that's what I'm tempted to do since everyone keeps telling me so, but if I don't bother, then no one else will. I thought she was your friend? Don't you care that the killer is found?'

She stared down at her cup for a few seconds, and then looked up again. 'Of course I care. But what's the point of chasing a lead if it's going to get you killed. I don't really know you all that well, Dr Melina, but it doesn't mean that I want to see you dead.'

'Sure, I understand your concern. But quitting is really not an option from where I'm standing. I know you must

217

understand that.'

I sipped from my cup and stared at the red carnations carefully arranged in the blue vase on the kitchen table.

'Nice flowers,' I said.

'Thanks.'

'From a friend?'

'Yes. How did you know?' She seemed a little alarmed.

'You already had a bunch of them when I first came to visit. You told me they were from a friend.'

She sighed. 'That's right. You do have a good memory.'

'It's inbred into my line of work.'

She smiled at my comment which wasn't meant to be a joke in the first place.

'There's something that bothers me,' I said.

'What?'

'I still haven't found that little address book you've told me about. And yet everyone seems to be looking for it. You know, now I'm wondering if that's the reason why someone broke into my home.'

'Well, it exists, all right. I saw it myself.'

'I never said it didn't exist, but I'm just wondering where the hell it could be.'

'The killer probably took it with him.'

'Yes, but why?'

'His name was in it.'

I emptied my cup of coffee. 'Yes, I suppose so, but I'm not too convinced that it's all that simple.'

'Nothing ever is, Dr Melina. Nothing ever is.'

She stared at me as if I was a child with a wild imagination and too much time on my hands. I wished I had more imagination, and time was something I never seemed to get enough of.

I stood from my chair, 'Okay, then,' I said, 'if there's nothing else you can help me with, I guess I better make a move on. Still got a lot of work to do before someone finds out what I'm up to and decides to put an end to it.'

She walked me to the front door.

We stood facing one another while the rain was beating behind my back.

'You be careful now,' she said while holding on to my right hand and patting it with her left. 'We just never know what type of lunatics are out there, do we?'

'I guess we don't.'

I took my hand back and stepped backward into the rain, flicking my umbrella open at the same time.

'Keep in touch,' she said.

'Will do.'

I turned around and followed the path to the front gate.

I didn't look back, but I could feel her stare locked in on me all the way to the car.

Forty minutes later, I eased the Hyundai into the parking lot of the VFSC. The rain had stopped, so I didn't bother with the umbrella. I checked my reflection against the sliding doors at the entrance of the building. With my black jacket and faded denims, I looked more like one of the bad guys than a law enforcer. I finger-brushed my hair to give it more volume. The rain had flattened it a little and made me self-conscious. I straightened my jacket and kidded myself I looked real neat.

I walked passed the main foyer, where I nearly killed myself on the polished floor with my wet feet. I glanced at the awards and trophies, and headed straight for the Liaison Office, room C47, at the entrance of the creamy-brown coloured building. I hoped to God, my ID was still valid. The paperwork to have it cancelled wouldn't have gone through yet.

I entered room C47, where a dots matrix printer was chucking out continuity labels as if all the crimes in the world were going through the VFSC. After clearing myself with the Liaison Officer, much to my relief, I made my way to the Department of Biology where John Darcy was working.

I entered the lab by pressing my ID card against the black plate next the entrance door. The door unlocked automatically. Security was second-to-none in these places. Once you entered the building, it didn't necessarily mean you had access to all the rooms unless you carried the appropriate pass.

John had his back on me, his right eye stuck into a compound microscope.

'Surprise visit,' he said without looking up. He must have

had eyes behind his head, like one of those alien creatures in a b-grade science-fiction series from the 60s.

John wore the obligatory white lab coat with its stripes—ink stains in a variety of blues, blacks and reds attached to his breast pocket. A good forensic scientist doesn't have time to be fashion conscious—he's too busy working around the clock, being obsessed with every tiny details of whatever case he is working on. And John was just that kind of person. His work was not just a job, but a vocation. He even had a laboratory at home which he assembled during his weekends from IKEA furniture and catalogue-imported equipment from the USA or from auctions he attended at least once a week. The guy was as obsessed with science as I was with criminology. And obsessive people lived on the edge of insanity—I was certain of that. One of these days, they were going to lock us both up and throw away the keys.

He turned around and slipped off his surgical gloves. His hair was unkempt, and he looked as if he was living on two hours sleep and five litres of coffee a day. He reminded me of what I must look like, other than the facial hair. His beard could have done with a little trimming, and it was obvious he had neglected shaving the neck area for a little while. I wondered if he still had problems with his wife. The previous year, things were not going too well at home, and I've never seen him so unhappy since then. When I met his wife, she gave me *the look* that woman do so well, and I couldn't help wondering if she thought there was a little screwing going on the side between John and me. She was dead wrong, of course, but it wasn't a debate I intended to have with her. So now I avoided visiting him at home altogether, even if it was a weekend emergency. I didn't want to become the other woman in someone's marriage.

'Can't keep yourself out of trouble, can you?' he said. Before I had time to reply, he added, 'if you're here for the result of that fingernail residue found on Evelyn Carter, you'll have to be a little more patient. The sample I was given was in a dreadful state. Frankly, it's lucky that I've managed to do anything at all with it.'

'So, what's the verdict?'

'Good morning to you too, Dr Melina. I thought you were off the case? I thought everyone was off the case?'

I stepped forward. 'Well, you know what it's like. If you can't count on your friends, who the hell do you turn to?'

He nodded. 'You know I have faith in you, Kristina, and that's why you keep coming back to me.'

'Only the best will do.' I paused and added, 'What's with the residue?'

'It's vegetable all right. The state of decomposition was a major problem. Okay, all the essential features are there, but all I can confirm is that this is some type of plant or flower. I've sent the sample to a friend in Sydney. He's got a library of hundreds of thousands types of plants on computer which he's collected over the last ten years. It's probably the most comprehensive database in Australia, if not the world. I told him it was urgent, but the guy is kind of busy and short tempered, but he'll do the best he can. And he added that if I called him and bothered him for the results, he would send them back straight away. He hates being told what to do on short notice. I remained polite with him, so I'm hoping we get some results within the next twenty-four hours. Whether it's going to help with the investigation or not, that's another question altogether.'

'Well, at least you've done what you could.'

I fished inside the pocket of my leather jacket and retrieved the labelled bag containing David's hair sample.

'I need you to do me another favour,' I said and dangled the bag in front of him. 'I need a DNA test done on this ASAP, and a comparison of the polymorphic sequences autoradiographs from the results and the one obtained from the semen found inside Evelyn Carter.'

He grabbed the bag from me. 'Sure thing. When do you need it by?'

'Is that a trick question?'

He smiled and said, 'You haven't changed. How long has it been? Six months?'

'Eight'.

'That long already? You should drop in more often. I miss the company of an intelligent woman.'

'Thank you, I'm flattered. Most people think I'm arrogant and a pain in the butt.'

'They're just jealous, that's all. It's human nature. Have the strength to forgive them. They're mere mortals.'

'And who are we?'

'Well, Kristina, do you really want me to get into it?'

I smiled and said, 'Okay, I trust your good judgement, but only because I'm biased. When can you get this done for me? It's really important.'

'Like everyone else, you want it yesterday. I'll give you a call as soon as I've done the comparison. You're on top of the list. And that's only because I like you.' I was just about to leave the lab when he added, 'Who's the owner of the hair?'

'Just a friend. Someone I'm fucking and who's fucking with me.'

John wore the expression of a kangaroo caught in headlights.

So much for telling Frank not to use the f-word.

I left the room before he had time to reply.

CHAPTER THIRTY-FOUR

'They found him in room 23 at the Highway Hotel in Chadstone,' Frank said. 'He hung himself. You better get your arse here on the double.'

Frank gave me the location of the motel and hung up.

I pushed the NO button on my mobile and had to catch my breath. As much as I hated the bastard, I never wished he ended that way. I couldn't believe I was on the edge of crying for someone who felt so obligated in making my life a living hell. Goosh was the last person on earth I expected to commit suicide. And me who thought he was living it up somewhere in the Bahamas. It just shows how little one knows the enemy.

I stepped out of the car in the pouring rain. When Frank called me, I was in the middle of the South Eastern Arterial on my way back to Richmond. I had to pull to the emergency lane when he told me the news. It was as if someone had just knocked me on the head with a cricket bat.

For what felt like infinity, I stood under the downpour, watching the traffic race past me, my mind wandering everywhere but in the present time. There had been so much hatred between us, and now that it was all over, I couldn't help feeling that it was my fault that he was dead. Had I pushed him over the edge? Had I been wrong about the accusations? Shouldn't I have just accepted his peace offering the other day, swallowed my pride, take the promotion he had offered me, and get on with my life? Was I the straw who broke the camel's back?

Frank was waiting for me at the Highway Motel in Chadstone, but I couldn't move on, not right away. We had to cover the crime scene, suicide or not. He requested it, and he knew I'd want to be there. And he was right, except that I hadn't expected myself to be so shocked by the event. I stood under the rain for another ten minutes, not knowing what to do. Was this some kind of wake up call that nothing ever lasts forever? As much as I often dismissed it, Goosh was a human being like I was. But only now that he had taken his life into his own hands, I finally realised the importance of what this meant. He had feelings like I did, and he must have hurt so much that he couldn't see himself facing another day. I hadn't come to that yet, not even close. Could I have been so wrong about everything? I continued to watch the traffic flow down the freeway, conscious that every single one of those people travelling were on their journey through life, not just another number in the crowd.

My mobile phone went off, but I left it in my jacket. The ringing, however, did wake me up from my slumber. It was time to face the truth head-on, no matter how difficult it might have been.

Finally I slid back behind the wheel, soaking from head to toe, my face and my fingers frozen from the cold. As strange as it seems, I could feel Goosh's soul was no longer amongst us. He was somewhere up there, looking down on the world, laughing on how insignificant we were with our little problems and our dramatised lives. Sitting on his cloud, he was presumably glad he jumped out before the ship sank. Maybe Frank had been right about the Titanic theory. Jump off while you still can.

On my way to the motel, I nearly killed myself at the Toorak Road and Glenferrie Road intersection. My mind was so worked up by the news I'd just received, that I run through a red light, forcing a white van to steer to the other side of the road, just avoiding a head-on collision with another car. I pulled to the side of the road for the second time, and I felt light-headed. I thought I was going to pass out. I opened the window fully and breathed in fresh air from outside. It was cold and humid, but it slapped me back into reality.

Someone came to the side of the car.

'Are you all right?'

A male voice, but I couldn't see the face. I was staring right in front of me.

'I'm okay,' I said.

The mobile phone went off again.

This time I picked it up without checking the caller ID on the LCD screen and said, 'Dr Melina.'

'What the fuck are you doing?' It was Frank.

'I'm coming.'

'It's gonna take you all day?'

'It's the weather. Isn't it raining where you are?'

'Well, hurry up. The whole media circus is already here. Jesus Christ, Kristina, this one's gonna make headlines around the country. You better get yourself mentally prepared for the evening news.'

'Give me five minutes, I'm nearly there.'

I ended the call without waiting for his reply.

The man who stood next to the car had vanished.

I have to be strong, I have to be strong, I repeated to myself as if I was reciting a mantra.

CHAPTER THIRTY-FIVE

When I pulled alongside the motel twenty minutes later, I noticed at least three media vans. The others were probably hidden behind police cars and ambulances. Blue and red lights were flashing as if were a natural disaster zone. A crowd had gathered around the motel, and it was virtually impossible to get past it. Even the rain wouldn't keep curious minds away. Crime was news, news was money. The television cameras were shooting footage galore, keeping it rolling just in case they managed to capture something worthwhile for the evening news.

The motel was the American type, slabs of cement joined together to make as many rooms as possible in a minimum amount of space. Each guest room had a symmetrical layout, simple lines, white walls and minimal ornament, typical features of today's architecture. Greenery was kept trimmed and tidy to uplift the banality of the construction. I never noticed the motel before, even though I'd driven up and down the highway a thousand times. Above the 'Highway Motel' badge, there was a red neon sign up high flashing the word 'vacancy'. Not likely for the next few hours, I thought.

For once my leather jacket and jeans came in handy. Journalists were used to seeing me arriving at a crime scene with my dress and matching jacket. I was a popular face among crime reporters, and they were usually very capable of sniffing me out before I even stepped onto the crime scene. Today I pushed through the crowd with my PERK in one hand and my Ray Bans on my nose.

Not a single journalist tried to ask me questions. I could have been one of them for all they knew. I certainly didn't look like a crime-scene examiner. And on top of that I was wet like a sewerage rat.

Blue-and-white police tape sealed the area. A middle-aged, slightly overweight, uniformed officer looked at me suspiciously as I pulled the crime-scene tape and entered the enclosed area. He wore a thick, brushed moustache and cropped hair. His shoulders were reasonably broad, and if he hated being a cop, he could have always got a job as a bouncer. He made me think of these guys who wore black leather pants and matching caps, and paraded at the Chapel Street Festival every year in October. He looked familiar, but I couldn't quite place him. Maybe I'd seen him in a club somewhere.

'Lady, you can't go in there,' he ordered as he paced towards me, 'get back on the other side of the tape.'

All eyes turned on me.

Someone said, 'Who's she with?'

'Freelance, no doubt,' someone else replied.

I checked the cop's blue name tag before he got to me: Constable Kevin Burnett.

I pulled my photo ID out of my leather jacket and attached it to my breast pocket. I'd only been kicked out of the VFSC three days ago, but no one knew about it, and I still had my ID with me. It got my access to the Department of Biology when I went to see John Darcy a couple of hours ago, so there was no reason why I wouldn't get away with it, especially when the expiry date on the card was still valid.

'I'm with the police, sir,' I said, pointing at my ID.

He looked at it and said, 'Jeez, I thought you were one of those reporters, Dr Melina. I didn't recognise you with the jacket and glasses. It's your day off or something?'

'Yeah, yeah, okay. Can you fill me in on the details and show me where the body is?'

'Sure, come this way.'

We crossed the motel courtyard. I saw Goosh's grey Lexus parked in front of room 23, where a crowd of police personal and other experts had gathered.

'Maid found the body when she came in to clean up the room,' Burnett commented. 'He hanged himself with the sheets from his bed. Doesn't look suspicious, but then no one's really had a good look yet. Frank Moore ordered everyone to touch nothing until you got here.'

I saw Frank talking to a short, fat man with thinning hair.

'Who's that guy,' I said, pointing to the short man.

'The manager. Says Goosh booked the room last night, then went out at around 9.30. Didn't see him coming back, but he did, otherwise he wouldn't be hanging from the ceiling.'

We got to the door of room 23.

'Okay, thanks for filling me in, Constable Burnett,' I said.

'You're welcome. Anything else you need, just come and see me.'

'Just make sure those vultures stay on the other side of the crime-scene tape.'

'Will do.'

Burnett returned to his post just outside the motel courtyard.

I moved in to where Frank and the motel manager were

standing.

'This is bad for business,' the short man was saying. 'Am I going to get compensated for that. Isn't there some type of victim of crime payment I'm entitled to?'

'I've already explained,' Frank said, 'this is a suicide, and even if it wasn't, you're not a victim. The only victim is the dead guy in room 23.'

'Yeah, but I'm going to lose income because of him.'

'Hey, I'm Dr Melina,' I interrupted, extending my hand to the motel manager. 'I'm in charge of this crime scene. And you're name is?'

'Richard Amardi,' the manager said and shook the hand I presented him.

'Richard, we're going to do our best to clean up this place ASAP, and we're out of here. If you think there's any money your entitled to, just give me a call, and I'll see what I can do.'

I passed him on one of my business cards.

'You're a lawyer?' Amardi asked.

'No, I'm an independent consultant, so I won't screw you around.'

Amardi looked at Frank and then back at me. He nodded in satisfaction.

'Okay,' he said. 'I'll give you a call then.'

'You do that,' I said.

And then he left us alone.

'Why the hell did you tell him he might be entitled to a compensation?' Frank asked.

'Avoid confrontation at all cost,' I said, 'agree with the guy, deal with him later.'

'Is that so?' He paused and looked at me from head to toe. 'What the hell happened to you? Don't you carry an umbrella any more?'

'Long story. Now, we're going to get in there or what?'

'Hey, don't get pissy, missy, you're the one who took your time. Plus you're not even supposed to be here in the first place, so I'm doing you a favour at the very likely risk of getting my arse kicked.'

I followed him inside room 23.

The body lay on his back. It was Goosh, all right, no doubt.

He was still dressed in his Italian-design business suit, his stomach protruding from his blue shirt. I tried to distance myself from what I was seeing.

Back on the job.

That's all it was.

Just a job.

Goosh's face was dark red with blotches of blue and purple in various places. There was bruising around the neck from the sheets he used to hang himself. An overturned chair lay next to him. A straight forward scenario. A stupid and sad way to die. Alone in a motel room, away from everyone and everything. I tried hard not to feel sorry for him. I'd done enough soul searching on my way here.

'Is that how you found him?' I asked.

'No, he was hanging from the ceiling,' Frank replied.

'Who moved him?'

'I did.'

'Why?'

'Because you were too fuckin' long.'

I placed the PERK on the floor, unlocked the latches and retrieved a pair of surgical gloves. I glanced around the room. Cheap furniture, vomit-green carpet, a television set screwed to the wall so that no one mistakes it for their own, unused coffee cups, coffee bags, tea bags, sugar bags, a plastic electric jug, a telephone, a large mirror, two side tables, two side lamps, an en suite in the far corner. Nothing I hadn't seen before. The rooms matched the style of the motel—cheap and nasty. Goosh was full of money, so why did he end up here?

'Did you touch anything else other than the body?' I asked Frank.

'Nope.'

'Good.'

I retrieved the Minolta from the PERK, loaded a new colour film and shoot an entire roll of the room. Nothing was disturbed, not even the bed. It looks as if Goosh had only entered the place to hang himself. In my notebook, I took details of the shots, including film speed and filters used.

Frank was beside the body, scrutinising it while I re-loaded a new film in the camera.

'Do you know much about hanging?' he asked, his attention

229

focused on Goosh's neck area.

'Enough to know what's what? Why do you ask?'

CHAPTER THIRTY-SIX

People do not hang themselves by accident, at least not commonly. And homicidal hanging is also very rare. Being the second most common method of suicide, it was easy to see why everyone had assumed Goosh had ended his own life.

'I don't know if I'm right on this,' Frank said, 'but does the bruising around his neck look like the type you'd expect from someone who hung himself?'

'Hold on a sec,' I said.

Gently, I rolled the body to its side. He was a heavy man, and I hated to be one of the two people who'd have to carry him out of the motel on a stretcher.

I traced the bruising with my finger while commenting, 'See, when a person hangs themselves, the rope causes a bruise in the form of an inverted 'V' on the neck. The veins are compressed by the rope, in Goosh's case the sheets, and pressure inside the head cause small bleeding sites. The face and neck are congested, which is why he is so discoloured.'

'Yeah, but is this suicide?'

'Take a look at the bruising around the neck.'

Frank followed my finger.

'A straight line,' he said.

'Exactly,' I said. 'When a person is strangled, the bruising is in a straight line. Look at the back of the neck.'

I was showing him a section just below the cranium which had excessive bruising.

'This was not caused by the sheets he used to hang himself,' I went on. 'The killer has used much more force than was necessary to kill Goosh. That's explains the deep bruising and contusions in this area of the neck.' I paused and added, 'Let's turn him around.'

Frank helped me to place Goosh on his back.

I passed one hand on Goosh's neck and felt his thyroid. It was loose.

'When someone is manually strangulated,' I explained, 'the victim usually puts on a fight, resulting in a lot of struggling and squeezing. This in turns causes damage to the internal and external structure of the neck. In such a case, the thyroid cartilage has been fractured. Exactly what has happened here.'

'Sonofabitch,' Frank said.

'There you have it, a clear case of someone trying to get rid of evidence—or more precisely, someone who knows too much. Do you still think I'm imagining things?'

'I never said you were, Kristina. That's why I told you to get away from Melbourne. I know I'm not going to hang around.'

We spent the next two hours collecting forensic evidence, including trace evidence of all sorts—carpet fibre, dirt, and everything that was virtually invisible to the eye. I packaged everything in paper rather than plastic to avoid mould growth from a wet or moist exhibit. Appropriate labels were attached to each items, identifying the case number, the item number and a brief description of what the items were.

I collected trace evidence with adhesive lifts and vacuum-sweepings. Blood stains on Goosh's clothes were collected by cutting samples and placing them in a folded piece of paper. The folder paper was subsequently placed in a labelled plastic bag. Other blood stains were scraped off with a clean scalpel, or sponged up with a wet cloth.

During the entire procedure, I continued to take photographs of anything which looked suspicious. I also entered accurate details in my log book.

Paper bags were placed on Goosh's hands to protect trace evidence which might have been caught under his nails or on the surface of his hands.

By the time we finished, the coroner arrived and whisked the body away to the morgue for the obligatory autopsy, which I had already decided I would not attend. Goosh had been a work colleague, whether I liked it or not, and I've had enough from having watched Evelyn Carter's autopsy a few weeks back. It seems that everyone I knew was getting killed. Who was going to be next? Me? Frank? Michael?

When we left the motel, the rain had stopped and the sun appeared shyly between the clouds. I felt light-headed, almost relieved. Now that the shock of Goosh's death had passed, I wasn't sure if I was happy or sad that he had left my life. One thing was certain—I would never have to put up with his chauvinistic attitude again. But death was still not something I would have wished on him, no matter how much he aggravated me.

I returned the PERK to boot of my car.

Frank was following closely behind.

'Let's go home,' he said. 'I think I've had enough for one day. We can work on the preliminary report tomorrow.'

'Sure,' I said.

My clothes had dried on me, but I could smell a mixture of dampness and sweat. I passed one hand though my hair. It was limply and dull.

I stepped in the car and inserted the keys in the ignition.

Frank was standing by the driver's door.

I wound the window down, 'What's up now?'

'We need to have a serious talk when we get to my place,' he said.

'I know.'

I watched him walk to his car. He looked older now than he ever had. He seemed to have lost more hair. His crown didn't help either. I wondered why he never bothered shaving it all off. He would have looked a hundred times better.

As I was watching him walking away, I felt this vacuum inside me. What would I do if something ever happened to him? All the years we've been working together, I've always taken him for granted, even though he had always been so nice and considerate to me.

I pulled into Princess Highway and jumped into the right lane.

Frank was following me close behind.

He probably always did, but I never really noticed until now.

CHAPTER THIRTY-SEVEN

'**I** don't care what you do,' Frank said, slamming the palm of his hand on the table, 'he's coming with me to Sydney.'

One side of me wanted to argue with him, and the other saw the reasoning behind his decision. I, too, feared for Michael's life as well as Frank's and mine.

We were sitting at the kitchen table over coffee. Michael was in front of the PlayStation. Sometimes things never seemed to change. I could have sworn I had been there before, arguing with Frank about what was best for Michael, while Michael was playing his game console in front of the television. *Déjà vu* to the max. My life was beginning to take on a circular pattern, and if the Lord of the Karma was right, this pattern would continue to re-occur throughout my life until I've learned my lesson and moved on. Problem was that I had no idea what the hell my lesson was supposed to be. Whoever had invented life forgot to enclose an owner's manual with it.

'What about his school?' I said for the sake of arguing. 'Isn't he behind enough as it is?'

'His school is nothing compared to his life,' Frank said. 'It's no good going to school if you're dead.'

'Come on, Frank, you're scaring me.'

'Why? Do you think this is a joke? Do you think I'm going to stay here and wait for someone to break into my home and put a rope around my neck? You're crazy, Kristina, you have to come with us.'

'We don't know if that's what happened to Goosh.' Of course we knew. The forensic evidence pointed squarely in that direction, weakening my stance to the point of sounding like a moron.

'No, but I'm not going to stand here and wait to find out,' Frank said.

I stood from my chair. 'Look, you do what you have to do, but don't ask me to come with you. You know it's not going to happen. Give me another week. If in seven days I haven't made any progress, I'll come and join you. Promise.'

'Sure, but it doesn't matter, because whatever I say, you're going to go ahead and do what you want anyway. I've known you long enough to know you're not going to change.'

That much he had right.

They decided to leave that same night. I was to drive them to Melbourne Airport in Tullamarine. The plane was leaving at 11.20 p.m., and it would only take an hour to get to Sydney. Their motel had been booked ahead on the other side, so the only thing they'd have to do is jump in a cab and try to get some sleep. I doubted they would after everything that had occurred that day.

As I helped Michael pack up his belongings, I wondered if I had made the right decision by sending him away. I certainly would feel more secured about his safety, there was no doubt about it. Still, I had never separated myself from him, and not seeing him for a week was going to be the longest time we'd been apart.

'This is so cool,' Michael said. 'Hey, your job is not that bad after all. I get to travel in the middle of the year.'

'Come on, Michael, you know it's not a holiday. I just want to make sure you're safe. You don't mind going away for a little while, do you?'

'Nope, I hate school, anyway.'

'That much I know.'

I zipped up his back pack.

'I'm going to miss you, you know,' I said.

He just stared at me for a little while.

'I know,' he finally said and gave me a hug.

I wanted to cry but I held my tears back.

'I love you, mum, you know I love you.'

'I know, darling.'

He was the sweetest man in my life, and he probably didn't even know.

We ate Double Whoppers with cheese at the airport's Hungry Jack's. Flight QF479 to Sydney was not due for another half hour, and we never bothered with dinner back in Richmond from fear of missing the flight. It's started raining again on the way to the airport, but then it never really completely stopped since that morning. I was dying for endless days of sunshine, where I'd have no obligations other than sitting at the beach with a good book. But unfortunately, I had no idea as to how I was going to achieve my goal. Whenever I get out of this mess, I told myself, I'm going to make sure my wish doesn't remain an unattainable dream.

A copy of Matthew Condon's *The Pillow Fight* sat on the table next to me. I bought it for Frank at the airport's bookshop as a thank-you gift for taking care of Michael, and also to show him that he wasn't missing out on much by not being married. The novel shows the sad but all-too-common situation of domestic violence, but this time the husband is on the receiving end.

'You take care of the preliminary report of Goosh's murder,' Frank said and took a bite from his hamburger. 'I've left my log book on my desk. If you need additional information, or your details are too sketchy, feel free to look through it.'

The log book was to the crime-scene examiner what the car was to the taxi driver. Without a log book, exhibits presented as evidence or testimony in a court of law would be disputed and more than likely rendered inadmissible. The log book served as part of the chain of continuity of collected exhibits.

With a napkin, I whipped off a sauce stain from Frank's shirt. He just looked at me doing it, not surprised, nor angry. We were both feeling the weight of his departure and the fear of not knowing for sure when we would see each other again. It was tearing me apart, but I choose to remain in control of my churning emotions in front of Michael. The last thing I needed was to break down and make their departure hell for all of us.

Michael was eating his fries at a hundred miles an hour, as if someone was going to take them away from him. As soon as he finished his serving, he began digging into mine. I didn't stop him. He could have had the whole lot if he wanted to. I found it hard to swallow food at all.

'What about your side of the story?' I asked Frank. 'I wasn't present at the crime scene from the beginning. What if everything I need is not in the log book?'

'I'll fax you any details you need for your report. Just call me on the mobile.'

'How am I going to explain my presence at the crime scene when I'd been ordered to step down?'

'I haven't told you.'

'You haven't told me what?'

'Did you get a letter from the VFSC telling you that your services were no longer required?'

'Not that I'm aware of.'

'Good, then you don't know anything, and I forgot to tell you.'

That was a change. Usually Frank wanted to do everything by the book, especially when I was the one who broke any of the rules. Not that I was complaining about his change of tactic. It suited my agenda perfectly.

Half way through my hamburger, the mobile went off. It was John Darcy from the lab.

'I've the results you wanted,' he said.

I checked my watch: 11.05 p.m.

'You're working late,' I said.

'I've had a shit-load of work that's been dumped on me this afternoon. I had to wait to do the test. I'm still at the lab.'

I thought about his wife, and of how his current working situation wasn't going to help them renew their marriage vows.

'That's the DNA test?' I asked. 'David's hair?'

'Correct.'

Frank threw me an inquisitive glance. I had never told him that I took a sample of David's hair and gave it to John for a DNA comparison test with the semen found inside Evelyn's uterus. I knew he would have been angry, so I'd decided to by-pass his expert's opinion on the subject.

'So what have you got?' I asked, feeling my heart beating

like a kettledrum.

'Well, if you're really fucking this guy, as you put it this morning, then you better be sitting down.' He paused for effect. 'It's a perfect match.'

I felt a pain in my chest. 'Are you sure?'

'Sure as anything. I conducted the test twice. I can send you copies of the polymorphic sequences autoradiographs.'

'That's won't be necessary.'

'Okay then, was that useful?'

'You bet.'

I pushed the NO on the mobile and swallowed my saliva.

There was no way in the world I was going to be able to have another bite of anything.

The first word that came to mind was 'betrayed'.

Then 'fear'.

Then 'murder'.

Then 'shit'.

'What going on?' Frank asked, 'Who was that?'

'Just a friend,' I lied.

'A friend? *That's the DNA test? David's hair?*' Frank put his burger down. 'What the hell is going on Kristina?'

I checked my watch and said, 'It's 11.15. Your plane is going in five minutes. Come on we better get going. I'll give you a call and let you know.'

I stood from my chair without giving them a choice, grabbed Michael's back-pack, and began pacing towards Gate One.

'Hey, hold on a sec,' Frank yelled out.

'Mum,' Michael said.

They finally caught up with me.

My legs were like rubber. I didn't know how much longer I would be able to stand on my feet.

'Okay, okay, fine,' Frank said, 'you don't have to tell me shit. But you better not be putting yourself in danger. Has that got anything to do with this guy from the bookshop?'

'Not now, Frank,' I said. 'I told you I was going to let you know.' Then I pointed towards Gate One. 'Look everyone is already boarding. Come on, quick, you're going to miss your place.'

We passed a metal detector. Just as well I'd left my handgun in the glove compartment of my car. The last thing I need was being tackled to the floor by a hundred-and-twenty pound security guard, his knee jabbing at my collarbone and his gun aiming at the back of my head.

We all hurried to the gate lounge. Travellers were already queuing for boarding.

When we got there, I gave Michael a big hug, 'I love you, honey. You take care of yourself, and if you want to call me, call me any time on the mobile.'

'I love you too, mum.' He kissed me on the cheek.

Frank hugged me. I never realised how his cigarette smell had been such a comfortable thing. 'Don't do anything silly,' he said. 'You're the best friend I've got, and I don't want to spend the rest of my life wondering where I went wrong.'

'I'll be okay.' I felt a lump in my throat.

Too much in too little time.

They joined the queue, and before I had time to fully realise what was going, they had disappeared from view. I stood like a statue for a full minute staring at an empty spot in front of me.

And then my legs gave in and I collapsed.

CHAPTER THIRTY-EIGHT

There was a white ceiling above my head, and I could smell disinfectant. For the next few seconds, I tried to figure out where I was and what had happened. I remembered Michael and Frank and the airport lounge. And then I didn't remember anything.

The sheets under me felt soft and clean. My fingers rubbed them gently, and then I felt blood rushing through them.

I tilted my head, but my neck hurt, like if someone's tried to strangle me. My right shoulder hurt as well. It felt bruised. I must have fallen sideways onto the hard tiled floor at the airport.

My eyes circled the room. The walls were white washed, and there was a red plastic chair in the top right corner directly in front of my bed. I was alone in the room, and I had no idea how long I'd been here. It was almost a relief. For a little while, I didn't even want to know who I was. I pretended my current life was something out of my imagination, that it had been a novel I read, or a movie I'd seen recently. My real life was that of someone who had a mild accident, and who was now resting in hospital, someone who had a loving family waiting for her and a warm house where everything was perfect. I had a little job which brought in enough money to pay my car off and my share of the mortgage. It wasn't a career job, just something to make a living, a past-time that gave me a sense of belonging.

As I continued to stare at the white ceiling above my bed, the realisation of what my real life was all about began to sink in. There would be no loving family or warm house to come to. Instead, my home was now in the bedroom of a friend's place in Richmond, and what passed as my family was in Sydney right now. I wondered how Michael was coping. He seemed quite cheerful when I left him at the airport, certainly better that I'd been.

And then it hit me like a kick in the jaw.

David.

The DNA result of the hair strand I took from him at the airport matched the semen found inside Evelyn. He fucked her, and he never told me. He never said he knew her, and yet he had acted perfectly innocent. Disgusted with myself for having been so naive, I recalled how every time I used to come and see him, he'd asked me how the investigation was progressing. No wonder.

I stood on my bed. The bruising on my right shoulder hurt even more. I had slept with this man, believed everything he told me. I had been happy in his arms for a while. Of course, I kind of expected that the test was going to be a perfect match, but until the result were actually confirmed, there was also some hope at the back of my mind that maybe I was being too paranoid.

Nothing was ever what it seemed, I should have learned by now.

www.ingramcontent.com/pod-product-compliance
Lightning Source LLC
Chambersburg PA
CBHW022012010726
47494CB00003B/1005